Fringe of Gold
The Fife Anthology

Professor Duncan Glen's local history books include *Illustrious Fife*, *Historic Fife Murders*, *Kirkcaldy: a new illustrated history* and *Splendid Lanarkshire*. He is also the author of *Hugh MacDiarmid and the Scottish Renaissance* and *The Poetry of the Scots*. His *Collected Poems 1965-2005* was short-listed for the Saltire Scottish Book of the Year.

Tom Hubbard conceived the idea for this book while he was Visiting Professor in Scottish Literature and Culture at the ELTE University of Budapest during 2006. He is now a Research Fellow at the National University of Ireland, Maynooth. His permanent home is in Kirkcaldy. His other Fife-related publications are *Michael Scot: Myth and Polymath* (2006) and *Peacocks and Squirrels: Poems of Fife* (2007), both from Akros. His first novel, *Marie B.*, will appear from The Ravenscraig Press in 2008.

FRINGE OF GOLD
The Fife Anthology

Edited by
Duncan Glen
&
Tom Hubbard

BIRLINN

First published in 2008 by Birlinn Ltd
West Newington House, 10 Newington Road, Edinburgh, EH9 1QS
www.birlinn.co.uk

Selection, Introduction and Notes © Duncan Glen
and Tom Hubbard 2008

ISBN-10: 1-84158-704-4
ISBN-13: 978-1-84158-704-2

Set in Bembo and ITC Benguiat by Vikki Reilly
Printed and bound in Great Britain by
Antony Rowe Ltd

Contents

Inverkeithing to Kinghorn

West Fife's Towns and Proudest Industry

The East Neuk

Across Country to Leuchars and the Tay

St Andrews

Introduction

Why a "Fife anthology"? There is a plethora of "Glasgow anthologies", and over the past three decades and more Aberdeen and the north-east have been well-served by editors such as James N. Alison, Cuthbert Graham, William Donaldson and Alistair Taylor. It's now Fife's turn.

Within the past twenty years groups of Fife-based writers have published their own magazines—first *Scrievins*, followed in due course by *Fife Lines*. Akros Publications flitted to Kirkcaldy in the mid-1990s and publishes *Zed 2 O* magazine as well as books and pamphlets. Helena Nelson runs her small poetry press, Happenstance, from Glenrothes. None of these ventures sought or seeks to publish writers exclusively from Fife, and the annual Stanza Poetry Festival in St Andrews embraces a healthy internationalism; however, as two editors with much experience of working together, it seemed to us that the time was ripe to focus on work emanating from the county or otherwise "Fifish" in content. We wanted to include native and adopted Fifers as well as overseas writers who had shown an active interest in this part of Scotland—hence the presence here of an American, Herman Melville, and a Hungarian, Lajos Áprily. Conversely, we have also been attracted to material which starts from a Fife base, then addresses itself to the wider world.

The structures and principles supporting this anthology are not difficult to discern. We have looked for good writing and, whether prose or verse, selected it without bias towards particular styles. The earliest work is a small poem written by an unnameable writer in the late thirteenth century; more recent is an extract from a work of 2005 by Ian Rankin. We have gathered verses by major known poets and by anonymous writers of popular rhymes. We offer good prose by local historians, great novelists and those who have been "afoot in Fife".

New major roads and a large and influential New Town have come to rural Fife, but such changes are often only marginal to the greater prospect. In 2008 it remains, as T. G. Snoddy wrote in the 1960s in his *'Tween Forth and Tay*, easy to veer "off the highway and away from the more heavily populated centres, away from the rush and fever of our modern ways. It is a road for loitering and looking." Again and again the traveller in Fife will be surprised by a "splendid panorama" and, to quote the final sentence of Snoddy's book, "What a deal of natural beauty and far-reaching history lingers about this simple countryside."

Geographically our anthology begins at the iconic cantilevered rail bridge and ends at a gateway to the sea at St Andrews. Having gone as far west as Kincardine, there is then a west to east logic to this physical route. But, like good stories, there are unexpected twists and turns, including a glimpse of a very clever cat in Aberdour, a hilariously snobbish General Alex Campbell writing to General Wemyss at Wemyss Castle, and Bob Dylan in St Andrews wordlessly receiving an honorary doctorate. As Robert Burns sang, "We hae tales to tell, / And we hae sangs to sing."

Fife has a rich history. In 1923 John Geddie wrote of Fife as always having "been in the swim of events" and of "its rich store of ballad lore and romantic and saintly traditions, its contributions of early or later date to literature, art, and philosophy; its intimate associations, all through its annals, with the great names and great events in the history and progress of the Scottish nation. Fife and its coasts are studded with places that have been the homes, or temporary residences, of Scottish royalty, and the scenes of happenings that have had a decisive influence on national as well as local destinies… was not Dunfermline the favoured seat of the Scottish Court before Edinburgh?" There are the serenely beautiful and richly productive agricultural landscapes, the fishing villages of the East Neuk and, as Alan Hall has written, "East from Dunfermline lie the skeletons and memories of West Fife's proudest industry—coalmining."

John Geddie saw Fife as a "'Kingdom' within a kingdom—almost an island within an island", but there are many ways in which the "Kingdom" is a microcosm of Scotland as a whole. As well as taking note of recent writing, we were highly conscious of the county's distant antecedents. Dunfermline offers a fascinating case study of traditions rediscovered and reconfigured in the twentieth and twenty-first centuries. We have included a passage from Patrick Geddes (1854-1932), the Scottish all-rounder (botanist, publisher, arts impresario, sociologist, "city designer") who in 1904 had proposed a more-than-university, based in Dunfermline, to the Carnegie Trust. Geddes aimed to restore to the auld grey backwater a role akin to its former status as the capital of a north-western European nation. Geddes's ambitious plans remained on paper, but later activists such as Elspeth King (from a Fife mining family) created a mini-renaissance in the town during the early 1990s. The Abbot House was restored, and about the same time the Robert Henryson Society was co-founded by an expat Fifer living in Glasgow, George Philp. These new beginnings were at once bold and modest, capable of development.

Geddes had advocated a philosophy of "Regionalism" as a counterweight to the metropolitan cities, be they London, Edinburgh or Glasgow. In Ireland, during the late 1940s, "Regionalism" was articulated by the Ulster poet John Hewitt, who championed geo-cultural units that could be complementary to larger national loyalties but which, unlike them, could provide an immediately graspable identity. In times of "over-centralisation" and "increasing standardisation" the region could offer "the security of a sheltering rock". (John Hewitt,

Ancestral Voices, Belfast, 1987.) The sheltering rock wasn't, however, merely a comfort zone, a cosy kailyard idyll. Hewitt was by no means the only Irish writer to present his local habitation in a spirit of challenge. In 1952, Patrick Kavanagh, best known for his long poem "The Great Hunger" (set in a very unpastoral Co. Monaghan), made this important distinction: "Parochialism and provincialism are direct opposites. The provincial has no mind of his own; he does not trust what his eyes see until he has heard what the metropolis—towards which his eyes are turned—has to say on any subject... The parochial mentality on the other hand is never in any doubt about the social and artistic validity of his parish. All great civilisations are based on parochialism... it requires a great deal of courage to be parochial." (Patrick Kavanagh, *A Poet's Country*, Dublin, 2003.) To be able to accept that the local is the only universal, we have to develop confidence in the strength of our parochial roots.

The present book, then, issues a challenge to contemporary Fife to become less provincial and more parochial in its cultural undertakings. To be sure, our anthology is not purely "literary", as we include topographical and architectural description, political memoir and accessible history, as well as the more obviously writerly forms of poetry and fiction. Publisher and editors were agreed that our selection should be as broadly-based as possible. We present here voices medieval and contemporary, many (most?) of which are better known outwith Fife than within it. We have rediscovered a few late-Victorian gems from almost-forgotten authors such as "Sarah Tytler" (Henrietta Keddie), David Grant and John Geddie. We have welcomed old favourites like "The Kelty Clippie" and "The Boy in the Train". Scots is well represented because poetry and prose in that language follow the contours of actual speech, not slavishly but creatively: the analogy is with the operas of Janácek, who deployed the cadences of spoken Moravian, upon which he built his own unique structures of sound. For those who visit Fife, and inhabit it, it is to be hoped that something in this book will echo in the inner ear.

Bridges, Ferries, Coaches
& the Railway

BRIDGING THE FORTH ESTUARY

In 1849 the Edinburgh and Northern Railway changed its name to the Edinburgh, Perth and Dundee Railway and recruited the young Thomas Bouch as its engineer. He was determined to come up with an answer to crossing the Tay and Forth estuaries and devised a system of transporting trains over water on floating platforms. His idea was not entirely original, nevertheless his name became associated with these "floating railways" which were considered to be marvels of ingenuity and invention, so much so that the directors of the North British Railway Company took his plans to bridge the two estuaries very seriously indeed.

Thomas Bouch's twenty-year-old dream assumed reality in July 1871 with the laying of the foundation stone of the Tay Bridge. And by December 1879 the Bouch family, ensconced in their comfortable Edinburgh West End home, had more reason to count their blessings than to worry about the storm raging over Scotland's east coast. The Tay Bridge, for which Thomas Bouch was knighted, had been in operation for nineteen months; Margaret Bouch had laid the foundation stone for the Forth Bridge in 1873; the Bouch's engineering son was supervising his father's designs for the bridge over the South Esk at Montrose.

Work was under way on the Forth Bridge which was to be the head of the household's ultimate achievement. Together, the three bridges would complete the long-dreamed-of route to the north, from Edinburgh to Dundee and Aberdeen, carrying the trains of the railway companies over the deep-sea inlet barriers of the east coast at last.

The Forth Bridge Company was formed in 1873 to carry out Thomas Bouch's design for a suspension bridge and the same year an Act of Parliament authorised construction and contracts were signed with Messrs W. Arrol and Co., of Glasgow. The plans looked so promising that, at the zenith of his career, Sir Thomas little expected the blow which arrived at his home in the form of a telegram three days after Christmas 1879: "Terrible accident on bridge one or more of highgirders blown down a.m. not sure of the safety of the last down Edinbr train will advise further as soon as can be obtained".

The extent of the disaster was all too evident by the cruel light of dawn. The Tay Bridge had crumbled into the estuary, sweeping the Edinburgh train and

1

an estimated seventy-five passengers to their deaths with the debris of brick and metal. Work on the Forth was immediately halted by a formal Abandonment Act pending investigations into the disaster. Public confidence in Sir Thomas and his assumed abilities was shaken to the core. His "floating railways" continued to operate and locomotives went on chugging over the three hundred miles of lines he constructed in Scotland and England. But the Tay Bridge collapse rendered these achievements virtually worthless and Sir Thomas retired shattered to his country house in Moffat, where he died on 1 November 1880 from a cold which he had no will to resist. He was buried at Edinburgh's Dean Cemetery.

It would, however, have taken more than a disaster even of this scale to halt a determined Victorian railway director in his tracks. Before 1880 was out the four railway companies which had raised the capital for Bouch's scheme—the Great Northern, the North-Eastern, the Midland and the North British—had instructed their consulting engineers, Messrs. Barlow, Harrison and Fowler to reconsider all the options for bridging the Forth.

A design submitted by John Fowler and Benjamin Baker, based on the cantilever and central girder principle, was modified to take account of the conflicting views of the consultant engineers and submitted to the director of the Forth Bridge Company in May 1881.

SHEILA MACKAY, *The Forth Bridge: a Picture History*, 1990.

THE FORTH BRIG

It's an awfielik size the Forth Brig richt enyeuch, apairt
fae onie conseederatioun o utilitie,
stress, strain, wather an wuin an siccan calculatiouns
the engineers o thon biggin generatioun
tuk tent o. True, lik the aurochs o the northern airt,
it's gy near had its tyme, and 'll hae had its day
in a wheen o years syne lik the dodo burd,
yuissless, lik the thocht o a road brig the noo, absurd.

Nae doot there's been a walth o wunder ower the makkin o the Brig,
folk fair taen up wi the thing an no the thocht,
tho for ma money—chippit fae the cairriage windae—the trig
thocht o the engineer is shairlie brocht
tae wunder ower the watters o the Firth wi the sicht
o the suin aistlins i the morn an wasterin at nicht.

T. S. LAW

HEY-DAYS OF STAGE COACHING

The era after the Napoleonic War and before the coming of the train was the hey-day of coaching. North Queensferry with its thirteen places "where spirit may be bought in small quantities and drunk upon the premises" was well-placed to benefit from the passing traffic. The principal inns were the Old and New Inns. The former no longer exists. It stood on the east side of the road at the head of Signal House Pier and had stables behind it. It was also known as Mrs. Malcolm's Inn. The latter still stands and is known today as the Albert Hotel... In the early coaching period the steepness of the Brae was a source of inconvenience. Before the improvements to the Great North Road the coach ran over the old road to Inverkeithing, i.e. up the Brae with its tortuous turns and its one in five gradient. In the opposite direction passengers got out of the coach at the top of the hill and descended on foot to the passage boat.

Several coaches passed through the village. One of the best known was the Defiance, run by a Captain Barclay on the route between Edinburgh and Aberdeen. He was coachman both on the inaugural run in 1829 and the coach's final journey in 1849. He was otherwise known as the "celebrated pedestrian" because he had once won a 1,000 guinea bet that he could walk 1,000 miles in 1,000 hours. There was nothing pedestrian about his coach service however. It had such a record for time-keeping that people set their watches and clocks by "Defiance time". The first ten miles of the journey, from Princes Street to South Queensferry, were covered in a miraculous fifty minutes. The whole route was timed to the last minute. Barclay bragged "She'll be in Aberdeen by 7.10 if naethin' happens tae Aberdeen".

> **PETER and CAROL DEAN**, *Passage of Time: the Story of the Queensferry Passage and the Village of North Queensferry*, 1981.

FROM A RAILWAY CARRIAGE WINDOW, FROM BURNTISLAND TO THE TAY IN THE 1890s

We will put ourselves in the place of a stranger travelling through the county by rail, and will indicate a few "bits" that may be seen from the line that might otherwise escape his notice. Leaving Burntisland for the north we observe on the left the rock where Alexander III was killed; then on the right Pettycur harbour, the old ferry-port of the Forth. We pass through a tunnel under the Witch-Hill, where the good folks of Kinghorn used to practise cremation. Close to the sea, we get a peep of the old kirk where they were commended for so doing, and of the ship-building yard where many a stout ship has been built. A ruinous keep,

Seafield Tower, is near Kirkcaldy. After crossing the Leven, and passing Markinch, an irregular village full of hills and hollows, we enter Stratheden, or the Howe of Fife—the Eden flows down from the Lomonds by Cupar, and reaches the sea at Guardbridge. The wide plain stretches before us to the foot of the Lomond Hills, which rise to the height of 1492 and 1713 feet. The Romans had a camp on them, and the battle of Mons Graupius is said to have been fought on their slopes. A valley on the West Lomond was a meeting place of the Covenanters.

The village on the left, at some distance from the railway, is the famous Freuchie, and from the woods beyond the smoke of Falkland may be seen rising. At Kingskettle, on the right, we notice two good churches. The Mount, wooded to the summit, the old home of Sir David Lyndsay (of Scott's "Marmion"), with its tall chimney-like monument to Earl Hopeton, is conspicuous on the northern horizon.

Leaving Ladybank for Perth we observe Kinloch House, surrounded by trees, formerly the farm of John Balfour. Lindores Loch next is worthy of attention. There is a fine view at Newburgh, where the Tay Bridge can be seen. The celebrated Round Tower at Abernethy, on the left, completes this section.

On the Dundee line, Pitlessie village at some distance is seen on the right, between Ladybank and Cupar; and near it Cults, where Sir David Wilkie, the painter, was born and where he spent his early days. At Springfield, on the right, is Crawford Priory, a very handsome building, the Fife seat of the Earl of Glasgow. After passing Cupar, the Church and old Castle of Dairsie close to the line, with the entrance to Dura Den, catch the eye. It was in Dairsie Castle that Spottiswoode wrote his *Church History*. The ancient Church of Leuchars, with its Norman architecture, stands on rising ground on the right; whilst St Andrews can be seen distinctly a few miles further east. Soon after we reach the Tay.

"KILROUNIE" [JOHN R. RUSSELL], *The Kingdom. A descriptive and historical hand-book of Fife* [1890s].

THE KINGDOM OF FIFE AS SEEN IN 1923

A "Kingdom" within a kingdom—almost an island within an island—Fife proclaims itself as a region apart—distinct, in position and character, from other divisions of the land. A glance at the map suffices to show that, using the name in the older and wider sense, Fife is set aside from its neighbours by strongly marked frontiers. It is shaped, as the learned George Buchanan pointed out more than three centuries ago, like a wedge thrust out between the two Firths that bound it, into the mists and waves of the North Sea; and this wedge begins to be bevelled to a sharp point at St. Andrews, where, also, its civil and ecclesiastical history starts and culminates. Across its base, to the west, the high range of the Ochil Hills is drawn, leaving little room between their skirts and the tidal waters of the Forth and Tay.

But little they know of Fife who know it only on paper or from without. One has to explore it to understand the success with which Nature has adapted it for the rearing of a special stock, with a history, customs, and character of their own. Neighbours all agree, and Fifers themselves have never denied, that they are a peculiar people, endowed with peculiar gifts and living in a favoured land. If, in early times, the sea and the hills cut it off from easy access to and from the surrounding provinces, Fife has always been in the swim of events, when any great crisis came in the affairs of Kirk or State; while in quieter intervals, never too extended in Scottish national annals, it gave itself to the practice of the arts of peace with a vigour and tenacity that became proverbial...

Fife has laid strong hands on the sea ever since Sir Andrew Wood of Largo captured Stephen Bull, the English admiral, and his three ships at the back of the May Island in 1499; or six centuries earlier, when King Constantine, son of that Kenneth MacAlpin who united the kingdoms of the Picts and Scots, was slain at Fife Ness while driving the invading Danes into the salt water; back even to that more dim and uncertain date when Saint Rule, or Regulus, landed at the "Boar's Promontory", bearing with him from Achaia the bones of Andrew the Apostle, whose cross—a white saltire on a blue ground—was straightway adopted by King Hungus, the Pict, as the symbol of Scotland and of victory, and whose relics gave a new name and sanctity to the site of St. Andrews. In these our days the bonds laid upon the subject waters are literally forged of steel. The Forth Bridge stretches an airy cobweb of brackets and girders, struts and stays, across the narrows of the "Queen's Ferry"; and, on the other side of the county, the Tay Bridge strides across the three miles of estuary which separates Fife from the coast of Forfar and the city of Dundee, making of these ancient sea-passages main links in the new, and short and easy, chain of railway communication that binds together the South and the North.

The Kingdom of Fife has, however, possessions in which its inhabitants take still more pride than in its mineral treasures, its busy seaports and factories, and its triumphs of engineering science. There are, for example, its rich store of ballad lore and romantic and saintly traditions, its contributions of early or later date to literature, art, and philosophy; its intimate associations, all through its annals, with the great names and great events in the history and progress of the Scottish nation. Fife and its coasts are studded with places that have been the homes, or temporary residences, of Scottish royalty, and the scenes of happenings that have had a decisive influence on national as well as local destinies... was not Dunfermline the favoured seat of the Scottish Court before Edinburgh? Did not Malcolm Bighead—the last King of Scotland who spoke Gaelic as his native tongue—live in the ancient tower whose fragments can still be seen in Pittencrieff

Rossend Castle

Glen; and did not the saintly Margaret, his wife, say her prayers and perform her penances in the cave beside the "Crooked Lin" hard by? Are they not buried within the precincts of the great Abbey Church which their son David helped to rear in the style of Durham Cathedral, along with a host of other kings and queens, including Robert the Bruce, and James III and James V of Scots, one of whom began, while the other completed, the Palace which adjoins and partly occupies the site of the renowned Benedictine Monastery? Were not some of these and other members of the line of Banquo—with happy, or much more often unhappy, fortunes awaiting them—born in this royal dwelling under the shadow of the Abbey Barbican, and among them Charles I, the "Martyr King", of whom, while still in his cradle, his sapient father said he was "a girnin' bairn" over whom "the Deil has cussin his cloak"?

Or, to extend the field of vision to places of lesser standing, although, to the Fife eye at least, by no means undeserving of note… Had not Annabella Drummond, the consort of Robert III, and mother of the royal author of the *King's Quhair,* her palace in Inverkeithing, of which some walls and vaults remain? Did not Queen Yolande, the bride of Alexander III, wait for the coming of her husband to the castle on Kinghorn Ness on that fateful night—"the worst that Scotland had ever known"—when he was flung from his horse while riding homeward from the Ferry along the shore rocks? Was it not at Rossend Castle that the poet Chastelard committed the culminating folly of hiding in the bed-chamber of Mary Stewart, that brought him to the block; and in the Kirk of Burntisland close by that Mary's son announced the design that bore fruit in the Authorised Version of the Bible? It was at Wemyss Castle, farther east, that Mary first saw and was taken by the goodly outer person of the "lang lad" Darnley; and at the East Neuk, beyond Crail, that Mary's mother stepped ashore on the Scottish soil where she was to meet a larger portion of sorrow than of happiness.

Many, also, are the filaments in the warp and woof of the story of the royal line that are attached to Balmerino and Lindores Abbeys, to Ballenbriech and

Ferry-Port-on-Craig, and other spots on the northern fringes of Fife. But towards St. Andrews all the threads in the history of the Scottish monarchy, and of the Scottish Kirk and State, seem to converge, and to be wrought into a pattern of strong and sombre colouring.

JOHN GEDDIE, *The Shores of Fife* [1923].

SPECIFICS

"I gaed to spend a week in Fife—
An unco week it proved to be—"
George Outram

I gaed to Fife for a tourin week.
I crossed the brig at Kincardine
and went as faur as I could at Newport. I sat wi miners
in Bowhill and wi fishermen in Crail.
I saw coal loadit at Methil and whisky in Markinch.
I watched the golfers at Lundin Links
and the electronic girls at Glenrothes. I saw trout leap
at Strathmiglo and an Englishman asked me the wey to
Auchtermuchty. I watched the lawyers perform in Cupar
and the shipbuilders in Burntisland. I walked the gress atween
the stanes o the cathedral of St Andrews and stood by
Mr. Morris's grave. I pondered on Carnegie's
steel, the richt saintly Margaret's iron will, the warrior Bruce's
missin hairt, and the maisterly Henrysoun's
twa mice in richt royal Dunfermline.
I stood unner the auld railway brig at North Queensferry
and missed the smell o linoleum at Kirkcaldy. I tried for high tea
at Peat Inn and had dinner in Falkland near the Palace.
I was sent to Freuchie
and there I settled doon, for a rest.

Where are you from they ask me. I tell them
whaur I've juist been. No, they say,
you're "from Glasgow"

like the English say I'm "from Scotland"
and the French say "from England".

DUNCAN GLEN

7

THE ANNUITY

I gaed to spend a week in Fife—
An unco week it proved to be—
For there I met a waesome wife
Lamentin' her viduity.
Her grief brak out sae fierce and fell,
I thought her heart wad burst the shell;
And—I was sae left tae mysel—
I sell't her an annuity.

The bargain lookit fair eneugh—
She just was turned o' saxty-three:
I couldna guessed she'd prove sae teugh,
By human ingenuity.
But years have come, and years have gane,
And there she's yet as stieve's a stane—
The limmer's growin' young again,
Since she got her annuity.

She's crined awa' to bane and skin,
But that it seems is nought to me;
She's like to live—although she's in
The last stage o' tenuity.
She munches wi' her wizened gums,
An' stumps about on legs o' thrums
But comes—as sure as Christmas comes—
To ca' for her annuity.

She jokes her joke, an' cracks her crack,
As spunkie as a growin' flea—
An' there she sits upon my back,
A livin' perpetuity.
She hurkles by her ingle side,
An' toasts an' tans her wrunkled hide—
Lord kens how lang she yet may bide
To ca' for her annuity.

I read the tables drawn wi' care
For an Insurance Company.
Her chance o' life was stated there,

Wi' perfect perspicuity.
But tables here or tables there,
She's lived ten years beyond her share,
An's like to live a dizzen mair,
To ca' for her annuity.

I gat the loun that drew the deed—
We spelled it o'er right carefully;—
In vain he yerked his souple head,
To find an ambiguity.
It's dated—tested—a' complete—
The proper stamp—nae word delete—
And deligence, as on decreet,
May pass for her annuity.

Last Yule she had a fearfu' hoast—
I thought a kink might set me free;
I led her out, mang snaw and frost,
Wi' constant assiduity.
But Deil ma' care—the blast gaed by,
And missed the auld anatomy;
It just cost me a tooth, forbye
Discharging her annuity.

I thought that grief might gar her quit—
Her only son was lost at sea—
But aff her wits behoved to flit,
An' leave her in fatuity.
She threeps, and threeps, he's livin' yet,
For a' the tellin' she can get;
But catch the doited runt forget
To ca' for her annuity.

If there's a sough o' cholera
Or thyphus—wha sae gleg as she?
She buys up baths, an' drugs, an' a',
In siccan superfluity.
She doesna need—she's fever proof—
The pest gaed owre her very roof;
She tauld me sae—an' then her loof
Held out for her annuity.

Ae day she fell—her arm she brak,—
A compound fracture as could be;
Nae leech the cure wad undertak,
Whate'er was the gratuity.
It's cured! She handles't like a flail—
It does as weel in bits as hale;
But I'm a broken man mysel
Wi' her and her annuity.

Her broozled flesh and broken banes,
Are wed as flesh an' banes can be,
She beats the tades that live in stanes,
An' fatten in vacuity.
They die when they're exposed to air—
They canna thole the atmosphere;
But her! expose her onywhere—
She lives for her annuity.

If mortal means could nick her thread,
Sma' crime it wad appear to me:
Ca't murder—or ca't homicide—
I'd justify't—and do it tae.
But how to fell a withered wife
That's carved out o' the tree o' life—
The timmer limmer daurs the knife
To settle her annuity.

I'd try a shot—But whar's the mark?—
Her vital parts are hid frae me;
Her back-bane wanders through her sark
In an unkenned corkscrewity.
She's palsified—an' shakes her head
Sae fast about, ye scarce can see't;
It's past the power o' steel or lead
To settle her annuity.

She might be drowned;—but go she'll not
Within a mile o' loch or sea;—
Or hanged—if cord could grip a throat
O' siccan exiguity
It's fitter far to hang the rope—

It draws out like a telescope:
Twad tak a dreadfu' length o' drop
To settle her annuity.

Will pushion do't?—It has been tried;
But, be't in hash or fricassee,
That's just the dish she can't abide,
Whatever kind o' *gout* it hae.
It's needless to assail her doubts,—
She gangs by instinct—like the brutes—
An' only eats an' drinks what suits
Hersel an' her annuity.

The Bible says the age o' man
Threescore an' ten perchance may be;
She's ninety-four;—let them wha can
Explain the incongruity.
She suld hae lived afore the Flood—
She's come o' Patriarchal blood—
She's some auld Pagan, mummified
Alive for her annuity.

She's been embalmed inside and out—
She's sauted to the last degree—
There's pickle in her every snout
Sae caper-like an cruety
Lot's wife was fresh compared to her;
They've kyanised the useless knir
She canna decompose—nae mair
Than her accursed annuity.

The water-drap wears out the rock
As this eternal jad wears me;
I could withstand the single shock,
But no the continuity.
It's pay me here—an' pay me there—
An' pay me, pay me, evermair;
I'll gang demented wi' despair—
I'm *charged* for her annuity!

GEORGE OUTRAM

Kincardine to Culross and to Rosyth

KINCARDINE

Kincardine, when we have made our way into it, does not afford large compensation. Its streets come straggling up to the neighbourhood of the Cross, and stare vacantly at each other. They are wide and clean enough, and have some marks of eld, but they are wanting in distinction as well as in cheerfulness. The sap of life flows slowly through the old barony burgh. It has seen better days. The very houses are built upon the ashes of its former prosperity—upon the ejected refuse of its five-and-thirty salt-pans. Gone, too, is all but the name of the potent spirit of Kilbagie that inspired the mirth at Pousie Nancy's.

Many of the houses date from the latter part of last century. It was then that Kincardine stirred itself up to great things in the carrying trade. A hundred years ago it would have as many as nine vessels on the stocks at one time. Its tonnage was more than half that of the port of Leith. It had vessels trading to the West Indies; it sent whalers to the Greenland Seas; a large share of the coasting traffic was in its hands. But these days are only a memory; and an air of deadly dulness has settled down upon it. Yet the inhabitants have enough of spirit left to resent their recent inclusion by the Boundary Commissioners within the realm of Fife. "Me a Fifer !" said the young lady of the tobacconist's shop whom we had incautiously complimented on the change. "I'll never be a Fifer. I was born in Perthshire." This prejudice is not unknown among the neighbours of the Kingdom.

JOHN GEDDIE, *The Fringes of Fife*, 1894.

THE HAMMERMEN OF CULROSS

From before 1599, when James VI granted the Culross Girdlesmiths their Royal Charter, they had the monopoly of making girdles in Scotland. These were the days when oatcakes and bannock scones were eaten by folks of all ranks, making the cast-iron girdle an essential utensil in the kitchen. For the next 150 years the girdlesmiths of Culross flourished, rendering the craft a closed shop. When being admitted to the Culross Hammerman's Guildry, each mastersmith was sworn only to apply their craft within the Burgh of Culross, and to only employ servants and apprentices from within the Parish. All journeymen were bound to Guildry laws banning them from the practice of any unlawful games and stipulating they attend church every Sunday. When the Girdlesmiths attended church, they did not sit amongst the congregation, but built a small gallery for their own exclusive use. The front panel of the gallery was impressed with their emblem, the crown and hammer, which also appeared on their girdles, the hallmark of their skill.

Many ancient traditions were part of the craft; only the mastersmith could use the tongs for lifting the iron plate from the forge onto the anvil, leaving the apprentices to hammer out the plate to the required size, either "twa fit" or "four fit." Another tradition was to allow the widow of a girdlesmith to carry on working at her husband's forge, as long as she met the standards required and adhered to the rules of the craft.

While most of the Culross villagers worked in the coal and salt mines, the girdle-smiths hammered their way to prosperity. Up until the middle of the eighteenth century, the Culross Girdlesmiths managed to fight off any competition, but were unable to match the Carron Iron works at Falkirk when they started to product cast-iron girdles in large quantities. Therefore the Culross hammermen disappeared along with their craft.

The Riding of the Marches. The Royal Burgh of Culross 400th Anniversary 1592-1992, Souvenir Publication, August 1992.

INSCRIPTION ON A HEADSTONE IN CULROSS

My sledge and hammer lie declined
My bellows too have lost their wind
My fires extincted, my forge decayed
My shovel in the dust is layed
My coal is spent, my iron gone,
My nails are drove, work is done
My fire-dried corpse lies here at rest
My sole, smokelike, soars to the blest.

THE PALACE LYING IN THE SANDHAVEN OF CULROSS

(*loquitur* Sir George Bruce, *Anno* 1605)

This sea-coal gutters but this room is sure
Where nothing else is: as this working flame's
My *faber fortunae,* my land and rents
Lie under the cold water and the sands
Which shift in answer to the tideless moon.

No gulls today, no voice of women here:
Now that the haar has fastened on the town
Abominations walk the land. They found
The *Agnus Dei* in the women's house
And vaults of glasses trained upon the sky.
O darkness, my delight: in black and red
My roofs are traced with matters of the stars.
I built this house upon the silt which wears
The shores of Scotland, salts our earthly loves.
No noise of gulls upon this fine east wind
Which levels men, and searches one and all:
No other shifts nor sweetens my dour sand.

PETER DAVIDSON

Culross Abbey

FIFE'S BRIDGES, WESTWARDS FROM DUNFERMLINE

From Dunfermline, where the original station site is now a retail park—the line was extended to Oakley in 1849, still later being continued to Alloa and Stirling, but that section was closed in 1979. Dunfermline's Coal Road, the route of a mineral tramway known as the Elgin Railway which opened in 1744, was crossed on light wrought iron lattice girders, probably the originals (*NT 0888*). The Charlestown mineral branch, opened in 1877 and using parts of an old wagonway, crossed a road at Dunfermline gasworks by a wrought iron plate girder span (*NT0986*); farther west about 1960 the old stone arch on the Charlestown branch was replaced by a new plate girder bridge on red brick abutments (*NT 0784*) to rid the A985 of a double bend. From this line there diverged a sea level route to Alloa, opened in 1906, and carried over a girder bridge south of Crossford (*NT 0785*). Since the closure of the Longannet mine complex this modest bridge has carried all the coal supplies for the huge Longannet power station, Scotland's principal source of electricity. This should soon change, due to the Scottish Executive's plan to reopen the line between Longannet and Stirling via Alloa, enabling coal from opencast workings in the west of Scotland and the deep seaport at Hunterston to avoid the long detour over the Forth Bridge and through Kirkcaldy.

ROBIN SMITH, *Fife's Bridges*, 2006.

HIGH VALLEYFIELD

Doon thonder a'thing was thick wi stoor,
Fine stuff it was, sir, pepper an saut
And by Christ ye didnae coaff or sneeze
For fear thon bugger went up.
That nicht I didnae fancy thon ata',
I'd been aff for a fortnicht wi the flu,
But doon that shank I went sir, a' the same.
I had a look,
Syne cam up in the cage wi Joe the Pole
Tae sign anither fortnicht's line.
It blew neist nicht at twa o'clock
Tho' we didnae ken whit day it was,
The hale o the Valley shook tae the foonds,
The plaister fell aff the press wa
And we a' ran aboot in oor nichtshirts.

Noo Joe the Pole, he dee'd there, no long back,
While I retired at sixty-three, bad lungs.
Forty-ane bastardin years I warked doon there,
Noo I dream I hear the picks ablo ma bed
Delvin the coal in the nicht. I speir them a'
Playin at cairds and here's me here.
Faithers and sons, brithers and kissins tae,
They were harum scarum and taen some drink
But guid boys a' the same.

Ma dochter luiks eftir me noo
They sealed it aff syne ca'd it sacrid grund
But this I'll say... there's plenty guid coal there yet.

WILLIAM HERSHAW

15

LIMEKILNS: SUNDAY MAY 9th, 1999

In the limbo of the harbour, a dog noses wrack,
pads through puddles, while gulls protest
and four spruced-up yachts wait for the tide.
In the distance, the two Bridges seem made of thread,
too fragile to sustain their connection.
On a scarf of grass a bearded roll-up smoker
sips a Special Brew, struggles with a crossword.
Houses look down from landscaped gardens.

A row of volvos is parked before the beach.
Their silent occupants sip tea from flasks,
stare across the Forth's grey boundary
at the misted patchwork of Lothian
and watch waves wash in like question-marks.

A. M. FORSTER

ADMIRAL BEATTY AT ROSYTH AND ABERDOUR, 1914-18

Aberdour House

While "everyone" knew that the Grand Fleet lay at Scapa, a plan to detach Beatty's command and base it on Rosyth in the Firth of Forth, much further south, was very secret; because, if the enemy knew, he might profit from the division of our forces, gaining considerable advantage thereby if he could overwhelm the Battle Cruisers with his own Battle Fleet, or part of it, before Jellicoe could bring effective support from Scapa.

As usual, Ethel [wife of Admiral Beatty] found what she wanted, Aberdour House, only seven miles from the dockyard, where for some years she lived almost alone except for Peter, aged five, and local social contacts, including naval wives in a similar but less opulent case. It is not surprising that her alternating moods of depression and euphoria returned, giving her the reputation of being somewhat "mental", and incurring displeasure from dour Scots because of her occasionally lavish hospitality while her husband was virtually confined to his ship. Then she made a gesture which disarmed some of the gossips. Having brought her yacht to the Firth of Forth she offered it to the Admiralty as a hospital ship. The offer was accepted and she then engaged one of the foremost surgeons of the day, Sir Alfred Fripp, to design the medical layout, particularly an operating theatre…

The Surrendered German Fleet in the Firth of Forth, November 1918
From the journal of Commander Ogilvie, then Lieutenant in the light cruiser
Inconstant: *Thursday 21st November 1918*

The Grand Fleet put to sea during the night to meet the portion of the German fleet for internment. H.M.S. *Cardiff* (Flagship of the 6th light cruiser squadron (Admiral Alexander Sinclair)) was detailed to lead in the German heavy ships. H.M.S. *Phaeton* (Captain Cameron, 1st L.C.S.) was to lead in the German light cruisers, and *Castor* (Commodore "F" Tweedie) the destroyers. These three ships left harbour first, *Cardiff* towing a kite balloon for lookout purposes, and the whole of the Grand Fleet followed.

The first to sight the Germans was Commodore "F" in *Castor*.

The time for meeting the enemy was approximately 9.15 a.m. Accordingly ships' companies were sent to action stations about 8.30 a.m.… The Germans should have been sighted bearing East, and as they were out for reckoning we had to move to the south eastward. This of course entailed a large number of signals and alterations of course. However, we finally got into position. I had had the morning watch on *the* day, 4 a.m. until 7.30 a.m. during which time we had been steering S73⁰E at a speed from 10-12 knots. We passed May Island at 4.45 having weighed at 2 a.m. It seemed most extraordinary crawling along at 10 knots as of course previously we always steam about 20 knots at sea, also zigzag…

It was quite a fine day, the sea being calm and the sun occasionally exhibiting itself. The visibility was only about 3 miles (6,000 yards). At 8.50 a.m. we sighted smoke on the starboard bow… when at 8.25 a.m. the smoke developed into a formation of German battle cruisers—looming out of the haze—we could hardly believe our eyes. *Cardiff* and *Seydlitz* were the first ships sighted. After the battle cruisers (5 in number) came 9 battleships led by *Friedrich der Grosse,* the German Fleet Flagship (2.0). Then came *Phaeton* followed by 7 German light cruisers (2.25) and lastly *Castor* followed by 49 German destroyers in parallel lines (2.36). No. 1 and myself clicked away with our cameras—without much hope as the light was so bad—at the same time, of course, keeping the [fire] control running in case of treachery. We steamed past the whole line and at 9.45 turned 16 pts and reduced to 10 knots to keep station on the starboard quarter of the procession. The German destroyers, surrounded by our own were then on the port bow… At 11.35 we "packed up" from Action Stations. Our one regret was that instead of *Nov* 21st it could have been *October* 21st, anniversary of Trafalgar. On arrival the German ships anchored off Inchkeith with a screen of Battleships and battle cruisers, and light cruisers round them anchored also… On arrival in the Firth of Forth, *Queen Elizabeth* with the C-in-C, Sir David Beatty, stopped, and the fleet steamed past, all ships massing their men on the forecastle and cheering him. The ships anchored outside Inchkeith as a guard to the surrendered German ships, and the remainder anchored in their old billets west of Inchkeith.

Thus closed what is, I am sure, one of the most dramatic incidents in the History of the Sea that the world has ever seen. Nothing can compare with the moment of sighting the "Surrender"—which seemed incredible to us—until the German Battle Cruisers were plainly discernible through the mist, led by *Cardiff.*

CHARLES BEATTY, *Our Admiral. A Biography of Admiral of the Fleet Earl Beatty*, 1980.

Dunfermline

SAINT MARGARET, QUEEN OF SCOTS

Shortly after the young brothers'★ arrival in Hungary Edmund died at the age of sixteen, and in due time Edward married Agatha, daughter of King Stephen. Thus the royal families of England and Hungary were joined. Edward and Agatha had three children, Margaret (born around 1045), Christine and Edgar. It was this Margaret who was to become the Queen of Scots and a Saint of the Roman Church.

Margaret having been brought up in a royal household was accustomed to the style and atmosphere of the courtly life. She lived and was educated in a small country split by warring tribes but united by the saintly rule and example of her grandfather King Stephen. Her mother was the daughter of a king; her father was to become heir apparent to the throne of England since his father King Edmund II had died in 1016, and half-brother Edward the Confessor was elected King of England in 1042. Like Margaret and King Stephen, Edward was canonised in 1161 by Pope Alexander II, so there are three saints in this short story! With this ancestry on both paternal and maternal sides and her courtly training, Princess Margaret was well prepared for life at the court of the King of Scots, where she was to preside for twenty-three years with firmness and compassion…

The traditional story of their arrival in Scotland is that they had intended to return to Hungary but their ship encountered a severe storm and was wrecked on the north shore of the River Forth. There they were received and welcomed by Malcolm, now King Malcolm III, and brought to the safety of his fortress home in Dunfermline, capital of Scotland. But another theory now held by scholars has a more likely explanation. Had Edgar intimated that he intended to retreat to Scotland where he would undoubtedly have gained the armed support of William's enemy Malcolm, William would have made a determined effort to stop him, and his mother and sister would have been in jeopardy. So he made it known that he was returning to his native Hungary (a natural decision for a defeated exile), but in fact he intended all the time to go to Scotland. Whether his ship was wrecked in a storm in the Firth of Forth or not, the important fact was that he and his family did land on the north bank of the river and were warmly welcomed by Malcolm. The year was 1069, the place near to the site of Rosyth Castle. The name Rosyth is probably derived from the words ross and hythe, meaning a spit of land and a jetty or landing-place respectively. If this

★The two young brothers were the exiled sons of Edmund Ironside in Hungary.

is the exact spot where Princess Margaret landed, then the bay beside it is well named Saint Margaret's Hope in memory of her.

It is said that on her way to Dunfermline, Princess Margaret rested against a large stone by the road-side until she had regained her strength sufficiently to continue her journey. In pre-Roman times there had been a Druid *cromlech* or circle of standing stones close to this spot, and it is believed that this stone is the last remaining fragment of that *cromlech*. The stone can be seen at the side of the road between Dunfermline and Rosyth, and is known as Saint Margaret's Stone. It is strange that the ancient pagan religion and the new Christian faith should be thus commemorated in the same stone.

Malcolm took the exiled family to his Tower or fortress. It had been built on a spur of land (a dun) with a narrow, steep approach; to the south was a broad stretch of marshland, to the west a dense forest, to the north a precipitous drop down to the lyn or burn that flowed around the base of the hill. It was a fine defensive position. The fortress itself was several stories high with at least twenty main halls or rooms and many smaller apartments for servants. The base was 11 metres by 10 (35ft 6in x 31ft 4in), the topmost part of the structure widening out considerably. The remains of the foundations of this fortress can still be seen in Pittencrieff Park.

The first time Malcolm had seen Margaret at the court of Edward the Confessor she was a girl of twelve, now she was a beautiful young woman, and on the day after Easter in 1070 they were married in the little Culdee Church in Dunfermline. There they made their home in Malcolm's Tower, as his fortress was called. There Queen Margaret gave birth to six sons and two daughters. There she began her true life's work… At the marriage of Malcolm and Margaret it became clear that the little Culdee Church was much too small, many of the distinguished guests at the royal wedding having to stand outside during the course of the service. But the site was specially precious and sacred to Queen Margaret. Soon afterwards, therefore, she decided to replace it with a fine, large church, more in keeping with the new forms of religion which she was seeking to introduce, and more suitable for the capital township of Scotland and the place of worship of the royal family. Work began at once and by 1072 her new church was completed and dedicated to The Holy Trinity. It was built over the old Culdee Church, and so the ancient site was preserved as a place of worship. At that time it was reckoned to be the largest and finest church in the land.

…In later years her son David I replaced his mother's church of The Holy Trinity with a magnificent abbey, the nave of which still stands as one of the finest examples of Norman architecture in Scotland.

STEWART M. MACPHERSON, *Saint Margaret, Queen of Scotland*, 1993.

Abbot House

ABBOT HOUSE

As the administrative headquarters of the first and richest Benedictine Abbey in Scotland, Abbot House is truly unique. It has borne witness to the intrigues of Church and State, survived fire and tempest, war and pillage and even outlasted much of the Abbey itself. Beneath its lovely garden lie the long-forgotten graves of pilgrims and craftsmen, and events washed over it. Little wonder then that it refused to burn in the great fire of 1624. Forging armour for Bruce's freedom fighters, casting iron for power looms, or training pilots to fight the Luftwaffe, Abbot House has seen it all.

From a Guide to Abbot House.

INSCRIPTION ON LINTEL AT THE ENTRANCE IN NORTH STAIRTOWER OF ABBOT HOUSE

Sen Vord is thrall and thocht is fre
Keip veill thy tonge I coinsell the

DUNFERMLINE ABBEY

This great Benedictine house owes its foundation to the saintly Queen Margaret, and the foundations of her modest church remain beneath the present nave, which is a splendid piece of late Norman work, obviously by masons from Durham. The site of the choir is now occupied by a modern parish church, but at the

21

east end of this the remains of St. Margaret's shrine, dating from the thirteenth century, are seen. King Robert Bruce is buried in the choir, his grave marked by a modern brass. Of the monastic buildings, the ruins of the frater, kitchen, pend and guest-house still remain, and are of much beauty and interest. The guest house was later reconstituted as a royal palace, and here Charles I was born.

V. GORDON CHILDE AND W. DOUGLAS SIMPSON,
Illustrated Guide to Ancient Monuments. Vol 6, Scotland, 1959.

Dunfermline Abbey

From *THE TESTAMENT OF CRESSEID*

Quod sho: "Fair chyld gae to my father dear,
And pray him cum to speak with me anone."
And sae he did, and said: "Dochter what cheer?"
"Allace" (quod sho), "Father my mirth is gone."
"How sae" (quod he); and sho can all expone
As I have tauld, the vengeance and the wraik
For her trespass, Cupid on her culd tak.

He luikit on her ugly lipper face,
The whilk before was white as lillie flour,
Wringand his handis oftimes he said allace
That he had levit to see that wofull hour,
For he knew weill that there was nae succour

22

To her seikness, and that doublit his pane.
Thus was there care aneuch betuix them twane.

When they togither murnit had full lang,
Quod Cresseid: "Father, I wald not be kend.
Therefore in secreit wyse ye let me gang
Into yone hospitall at the tounis end.
And thither sum meat for cheritie me send
To leive upon, for all mirth in this eard
Is frae me gane, sic is my wickit weird."

Then in ane mantill and ane baver hat,
With cup and clapper wonder privily,
He opnit ane secreit yett, and out thereat
Convoyit her, that nae man suld espy,
Into ane village half ane mile thereby,
Deliverit her in at the spittaill hous,
And daylie sent her part of his almous.★

ROBERT HENRYSON

THE RETOUR O TROILUS

Ill-thriven laund, eenou ti me sae deir,
Cauldrife an courin fae the daithlie drow:
Lang-cowpit waas, owre mony ghaists ablow;
An yit I mynd the bluid-reid wine flowed here.

Why suid my youth feel auncient as thir stanes,
Why suid my prieven virr sae faa fae me,
Why suid my een, aye vieve efter the years
O cruellest sains o fechtin, cryne fae this sicht?
Here at the burn that mirrors me throu time
I leuk upo mysel as yince I wis,
Like faither ti a son, leevin ti daid,
The past o Troy an Troilus. In this glen
I cam late ti manheid: she, the forehand

★'The "secreit yett", or postern gate, refers to a gate in the south wall of the Monastery, Priory Lane, long since removed. "Ane village half ane mile thereby" undoubtedly refers to the Nethertown, and the "spittail house" to St Leonard's Hospital.' Ebenezer Henderson, ed., *The Annals of Dunfermline*, Glasgow, 1879, pp.169-170.

o aa the queans that ti my breist hae won,
The rare Cresseid; she, whase flichterin hairt
Felt delicat as ony timorsome mavie
That liltit owre oor heids; she, whase quick muivement
In guidin me ti a neuk, wis sib ti the con
Wha derts athort the pad, then vainishes…
Here at the sacrit crag upon whase brou
Oor forefowk biggit the dun an steidit Troy,
We were twa glaikit bairns: the merest smitches
That an ever-twynin linn
Kests on the seg as, tentless, it hauds forrit.
Aye bydes the auld Troy fir Troilus. In this cave
A queen made her orisons, an we oor luves;
Whaur noo it's daurk, then glintit my leman's een,
Whaur noo it's foustie, then fufft her body's scent,
Whaur noo hing cobwabs, she cleikit me in her hair.

Thon wis the folly that first made me wyce,
Chynged the heich-heidit halflin wha kent aa
—Or sae he thocht—aboot the courss o the state,
The macklik policies o peace an weir,
Wha laucht at ither men whase caa ti airms
Wis ti the airms o a mere paramour:
This wis your Troilus, buirdliest chiel o the land,
The rival o the gods, an no yit twinty!
I staun the day, at the hinner-en o youth,
Amang the wrack o a kinrik an its fowk:
Ithers hae peyed mair deirlie nor mysel
Fir weivin o mishanter an mistak,
That skufft us fae oor umwhile eminence
Ti the untentit airts ayont the port:
Rickle o bleckened banes i the aise-midden
Or gruggilt beauty i the lazar-houss.

Cuid I but see the thristin o new life
Up throu the cleavin o the palace flair,
Ti spreid o emerant i the simmer sun—
Yit I maun leave, an come here nevermair.

But I can hear this ferlie: a deid-bell.
There's mair come back ti murn here nor mysel,

Aa wabsters, an the last o their trade in Troy,
In slaw processioun:
Yin o their feres is ti be yirdit sune.
Nane sall gang pairt o the road and then gie owre,
Nane but sall cairry the corp, or else attend it,
Ti the kirkyaird aa the wey.
                                        Abune us nou
The crummlin temple floats upon the haar.

Owre mony ghaists, fir me ti gang my lane;
Owre mony ghaists, the kinrik's, an my ain.

TOM HUBBARD

THE BINK

Here on ma bink she sat i the lang day's waarmin
i the suimmer suin, or the merle wi its chirlin wheeple
mirlit i the bonnie garth o the glen wi cheer
cuid lowse Auld Tyme fae kanglin dool an care;
in tid wi Tyme itsel, an merle-lyke, charmin
masel alow Dunfaurline's Abbey steeple,
knappin a byeuk o verse fae her dentie mou,
she sat, as gentle as the croodlin gloamin doo.

But it's cauld noo, oh, but it's cauld alow the winter muin,
an the dirl, dirl, dirl o the Abbey bells dings doore
ower the snoovein snaw; and I'm as lanelie as a tinkler's shuin
for his socks as he traiks braid Scotland's shires attoore.
Eeh! but it's cauld, cauld. Gin I were a man I'd be as seik's
a duag, but a bink?—wae's me for her twaa waarm cheeks.

T. S. LAW

ODD GOINGS-ON IN DUNFERMLINE TOUN

In yon gusty toun on the slope, folk
slip aff it, disappear,
gang in an oot o' doors
fast, like in auld films,
uphill thin man roon corner,
doonhill fat man intae shop,

25

lassies intae trees,
auld men intae ruins,
rinnin boys intae the grun,
auld wife gangs heilster gowdie
wi a puckle leaves,
is blawn richt ower the kirk steeple.
John Bell walks straucht through
the shut gates o' Pittendreigh Park,
never heard tell again an naebody speirs why?

GEORGE BRUCE

BEGGING PEACOCK, DUNFERMLINE

A beau, a blue and mobile island
behind the car park, by old postern doors,
stepped forward gingerly to take a chip
I stepped forward gingerly to throw.

One had moulted high on rooftops,
could fly less cumbered than the full-clad bird
whose tail-coat, fashionable as absurd,
followed where he placed his gnarled grey claws.

Out of bounds, discarded feathers
visible at distance as white haulms,
green shot with garnet, ivory, apricot,
a medieval picnic spread on stones.

The begging peacock tempted us to move
from postmodernity to seedy splendour.
We scoured precincts in a late-night wander,
our fingertips hot from the touch of food.

SALLY EVANS

From *MOBY-DICK: OR THE WHALE (1851)*

Chapter 65: The Whale as a Dish

That Mortal Man should feed upon the creature that feeds his lamp, and, like
Stubb, eat him by his own light, as you may say; this seems so outlandish a thing
that one must needs go a little into the history and philosophy of it.

It is upon record, that three centuries ago the tongue of the Right Whale was esteemed a great delicacy in France, and commanded large prices there. Also, that in Henry VIIIth's time, a certain cook of the court obtained a handsome reward for inventing an admirable sauce to be eaten with barbecued porpoises, which, you remember, are a species of whale. Porpoises, indeed, are to this day considered fine eating. The meat is made into balls about the size of billiard balls, and being well seasoned and spiced might be taken for turtle-balls or veal balls. The old monks of Dunfermline were very fond of them. They had a great porpoise grant from the crown.

The fact is, that among his hunters at least, the whale would by all hands be considered a noble dish, were there not so much of him; but when you come to sit down before a meat-pie nearly one hundred feet long, it takes away your appetite.

HERMAN MELVILLE

CITY DEVELOPMENT: DUNFERMLINE AS TOWN AND CITY, 1904

There are more immediate reasons for the development of smaller cities. They lie in the hygienic, the intellectual and aesthetic, the moral and practical advantages of country life over city life, particularly for the young. The environs of every large city show how willingly paterfamilias faces a long and fatiguing double journey in addition to his daily work in order to give his children even a tincture of rustic upbringing; and the same principle is still more manifestly at work in the Garden City movement...

Looking, then, at the position of Dunfermline upon the map, so conveniently situated upon great lines of communication also, we see that it may readily combine the advantages of an ancient and revived Culture City with those of a modern Garden City, and these independently even of the new maritime city and garden city projected in the immediate neighbourhood.

Here, in fact, at Dunfermline (especially assuming some future lowering of railway fares, of which the Hungarian zone system and other improvements give promise) we have the most convenient residential centre within easy reach of Edinburgh. For the large class of retired people, and for those whose main concern it is to educate their children, Dunfermline, especially in view of the progress and initiative of its schools now being provided for, should be able to exercise a permanent attraction.

The Park is but the centre from which must increasingly radiate the lines of an enlarging web of civic improvement, not only extending town into country but fully diffusing country into town. With its charming and sheltered walks, and those afforded by the natural extension of the park, through and beyond St

27

Margaret's Glen, and gradually for miles beyond, we have ideal conditions for the invalid, the convalescent as well as for the tourist and holiday-seeker, with substantial economic import to the city.

PATRICK GEDDES, *City Development. A Study of Parks, Gardens, and Culture-Institutes. A Report to the Carnegie Dunfermline Trust,* 1904.

DUNFERMLINE IN MY BOYHOOD

Dunfermline has long been renowned as perhaps the most radical town in the Kingdom, although I know Paisley has claims. This is all the more creditable to the cause of radicalism because in the days of which I speak the population of Dunfermline was in large part composed of men who were small manufacturers, each owning his own loom or looms. They were not tied down to regular hours, their labours being piece work. They got webs from the larger manufacturers and the weaving was done at home.

These were times of intense political excitement, and there was frequently seen throughout the entire town, for a short time after the midday meal, small groups of men with their aprons girt about them discussing affairs of state. The names of Hume, Cobden, and Bright were upon every one's tongue. I was often attracted, small as I was, to these circles and was an earnest listener to the conversation, which was wholly one-sided. The generally accepted conclusion was that there must be a change. Clubs were formed among the townsfolk, and the London newspapers were subscribed for. The leading editorials were read every evening to the people, strangely enough, from one of the pulpits of the town. My uncle, Bailie Morrison, was often the reader, and, as the articles were commented upon by him and others after being read, the meetings were quite exciting.

These political meetings were of frequent occurrence, and, as might be expected, I was as deeply interested as any of the family and attended many. One of my uncles or my father was generally to be heard. I remember one evening my father addressed a large outdoor meeting in the Pends. I had wedged my way in under the legs of the hearers, and at one cheer louder than all the rest I could not restrain my enthusiasm. Looking up to the man under whose legs I had found protection I informed him that was my father speaking. He lifted me on his shoulder and kept me there.

…The change from hand-loom to steam-loom weaving was disastrous to our family. My father did not recognize the impending revolution, and was struggling under the old system. His looms sank greatly in value, and it became necessary for that power which never failed in any emergency—my mother—to step forward and endeavor to repair the family fortune. She opened a small shop in Moodie Street and contributed to the revenues which, though slender, nevertheless at that time sufficed to keep us in comfort and "respectable."

I remember that shortly after this I began to learn what poverty meant. Dreadful days came when my father took the last of his webs to the great manufacturer, and I saw my mother anxiously awaiting his return to know whether a new web was to be obtained or that a period of idleness was upon us. It was burnt into my heart then that my father, though neither "abject, mean, nor vile," as Burns has it, had nevertheless to

> Beg a brother of the earth
> To give him leave to toil.

And then and there came the resolve that I would cure that when I got to be a man.

ANDREW CARNEGIE, *Autobiography*, 1920

THE AULD GREY TOON. A STORY OF URBAN DECLINE

When I last looked at the ruins of the old co-operative society store in Randolph Street, Dunfermline, I never imagined they might have a role to play in the fate of the nation. Last week we were invited to believe they had. In some political version of chaos theory, Labour's loss of the Dunfermline by-election was ascribed to "local issues", including higher tolls on the Forth Road Bridge and Dunfermline's "ailing town centre". Hence Dunfermline's sad High Street may be the beginning of the end for Gordon Brown.

Who knows? But the ruins of the co-op were certainly strong evidence of the ailment. Through the 1990s they stood tall, shuttered and abandoned on both sides of the street, the kind of buildings you might find near a closed railroad depot in a small American town. Nobody knew what to do with them. And yet the buildings had once been so busy, so central to this town (as other co-ops were to other towns) that the co-op was known simply as "the store", again like something out of the American west. In the tea-room on the top floor my grandparents celebrated their golden wedding with "store" steak pie. For years I remembered my mother's "store" dividend number. The Scottish Co-operative Wholesale Society supplied own-brand goods to local co-operative societies across the country. Store tinned rice pudding, store mops, store custard creams, store slicing sausage ("I love a sausage, a co-operative sausage" was a street song, to the tune "I Love a Lassie"), all of them often delivered in store vans to the outlying villages.

But the co-op is only one small part in the story of Dunfermline's decline and the disappearing purpose of so many similar towns and high streets throughout

Britain. The fact that it has happened to Dunfermline is proof that nowhere is immune to the onward march of Wal-Mart and Tesco and new patterns of human behaviour, because Dunfermline is an old town and was once a handsome one, and not the kind of thrown-together product of Victorian industrialism that looked shameful and disposable to the town-planners of 40 years ago. Its roots are medieval. King Malcolm III, who defeated Macbeth, had his home in Dunfermline. Robert the Bruce is buried in its abbey. Charles I was born in its palace. This part of town, the royal-religious quarter, has buildings dating in part from the 12th century. In later centuries the settlement spread out from here along a ridge that runs west to east. Coal was discovered early, but that lay on the outskirts. At the heart of the town lay the cottages, and later the steam-driven factories which produced the finest table linen in Britain. By the 19th century it had a nickname: "The Auld Grey Toon."

I was educated here, at a school that boasted origins in the 15th century and the poet Robert Henryson (then known as a "Scottish Chaucerian") as one of its first masters. From the classrooms on the north side you looked up to the ridge and its horizons of factory chimneys, church spires, and the French-Baronial tower of the City Chambers. To the west lay the Glen, a private estate that had been prettified in the early 20th century into a public park. To the east lay the original Victorian public park, laid out by Joseph Paxton, and behind it the smoke of the locomotive sheds just over the hill. Between these two stretches of green, and invisible to the eye, ran the High Street, where almost everything happened. It is worth remembering what the centres of small and medium-sized towns actually provided and how hard it would have been to live without them.

Until the 1970s, Dunfermline's town centre held banks, the law court, the local newspaper office, four cinemas, a dance hall, the centre of local government, hotels and inns, a grand post office, two bus stations (the two railway stations were further off), several newspaper cryers (Edinburgh's *Evening News* and its *Dispatch*, Dundee's *Telegraph*), magnificently appointed public toilets and libraries, large churches, cafés, public baths. As to shops: a bookseller, various tailors, greengrocers, licensed grocers (the poshest, Bruce and Glen, smelled of newly ground coffee and stale wine), haberdashers, confectioners, butchers, bakers, milliners, electricians, ironmongers. All of these had a loyal clientele—people who would, say, disparage the mutton pies of Allen's in favour of Stephen's. On a Saturday, the High Street was filled with people and it was tedious to frown into shop windows as your parents chatted (again, again!) to couples they'd met by chance, and who may not have been seen since 1948.

As a teenager, I privately disparaged the High Street as "provincial". Now I see how much I owed it; my first long-trousered suit from Burton's, a prized jacket in black corduroy from Russell's, afternoons in Joe Maloco's drinking coffee and looking at girls. Scott's Electricals had a record department with listening booths, like the one where Vic works in A Kind of Loving (or the adulterous wife in Strangers on a Train), and it was there that I first heard and bought the Everly Brothers. The bookshop, Macpherson's, lay down the Regal Close next to the town's biggest cinema and rambled over several rooms. Shelves outside held the second-hand stock; I once picked up a leather-bound collection of Rupert Brooke for a pound.

It would be easy to say that what ended this life was the exhaustion of the mines, the collapse of the linen industry, the closure of the nearby dockyard. But it wouldn't be true. What ended it wasn't poverty but rootless wealth. In the 1980s the shopping and entertainments habits of Dunfermlinites moved east with their cars, to the multiplex and superstores that were built just off the M90. The High Street filled up with charity shops, its decent Georgian and Victorian architecture largely demolished and replaced with what the Penguin series, *The Buildings of Scotland,* describes as "developers' shanty-town".

Today, out near the motorway, you can stand in the car park of Tesco's and look back across the housing estates to Dunfermline's remaining spires, remembering that beneath your feet was the place of Sunday walks: high farmland and curlews now replaced by a cornucopia of imports—and an empty, dead town in the west.

IAN JACK, *The Guardian*, 18th February 2006.

Inverkeithing to Kinghorn

INVERKEITHING, 1963

After the Union of the Parliaments in 1707, to evade customs duties levied on imports, merchants and fishermen alike took to smuggling on a grand scale. Most of the inhabitants of the Fife coast involved themselves in the game of "free trade". The "Kingdom of Fife" had always a sea-going population, and a greater percentage of the people of Fife than of any other county served in the Navy during the Napoleonic Wars. The brilliant eighteenth-century admiral, Samuel Greig, of whom it has been said that he created rather than improved the Russian fleet, spent most of his life working indefatigably at every department of the Russian Navy and its economy until it was one of the most formidable in Europe. He was a native of Inverkeithing.

Inverkeithing has many seventeenth-century houses; Fish Teas can be had in one inscribed *1688 God's Providence is our Inheritance*. Three streets part at the Mercat Cross, given to the town in the fourteenth century by Annabella Drummond, Queen of Robert II. St Peter's Church still has its twelfth-century tower and contains a font carved with stone angels gripping heavy coats-of-arms, a gift from the same queen. Because she sometimes resided there the Grey Friars Hospitium has also been called the Palace. It is still something in the nature of a hospice, a municipal one graced with such civic notices as *County Library, Milk at Clinic from Now On, No Spitting Please Surely You are all Old Enough to Know Better* and *Don't take Papers away till they are Read*. The monks would surely have approved.

LESLEY SCOTT-MONCRIEFF, *Scotland's Eastern Coast. A Guidebook from Berwick to Scrabster*, 1963.

THE BONNY EARL OF MORAY

The slaying of the Bonny Earl of Moray in 1592 is without doubt the most celebrated single incident in the long history of the parish [of Dalgety]. The victim was James Stewart, the son of Lord Doune, who became the first Earl of Moray in the present line. This title came to him in 1581 through his wife who was the elder daughter of the previous earl, the famous Regent Moray. James VI recognized James Stewart's right to the title and indeed conferred an annual pension on the couple. (Although a street, Regents Way, commemorates his name, the Regent Moray, half-brother of Mary, Queen of Scots, had no connection with the parish.)

The granting of this title, and the lands in the north which went with it, brought upon the young earl the hostility of George sixth Earl of Huntly, one of the most powerful magnates in Scotland. Huntly, who was chief of the Gordons and "the cock of the north", resented Moray's attempt to move into what he thought was his fiefdom. The result was the onset of a bitter feud. But Huntly was not the Earl of Moray's only enemy. Lord Thirlestane, the king's chancellor, was another, and, it was alleged, so too was the king. Although it was said that the Queen, Anne of Denmark, thought highly of Moray, it is hardly likely that he was, as the ancient ballad put it: "the queen's love". More seriously, however, he was suspected of plotting treason, along with his cousin, the notorious trouble-making Francis Stewart, Earl of Bothwell.

In February 1592 James VI issued a warrant which seemingly was used to justify the arrest of the earl who was residing at that time at Donibristle. Incredibly the person who undertook this task was the Earl of Huntly, the arch-enemy of the Bonny Earl. With a large party of retainers, he left Holyrood and pretended to be heading for Leith, where a horse-race was to be held. But he soon changed direction and turned towards the Queen's ferry. Arriving at Donibristle on that fatal 7th day of February, Huntly found that Moray's dwelling was very ill guarded. The Bonny Earl had with him only Patrick Dunbar, the Sheriff of Moray, and a few followers. Donibristle was then just a humble manor-house. We can see from the inset view in the death portrait that it consisted of a small complex of buildings of no great height within a low, walled enclosure. It was part house and part farm, with some of the structures serving as stables and byres, and at one extremity a barn and adjacent stackyard. By no means could it be described as a place of strength. Huntly sent forward a messenger, a Captain John Gordon, to parley, but Moray refused to surrender himself. Then a shot rang out. One of Moray's men had fired and shot the messenger, felling him with a seemingly fatal wound. The battle was on. It was one though that could have had virtually only one outcome. With fuel in plenty at hand, the attackers stooked up corn from the nearby yard and set the house on fire.

For the inmates it was an appalling dilemma—whether to remain inside and be burned to death or to emerge and be hacked down. They decided to try to break out. Dunbar went out first, hoping that in the darkness he would be taken for the earl, his master. As Dunbar fell to the swords of the Gordons, the Bonny Earl ran out from a gate at the seaward side of the house. The Earl then sought a hiding-place among the rocks down at the shore, and in the dark of night he might well have succeeded. Unfortunately for him, however, the silken threads of his tippet or hood had caught fire, thus revealing his hiding place. The pattern of events is not all that clear, there being different versions of the tale. One later version says that Moray was stabbed by one of Huntly's men, who then, supposedly, forced his chieftain to strike a blow himself. The supposed dying words of the Bonny Earl "You hae spilt a better face than your awin" make a good story but are of dubious veracity.

The good looks and the accomplishments of the Bonny Earl (this "lustieth youth" according to one contemporary) are commemorated in the famous ballad.

> He was a braw Gallant,
> And he rid at the Ring,
> And the bonny Earl of Murray
> Oh, he might have been a King.

There are plenty of indications that the murdered earl was a popular figure. The people of Edinburgh were enraged, the more so since they were mainly Protestant, and the deed had been carried out by the Gordons, a staunchly Catholic clan. Also out for vengeance was Lady Doune, the mother of the victim. She brought her son's corpse, and that of his friend Dunbar, to Edinburgh to display them to the people at the market cross.

James VI, however, unwilling to make an enemy of so powerful a subject, kept out of her way, and took no effective steps to punish the Earl of Huntly. Huntly, a longtime royal favourite, was needed by the king to maintain the balance of power within his fractious realm. One of the minor participants was, however, made to suffer for the misdeeds of his master. This was Captain John Gordon, who had been badly wounded at the onset of the affray and left for dead. Ironically it was Lady Doune who took him in and saved his life. This was no humane gesture on her part. Her purpose was to mend his wounds and succour him, so that he could be put on trial. Thanks to pressure from the Protestant faction, John Gordon was brought to a speedy trial and execution at the cross of Edinburgh.

One sacrificial victim was not enough for Lady Doune, however. Nor was she the sort of person to give up very easily. She refused to bury her son's corpse. Thwarted in her demand for vengeance, Lady Doune did not long survive her son. As one commentator observed, Lady Doune, "seeing no justice like to be obtained for the murder of her son, left her malediction upon the king, and died in displeasure". Meanwhile the earl's body remained unburied. Preserved in a lead coffin it lay in the kirk at Leith as a ghastly reminder of his untimely end and of the need for vengeance. Eventually, six years after the murder, the Privy Council commanded the Stewart family to have the corpse buried "in their ordinary place of sepulture" within twenty days under pain of rebellion.

When she had been banned from displaying her son's body, Lady Doune had commissioned a portrait depicting the corpse of the Bonny Earl, all slashed and bloody. This life-sized "vendetta picture", which was painted on fine linen, was presented to the king. Set inside a scroll, apparently coming from the dead man's mouth, are the words: "God revenge my cause". Inset in one corner of this unique picture is a group of blazing buildings: presumably Donibristle House, stables, and associated farm buildings. Many years later the two families were reconciled: ironically through the good offices of the king. Indeed the new Earl of Moray set the seal on the reconciliation by agreeing to marry Lady Anne Gordon, the daughter of his father's assassin.

Yet it would have been impossible to forget what happened on that dark winter night, and the ballad has ensured that succeeding generations also know something of the tragic end of the Bonny Earl of Moray. Although the oldest version in print appeared only in 1733, this lament undoubtedly would have been composed at or near to this time of feud and bloody vengeance.

ERIC SIMPSON, from *Dalgety Bay. Heritage and Hidden History,* 1999.

THE BONNY EARL OF MORAY

Ye Highlands and ye Lawlands.
    Oh, where ha'e ye been?
They ha'e slain the Earl of Moray
    And they laid him on the Green.

Now wae be to thee Huntly,
    And wherefore did ye sae;
I bad you bring him wi' you
    But forbad you him to slay.

He was a braw Gallant,
    And he rid at the Ring;
And the bonny Earl of Moray,
    Oh! he might have been a King.

He was a braw Gallant
    And he play'd at the Ba',
And the bonny Earl of Moray,
    Was the Flower amang them a'.

He was a braw Gallant
    And he play'd at the Glove,

> And the bonny Earl of Moray,
> Oh! he was the Queen's Love.
>
> Oh! lang will his Lady,
> Look o'er the Castle-Down,
> E'er she see the Earl of Moray
> Come sounding through the Town.

ANONYMOUS

FORDELL, JULY 1856

The people employed at Fordell Coal-works observed Friday last as a holi-day, being the anniversary of the emancipation of miners from slavery in this country, in 1788. They assembled at the works, and marched in procession to Fordell House, the seat of G. W. M. Henderson, the proprietor of the works, accompanied with two instrumental bands, and eight banners, bearing suitable inscriptions. On their arrival at the house they received as usual, by the kindness of the proprietor, a substantial refreshment; and after expressing a wish that he might enjoy long life, prosperity, health, and happiness, and disposing of several other toasts, dancing commenced on the lawn, and was kept up with great glee nearly two hours, when they again formed in procession, and returned to a park in front of the manager's house. After giving Messrs. Cole and Robertson three hearty cheers, and received another refreshment, dancing was resumed, and kept up with much spirit till late in the afternoon, after which the proceedings terminated with a ball in the school-room. We were sorry to see a number of the men very much intoxicated, but glad to learn that they did not belong to the works, but had come from other places, and mixed with the workers, for the purpose of getting a guzzle.

Dunfermline Journal, 25 July 1856. Quoted by **ERIC SIMPSON**,
Dalgety Bay. Heritage and Hidden History, 1999.

ST BRIDGET'S SEVENTEENTH-CENTURY KIRK

After the Reformation, the little parish kirk, situated along the shore from Doni-bristle, underwent some alteration. As there was not too much space within the existing four walls, the more important landowners were anxious to find fitting accommodation for themselves and their families. Some had small lofts or galler-ies built, where they and their families could sit perched high above the rest of the congregation. Others constructed aisles, which projected outward from the

St Bridget's Kirk

main part of the kirk. We find in 1646 the laird of Fordell securing permission to build a loft on the north side of the kirk "becaus he had ane great familie".

It was Alexander Seton, first Earl of Dunfermline, who built the most notable of these additions. This is the two-storey building at the west end of the kirk, which has a burial vault on the ground floor and a handsome "laird's loft" above it. The Seton aisle, which can be compared to a small tower house, dwarfs the simple kirk which it adjoins. When Alexander Seton died in 1622, his body was conveyed across the Forth to Dalgety House, which was his favourite residence, and duly buried at St Bridget's with great pomp and ceremony. (To gain some idea what a seventeenth century nobleman's funeral procession would have looked like, see a depiction of a similar ceremony in the Museum of Scotland in Edinburgh.) The earl's remains were placed, as he had requested, in "ye little ile biggit be myself at the kirk of my house at Dalgetie." When three hundred years later the vault was opened by masons in the employment of the Earl of Moray, six large lead coffins were found. One was identified as being that of Chancellor Seton. Another, an unusually large coffin, held the remains of the third Earl of Dunfermline, who died in 1672. Also identified was the coffin of the first earl's widow, Dame Margaret Hay, Countess of Dunfermline and Callender, whose body had been conveyed from Fyvie Castle in Aberdeenshire so that she could be buried beside her late husband.

Although unroofed and windowless, the Seton loft is still an impressive structure. One can readily picture the Seton family retiring from their gallery into the handsomely furnished main chamber, with its fine, panelled stone walls. This loft received further adornment when Chancellor Seton's widow installed stained glass windows. But the kirk session did not welcome ornamentation of this kind. In 1649 the Countess of Dunfermline and Callender was rebuked by the kirk session, who saw this as a statement of theological defiance. This austere body of men insisted that she remove these windows with their "idolatrous and superstitious images". Next to the main chamber, there is a small retiring room with a fireplace. There the laird's family could warm themselves and take refreshments on the cold winter Sabbaths, while the more humble parishioners just had to thole the cold in a bare and unheated kirk.

ERIC SIMPSON, from *Dalgety Bay. Heritage and Hidden History*, 1999.

SIR PATRICK SPENS

The king sits in Dunfermling toune,
　　Drinking the blude-reid wine:
"O whar will I get a guid sailor,
　　To sail this schip of mine?"

Up and spak an eldern knicht,
　　Sat at the kings richt kne:
"Sir Patrick Spens is the best sailor
　　That sails upon the se."

The king has written a braid letter,
　　And signed it wi his hand,
And sent it to Sir Patrick Spens,
　　Was walking on the sand.

The first line that Sir Patrick read,
　　A loud lauch lauched he;
The next line that Sir Patrick read,
　　The teir blinded his ee.

"O wha is this has don this deid,
　　This ill deid don to me,
To send me out this time o' the yeir,
　　To sail upon the se!

"Mak haste, mak haste, my mirry men all,
　　Our guid schip sails the morne:"
"O say na sae, my master deir,
　　For I feir a deadlie storme.

"Late late yestreen I saw the new moone,
　　Wi the auld moone in hir arme,
And I feir, I feir, my deir master,
　　That we will cum to harme."

O our Scots nobles wer richt laith
　　To weet their cork-heild schoone;
Bot lang owre a' the play were playd,
　　Thair hats they swam aboone.

O lang, lang may their ladies sit,
　　Wi their fans into their hand,
Or eir they se Sir Patrick Spens
　　Cum sailing to the land.

O lang, lang may the ladies stand,
　　Wi thair gold kems in their hair,
Waiting for thair ain deir lords,
　　For they'll se thame na mair.

Haf owre, haf owre to Aberdour,
　　It's fiftie fadom deip,
And thair lies guid Sir Patrick Spens,
　　Wi the Scots lords at his feet.

ANONYMOUS

A CAT IN ABERDOUR

In 1819 a favourite Tabby belonging to a shipmaster was left on shore, by accident, while his vessel sailed from the harbour of Aberdour, Fifeshire, which is about half a mile from the village. The vessel was a month absent, and on her return, to the astonishment of the shipmaster, Puss came on board with a fine stout kitten in her mouth, apparently about three weeks old, and went directly down into the cabin. Two others of her young ones were afterwards caught, quite wild, in a neighbouring wood, where she must have remained with them until the return of the ship. The shipmaster did not allow her, again, to go on shore, otherwise it is probable she would have brought all her family on board. It was very remarkable, because vessels were daily going in and out of the harbour, none of which she ever thought of visiting till the one she had left returned.

CHARLES HENRY ROSS, *The Book of Cats*, 1868.

ST FILLAN'S KIRK, ABERDOUR

"Just to enter St Fillan's is to worship". Small, rectangular church whose Romanesque nave and chancel were built *c*.1140. The simple chancel survives, a joy to behold. The aisle, necessitating the formation of the fine arcade, and the porch were added c.1500. Later additions included the 16th-century Gothic window in the west gable, the sturdy belfry with pyramid roof, 1588, and the north aisle (now used by choir) in 1608. Neglected, it was deroofed c.1790, and derelict until restored with care in 1926 by W. Williamson.

GLEN L. PRIDE, *The Kingdom of Fife. An Illustrated Architectural Guide*, 1990.

Inchcolm Abbey

INCHCOLM ABBEY

Sometimes described as "The Iona of the East," the remains of this monastery stand on a green island in the Firth of Forth. It was an Augustinian house, founded about 1123 by Alexander I. Caught in a gale, he was driven to Inchcolm, and took shelter in a hermit's chapel. This has been thought still to survive in a small and rude cell west of the abbey. The monastic buildings, which include a fine thirteenth-century octagonal chapter house, are the best preserved in Scotland. The nave of the church is Norman, but it was gradually extended eastward, until a complete new cruciform church took the place of the early one, which was then converted into a dwelling house. In the original choir was discovered the finest example of thirteenth century wall-painting left in Scotland, showing a funeral procession of clerics. The abbey was much harried by English fleets, and the canons were frequently obliged to flee to the mainland. West of the abbey is a fine hog-backed stone.

V. GORDON CHILDE and W. DOUGLAS SIMPSON,
Illustrated Guide to Ancient Monuments, Vol 6, Scotland, 1959.

INCHCOLM

This morning I saw
on the waters of the firth a diving
bird I never saw before, turning a nimble
loop to enter the wave, and the wonder
of green light filtering down.

What was it like
for the king—Alexander, when the boat
nearly foundered, and all might be tossed
in the swirl of the sea? Did he kick
his boots free? Did he call out by his
birth-right for men to assist him?
And how did they come to land?

None of these
things is reported with surety. But fear,
if he felt it, was followed by gratitude—
the gift of an abbey for the Inch of
St. Colme. "Lord, I was drowning. What
better can I build than this?"

Then chancel
and chapter-house rose on the island.
Stone flourished on stone. Upon the table
slab of the altar five wounds were cut
like stars.

"It is foolish
to shrink from what cannot be avoided." Such

safety was the bread they broke to sustain
them. "Quicquid mali finxerit lingua"—
whatever evil the tongue composes
conscience may overcome.

What warmth
of the spirit must have wound itself
round them—only one social fireplace
beyond that in the kitchen—though something
burned in the wall of the Choir, when
Richard the Bishop had his heart interred,
so his ardour became part of the fabric
of the building.

Today we have
come to the natural harbour on the lee
side of the isthmus, climbed iron rungs
to the pier-head, and followed a path
by the narrow neck of land to stand
in the grave-yard, the Relig Oran,
surveying what replaced Colme's
daub and wattle traces.

Kings of Scotland
and Norway, Danes that were slain
at the "bickering" of Kinghorn, all
have their rest here: some at a stiff
price, and some with due reverence.

It is still broad
day when I take the night stair from
the ruins of the Church, and climb with my
sleeping child in my arms to the Dormitory,
talking and singing, though she sleeps,
and sitting for a while in the recess
at one of the windows.

The last day of January,
and the weather being mild, the water will
offer no menace as as we make our return, not even

when we pass by Aberdour, crossing the Deep of
that impious Mortimer, long consigned in his shroud
of lead, well short of the island for which
he possessed, by gift of his forebear,
the right of interment.

But now there burns
in my arms a burden lightly borne—her
hair like a cresset or candle in the dark,
her hair like a badge or blazon—my
darling girl.

Within this high-vaulted
chamber I show you to shadows: the dreaming
forms of those who sleep like mist, who looked
in their own way for what holds true beneath
the bewilderment of surfaces.

It was a cold, uncertain,
isolate existence; lived besides in a tangle
of dogma, that wrapped in despite: rock,
grass, flesh, sea-thrift and sea-bird.

I hold you here
against distortion; knowing that love
is work, is hard we know as breaking stones,
and desperate distance even when
the breath comes close.

But patience
with yourself; patience with the love
of others is a law worth learning, a thread
of blood I give you as a bond; and the water
of the world to enter and feed there as in
your natural element, taking your place
and composure, folding life around you,
your father's breath like a tide
on the margin of sleep.

ALEXANDER HUTCHISON

43

BOSWELL AND DR JOHNSON ON INCHKEITH

In crossing the Frith, Dr. Johnson determined that we should land upon Inchkeith. On approaching it, we first observed a high rocky shore. We coasted about, and put into a little bay on the north-west. We clambered up a very steep ascent, on which was very good grass, but rather a profusion of thistles. There were sixteen head of black cattle grazing upon the island. Lord Hailes observed to me, that Brantome calls it L'ile des Chevaux, and that it was probably "a SAFER stable" than many others in his time. The fort, with an inscription on it, MARIA RE 1564, is strongly built. Dr. Johnson examined it with much attention. He stalked like a giant among the luxuriant thistles and nettles.

JAMES BOSWELL, *Journal of a Tour to the Hebrides*, 1785.

INCHKEITH: AN ISLAND OF DERELICTION, 1984

Before going off to canoe in the Caledonian Canal last summer I had a quick paddle out to Inchkeith to see everything was in working order. It was, fortunately, and Inchkeith proved its usual variety of interests. It was not a solitary trip.

You could almost judge the distance by the bird life. There was a diving world of gannets first, then the flurry-scurry of solemn puffins, then the cliff-cacophony of gulls. Porpoises surfacing just behind the canoe nearly gave the dog and I heart failure. The cormorants were hung out to dry on the skerries as we turned in to the harbour.

Alongside was the Sea Cadets' boat, a fishing boat and several yachts. A skin-diver was splashing along and four boys were birling about in a dinghy. It was like something out of Arthur Ransome and one could almost believe in Inchkeith as a children's adventure playground.

But that was an oily-calm day on a Sunday morning in the holidays. A cliff-girt island at the mercy of the weather, covered in derelict fortifications and diseased birdlife is hardly a promising place for that sort of proposed development, especially in today's economic climate. Those of us who live on or by the Firth of Forth had a quiet chuckle when the sales blurb suggested it would make a pleasant place to stay and commute to Edinburgh. It is the seabirds who do that, with fatal results. Rummaging in Edinburgh's rubbish results in botulism and in dry summers like the last one the result is gull corpses all over the island. I counted over 50 dead birds while walking up to the lighthouse.

When Carlyle visited Inchkeith he mentioned the keepers having families with them and pasturing cows. It was *L'ile des Chevaux* to the French troops garrisoned there in the sixteenth century because their horses thrived on the grass. I don't think horses or cows would appreciate it now and the keepers' families have lived in Edinburgh for many years. The light is going to be made automatic so even the cheery keepers will depart. It will then be left to the white-washing seabirds. Perhaps it should be made into an effective, controlled bird island. Whatever happens the gulls desperately need to be culled.

Lighthouses are oddly pleasing objects, which is just as well considering their conspicuous nature. Inchkeith flickers its light across my bedroom window of nights—or blasts us with its scrawny new foghorn. When the foghorn started in 1899—it blared continuously for 130 hours before being turned off the Fife shore to face the sea.

Our resident starlings are excellent mimics (they can even make the sound of the garage door skarting across the concrete drive) so when I noticed one doing a very good peewit imitation I grabbed a tape-recorder and switched on. After a few minutes the bird flew off and I rewound to play what I'd picked up. It came loud and clear all right —the blare of Inchkeith! It takes several diesels to build up the pressure for this blast so it is best heard from some miles away.

The first mention of a light is 1635 when, at a May Island submission for a light, Inchkeith was also mentioned. The May got theirs the next year. Inchkeith had to wait 170 years. When they did begin, no time was lost, for construction started in May 1803 and the light was lit in September 1804. Perhaps because of its closeness to Edinburgh, quite a few innovations were introduced at Inchkeith over the years. The optics and mechanics are a bit beyond me, but R. W. Munro's *Scottish Lighthouses*, 1979, is the easiest source book in general and Inchkeith, both generally and for its light, is covered in a booklet by David Marshall, *L'ile des Chevaux,* which was issued in 1983.

The name Inchkeith probably derived from connections with the Earl Marischal family. A Caithness chief was granted the island in 1010 for his help in defeating the Danes. It was forfeited from them in the reign of James V and given to Sir Andrew Wood of Largo, who was governor during the "Rough Wooing" by Henry VIII of England. It remained a defensive base from that time to fairly recently.

Mary Queen of Scots was hustled off to France rather than marrying Henry's son Edward (one of the interesting IFs of history, had it come off) but Edward's "Protector" Somerset seized Inchkeith during his Pinkie campaign and French troops had a bloody time regaining control. A dated stone of 1564 marked its rebuilding, and though little remains this stone now is inserted over a gateway in the lighthouse's courtyard.

It changed hands many times and really only became a military base again in 1860 when batteries were built and these were increased early this century so that Leith, Inchkeith and Kinghorn formed an unattractive array of guns for any sea marauders.

As my home stands on the site of one of the shore batteries I feel a certain involvement with this history. (A neighbour has turned a bunker into an underground billiard room!) Inchkeith was more used during the Second World War, since when time, decay and vandalism have left the island neglected, overgrown and derelict.

On a previous paddle out to Inchkeith I jokingly said I'd bring back a ladder or something to complete a stile over the garden fence. We came back towing a fishing boat's companionway and several other beachcombed items. Inchkeith is still a fearsome place for shipping. The skerries facing Lothian are particularly bad, being completely covered at high tide. Now they are marked by the hulk of the *Switha* which ran aground there a few years ago.

Inchkeith is a sad place now: "a suitable place for treatment," as they say.

HAMISH BROWN, *Weekend Scotsman*, 1984.

PIERRE DE CHASTELARD AND MARY, QUEEN OF SCOTS

Rossend (or Burntisland) Castle has been through many vicissitudes and it is fortunate to have survived long enough to be excellently restored by two partnerships of architects, now the Hurd Rolland Partnership, for use as their offices… The road up to the castle passes the railway line as it makes its way through a cutting made into the castle rock. A little further up is a heavy two-arched gateway; even the heavier arch is, I have learned, no older then the mid-nineteenth century and the date on the other clearly says "Rossend 1932"… A side path begins alongside uncared-for back gardens and goes round behind the castle to a terrace on the edge of the rock that gives a view straight into the great shed and engineering activities of the company that builds constructions for the oil industry.

I found it difficult to envisage the geographical layout here when the young Mary, Queen of Scots walked by the shore of this promontory, as monks had done before her. It is easier to envisage her indoors and dancing with gentlemen of France and Scotland. When the Queen, not out of her teens we have to remind ourselves, returned to Scotland from the less Calvinistic French court, with her came a young poet, Pierre de Chastelard. For the Queen he played the poet and she accepted his poems. John Knox described their relationship in the worst possible terms. It does seem that the young man did hide himself in the Queen's bedroom at Holyrood and that he repeated this folly at Rossend. Execution followed in St Andrews and Knox wrote, "Such was the reward of his dancing." Another historian of the kirk, David Calderwood, wrote succinctly, "poore Chattelat was convoyed to Sanct Andrews, putt to an assize, and beheaded, the 22d of Februar 1563." Knox, who cannot be trusted in such matters, says the man confessed his guilt, but other witnesses say he rejected a religious confessor and, head held high and quite straight-backed, climbed onto the scaffold where he read a poem on death by the great Ronsard.

Je te salue, heureuse et profitable Mort
Des extrêmes douleurs médecin et confort.

I greet you happy and profitable Death
The healer and comforter in extreme pain.

We are also told that, looking to the place where he thought the Queen was, his last words were, "Adieu! Most beautiful and most cruel princess of the world." Or more dramatically sorrowful, "O cruelle dame."

DUNCAN GLEN, *Illustrious Fife. Literary, Historical & Architectural Pathways and Walks*, 1998.

FROM A LETTER TO THE SPEAKER OF THE HOUSE OF COMMONS

The greater part of the army is in Fife, waiting what God will further lead us. It hath pleased God to give us Burntisland, which is indeed very conducive to the carrying on of oure affaires. The town is well seated, pretty strong, but marvellous capable of further improvement in that respect without great charge. The harbour, at a high spring tide, is near a fathom deeper than at Leith, and doth not lye commanded by any ground within the town. We took three or four men-of-war in it, and I believe 36 or 40 guns. Commissary-General Whaley marched along the seaside in Fife, having some ships to goe along the coast, and hath taken great store of artillery and divers ships. The enemy's affaires are in some discomposure, as we hear. Surely the Lord will blow upon them.

OLIVER CROMWELL, 1651.

MARY FAE BURNTISLAND

Mary Somerville, mathematician, astronomer, classicist, 1780-1872

It wull ivver be thus
(Cum bio-chips in heids or genetic enhancement):
Ee o the individual
Spyin life-creation,
The shiver-reek o jist bein
Reels baith spirit an intellect.

"Didna aye gang tae the Kirk
When she gaed up the Kirkgate",
But ye wir near eneuch
On san, fuit soakin

A see yersel—
Ocean breaths
Maun mak ye stert.

No fer wumman
Aw thon learnin;
Whaur the minds o men fail
Sea an land tak ower.

ANDREW McNEIL

Quhen Alexander our kynge was dede,
    That Scotlande lede in lauche and le,
Away wes sons of ale and breid,
    Off wyne and wax, of gamin and glee.
Our golde was changit in to lede.
    The fruit failyeit on everilk tree.
Christ succoure Scotlande, and remede,
    That is stad in perplexitie.

Quoted by **ANDREW OF WYNTOUN** (c.1355-c.1395) in
his *Original Chronicle of Scotland.*

KINGHORN: DEATH OF A KING

To the castle of Dunbar, across the Forth, there arrived on a night in March nearly 700 years ago a seer named True Thomas of Earlston. Challenging him to exercise his powers of prophecy, Patrick, Earl of Dunbar, jestingly asked him if the morrow would see any event of note. Thomas made this answer: "Alas for tomorrow, a day of calamity and misery! Before the twelfth hour shall be heard the sorest wind and tempest that ever was heard of in Scotland."

By noon the next day news came to Dunbar that King Alexander III had fallen to his death from the cliffs at Kinghorn on the south coast of Fife. He had left Inverkeithing on horseback on his way to the Tower of Kinghorn. His attendants had advised him against riding along the top of the cliffs in the dark, but he refused their advice to halt at Inverkeithing and galloped on through the dusk. On the crest of the 150-foot-high precipice of Kinghorn Ness near Pettycur his horse stumbled, and the King was thrown over the cliffs. His attendants found him dead, his body caught on a wedgeshaped piece of rock 40 feet above the beach.

His death was indeed a sore blow for Scotland, precipitating a bloody conflict for the throne. The simple cross that was set up to mark the tragic scene has long since gone, and the present memorial to Alexander—a tall cross by the sea's edge—was unveiled by the Earl of Elgin in 1887. This memorial is one of the chief items of interest at Kinghorn, which long ago lost its ancient castle and also lost the tower of St Leonard's, which after the Reformation was used as Town House and jail and was removed to make way for the present Town House.

At one time Kinghorn was described as "one of the meanest and most irregular towns in Fife" but in the last century the burgh was rebuilt and repaved, and it is today a neat Forth-side town, which, despite thriving local industries, is still recognised as one of the holiday resorts of Fife.

The Kingdom of Fife and Kinrossshire, edited by **THEO LANG**, 1951.

From *AN ELEGY ON PATIE BIRNIE*

In sonnet slee the man I sing,
His rare engine in rhyme shall ring,
Wha's laid the stick out o'er the string
    With sic an art,
Wha sang sae sweetly to the spring,
    An rais'd the heart.

Kinghorn may rue the ruefou day
That lighted Patie to his clay,
Wha gart the hearty billies stay,
    And spend their cash,
To see his snowt, to hear him play,
    And gab sae gash.

ALLAN RAMSAY

West Fife's Towns & Proudest Industry

From *LICHT ATTOORE THE FACE**

Ay,
thare were the faces I myndit,
faces set as onie new aix-aidge is set,
as broken redd is set at the wark,
hard-aidged an sherp, ticht, clean;
and een watchin, quick, judgein,
hainin for daein, the kennin ot
yin wi the movement o the heid
as the licht is attoore the face
fae tree tae strap tae cundie or pack.
And efter the wark,
at piece-timm, the faces
cleir and easie as suimmer air,
innocent as bairns haein a byte
efter a dook in the burn,
thon ease ower something duin,
for piece-timm is the tyme o peace o myn,
mair sae whan the wark is furrit,
an tyme, lik toom hutches,
bydes its wheesht
for better days an nae bother.

Paer fellas,
that you deed thon wy,
blattert wi a mash o soond an stoond,

wi the grace o kennin an daein
cut shorte as bairntyme
is cut clean across wi manheid;
man's ancient tyme
gethered-up in fire at ye,
thae geological millennia
o physics an chemistrie roosed-up,

*The poet laments his fellow-miners (neebors) killed in the Lindsay pit explosion in 1957.

deevin the still, black centre o doom
wi blast an wrack,
a seik, ondeemas doom
that shairlie is nae weerd
for paer guid-hertit folk
suid aye gan doon as caunnilie
as easement made ye the kyndlie men;

gan doon as quate's the lang, lang years
can dwyne awo as soondless
as saun gowd-picklin
that a bairnie's fingers
whaur the rocks can echo
the saft tyde syllables
o the day-lang, lyfe-lang suimmer sea,
gan doon tae an easement
wi yer deid saft on yer broos
as a mither's fingers on her bairn's powe.

Nane o ye
had yer fuhll o Tyme,
but Tyme foued itsel
wi ilka yin o ye
in a greed o pooer nae man
can weel contend wi,
wi a gudgein o the takkin
nae man can weel content,
a sklander o "gie-me"
as selfish as the lang years
you and oor kyn gied aa
for nocht, for aa was wrocht.

Paer fellas,
that you deed thon wy.

T. S. LAW

THE CULTURE OF FIFE MINERS

Towards the end of the 19th century and into the 20th century, coal was still the
mainstay of industrial power. New deep mines were sunk, some near existing

towns and villages, leading to in many cases an expansion of existing towns and villages. Fife prospered at this time although the struggle was sometimes bitter. Fife coalfields were the first to achieve the eight hour day in 1870. Research any of the cultures of the miner in this period and the story will be the same; only the characters change. During this time you will find the miners active in developing a range of sports like forming quoits pitches. Curling was another sport miners pursued. In my small mining village we had two curling ponds. Football, even from its infancy, was a culture in which miners led the field. In Fife nearly every town and village has a history of achievement in football involving miners. Pigeon racing was a very popular sport with miners. Every village had its Pigeon Club and some still exist today. Whippet racing was another sport very popular in the early 20th century. It led on to greyhound racing between 1930-1960, there were eight flapping tracks in Fife. Now there is only one. As the pits closed so died the sport. Most collieries supported a pipe band, to which miners subscribed through their wages. Fife had many famous colliery bands in their heyday. Brass bands, though not as prolific, were also supported and were part of miners' culture. As you read this overview of the cultural history of the Fife miners you will realise the effect and speed of the disappearance of mining in Fife. There are no pits left in this area. Soon there will he no miners left to tell the story. We would like to build a Heritage Centre in Fife to inform and educate our children and grandchildren of a way of life that is no more and should be remembered with pride.

DAN IMRIE, from *A Mining Disaster 1901-2001*, 2001.

A LAKOTA SIOUX IN COWDENBEATH HIGH STREET
23rd AUGUST 1904*

I hae seen it aa afore:
juist anither mining toun.
I kenna its name,
for I am faur fae ma ain kintra.

The shawled wimmem
shriek crousely,
trauchled by thair
peely-wally bairns.

Outside the pubs
the men in thair bunnets

---

*William Cody's *Wild West Show* visited Cowdenbeath on this date.

douk moustaches in wersh beer,
cough, spit and blaspheme.
They stowe the causeys,
hing out o winnocks,
shin up biggins like raccoons,
pale-faces wi coal-stour war pent.

A big white cuddie up-ends:
the great Buffalo Bill hisel
is neir flung on his erse
when a hauflin runs out afore him.

Thay raip the yirth, get peyed
back in disaster, puirtith and daith,
these brithers o mine wha cheer us on
tae re-enact our genocide.

WILLIAM HERSHAW

6 COWDENBEATH KOIPU

a fiver ivry time
oan ir aff the leash
jesus christ doun Rose St
25 quids wurth

> ye seen ir pushin a pram doun Drylie St
> ye seen ir oan ir weddin day
> ye seen ir mither
> ye seen ir wi ir curlers in, daen dishes
> ye see it aw, then

doun Beath pokey
aw ma teesh fell oot
Am sayin nuthin
mibbe get aff

> see Stenhouse Street
> aw A iver did wis
> die

53

stick in it the skaill, son
ir ye'll no get oan a guid project
when ye leave

> here's me doun ti ma last
> staunin outside Woolies
> awbdys walkin past mi
> ignorin mi
> the bastards

IAN W. KING

THE OLD ARCADE

In these years Cowdenbeath was rapidly changing from a straggling village into a compact mining town. Old property was being pulled down. New buildings were going up everywhere. Right in the centre of the town an arcade had appeared with shops on either side, a hall at the foot, and a hotel above the shops. The entrance to the hotel was half-way down the arcade. Grandmother Greig's place of business had had to change with the changing town. Her old quarters were demolished and from 1902 onwards she rented the hotel above the grand new Arcade... Actually the Arcade was a rickety structure of cheap red brick with a grey cement facing. Almost as soon as it was built it began to need heavy repairs and to look grimy and old. The most startling feature about it was the "pug" engine from the pit that went shunting to and fro at all hours of the day and night immediately below the hotel windows. The hotel was built where the level crossing cuts across the main street of the town. Strangers unaccustomed to the noise of the pug had small chance of an unbroken sleep.

But from my third to my eighth year (while it was my home) that second description gives no more idea of how the Arcade looked and felt to me than the first does. From a child's angle it was a superb place. All kinds of exciting things were always happening. Particularly in the hall at the foot of the Arcade, I could never be sure what new magic I would find there. At that time touring companies were much in vogue. These were the great days of melodrama. *East Lynne* was drawing oceans of tears all over the country. The mining folks enjoyed a good cry as well as the next. They crowded into the Arcade hall and by their patronage made it just worth while for companies travelling between Edinburgh and Perth to make Cowdenbeath an irregular place of call.

Between the visits of the theatre companies the hall was let to any organization that could pay the rent. It sheltered with equal readiness religious meetings, bird shows, wedding parties, funeral suppers, trade union lodge meetings, temperance lectures, the Clarion Scouts and the then-active Social Democratic Federation. I patronized any of these gatherings that took my fancy. My mother was busy in the hotel upstairs. My father who had leased the hall was equally busy downstairs. No one had much time to pay attention to my comings and goings. I was able to run about pretty much as I pleased; and to collect a most dazzling range of acquaintances...

It is customary now to decorate nursery schools, and the infants' department in ordinary schools, with gaily coloured toys and pictures. There was little or none of that when I went to school. That was in the years just before the war. School was a drab, grey routine of unexciting tasks. But the stern old gods that frown down from our northern skies were cheated in my case. The Arcade was my real nursery school. Its actors and actresses, rats and ventriloquist's doll, its toy shop and Chinaman with a real pigtail, form in my memory a frieze of as grotesque and brightly coloured pictures as any child's artist could devise.

JENNIE LEE, *This Great Journey: A Volume Of Autobiography*,
1963.

THE KELTY CLIPPIE

She's just a Kelty clippie, she'll no tak' nae advice
It's, Ach drap deid or Ah'll bile yer heid or Ah'll punch yer ticket twice
Her faither's jist a waster, her mither's oan the game
She's just a Kelty clippie but I love her just the same

I've traivelled thru' this country from shore to shining shore
From the swamps of Auchterderran tae the jungles o' Lochore
But in all these far-flung places there's nane that can compare
Wi' the lily of Lumphinnans, she's ma bonnie Maggie Blair

Frae the pyramids up in Kelty tae the mansions in Glencraig
We've trod the bings together in mony's the blyth stravaig
Watched the moonlight over Crosshill, trod Buckhaven's golden sand
And mony's the happy hoor we spent in Lochgelly's Happy Land

I remember on the 8.15 that night o' romantic bliss
I says, Ho Mag, nip yer fag, gie's a wee bit kiss
She didnae tak' this kindly, didnae like ma chaff
Being a contrary kind of bird she said, Come oan, get aff

She hasnae got nae culture, she drives me roon' the bend
Sittin' in her big armchair readin' the People's Friend
Her lapels are full of badges frae Butlins down at Ayr
And she goes to the bingo every night with the curlers in her hair

But things is a wee bit better noo, I've gone and got the ring
I won it frae Jim at the pitch an' toss, last night at the Lindsay Bing
Wi' her wee black hat and her ticket machine ma hairt she did ensnare
She's the lily of Lumphinnans, she's ma bonnie Maggie Blair

JOHN WATT

A PIPER OF LOCHGELLY, 1812

About a century ago a drunken piper, returning from Lochgelly Fair, was arrested by the intoxicating vapour. Instead of availing himself of the propitious moment to learn the probable duration of Christmas doles, penny weddings, and other customs in which it may be supposed a person of his calling would be especially interested, the infatuated mortal only testified his exhilaration by a tune upon the bagpipe… A signal punishment, however, awaited him for the unhallowed use to which he had applied the divine *afflatus*. The instrument with which he had perpetrated the profanation was destined, alas! never more to pass from his lips. The night was stormy; but the louder the wind blew, the louder did the enchanted bagpipe sound along the strath. Such a piping was never heard either before or since… Nor did the music cease till sunrise, when a peasant going to his work found the piper lying dead at the mouth of the cave, with the chanter between his lips.

JOHN SIMPKINS, *County Folklore: Fife*, 1912.

HILL OF BENARTY

Happy the man who belongs to no party,
But sits in his ain house, and looks at Benarty.

Sir Michael Malcolm of Lochore, an eccentric baronet, pronounced this oracular couplet in his old age, when troubled by the talk about the French Revolution. As a picture of serenity and neutrality in an old Scotch country, it seems worthy of preservation. On the top of Benarty, which rises above the former bed of Loch Ore (for the lake is now drained, and its site converted arable land), there were formerly held games, which all the shepherds of Fife and other neighbouring counties attended. They brought their wives, daughters, and sweethearts, and having a plentiful stock of victuals, kept up the fête for a few days, bivouacking upon the ground during the night. The chief games were the golf, the football, and the *wads* [a pledge or hostage]; and what with howling, singing, and drinking, after the manner of an Irish *patron,* they contrived to spend the time very merrily. The top of Benarty is flat, and sufficiently extensive for their purpose.

From *Popular Rhymes of Scotland*, 1826, edited by
ROBERT CHAMBERS

From *GAGARIN WAY*

Tom (*to Frank*) There's a street called Gagarin Way in Lumphinnans.

Frank Is there?

Gary Yuri Gagarin the astronaut.

Frank Cosmonaut.

Gary Ay?

Frank (*to Gary*) The Soviets called them cosmonauts. (*Pause.*) The twelfth of April, nineteen sixty-one.

Gary (*to Frank*) Ay?

Frank (*to Gary*) The twelfth of April, nineteen sixty-one. (*Beat.*) The date that Yuri Alekseyevich Gagarin orbited the earth. (*Pause.*) It was my sixteenth birthday.

Eddie Aye? (*Beat.*) Ya cunt, how the fuck did your mum manage tay arrange that?

Pause.

Tom (*to Frank*) It shows the influence though. (*Beat.*) Doesn't it?

Frank Influence?

Gary Of communism.

Frank Does it?

Tom Why Gagarin Way... if it isn't?

Eddie First primate way a surname in space.

Gary First Soviet in space.

Eddie Gagarin Way. (*Beat.*) Armstrong Road. (*Beat.*) Aldrin Avenue. They'll be fucking everywhere.

Gary First Soviet in space.

Tom (*to Eddie*) Why else would they do it?

Eddie Well, never having known the spiritual communion ay squatting underground in the dark, hacking at a two-inch seam, I dinnay think I'm qualified tay comment on their motivation. *(Beat.)* But I suppose... when the sputnik went up the locals thought we werenay far away fay worldwide Soviet domination... they've thought, ya cunt, we better get a street named after one ay them before the Red Army rolls in and starts whacking suspected capitalist collaborators.

Gary *(to Tom)* They did it because he was a hero of the Soviet Union.

Eddie They backed the wrong fucking horse.

Pause.

Frank The wrong horse. *(to Tom)* Was that your conclusion?

Pause.

Tom When I was doing it... the dissertation... I went... I arranged this interview... up in Cowdenbeath, in this sheltered housing place, with a few of these old union guys. I thought they were all going to be like Joe Stalin's best mates.

Frank Joe Stalin killed all his best mates.

Tom I'm talking to all these old guys and I start being like all professorial... like... saying to them, do you not hold that much of the radicalism of the miners grew from the fact that they were forced to work underground and were therefore further alienated by the oppressive nature of the darkness... They all just looked at me like I'm daft... one of them goes, no, son, you have to go underground, that's where the coal is. *(Beat.)* I felt a right idiot. *(Beat.)* There was this other bloke who told me he got blacklisted from the pits... I said, were you victimised because of your political activities?... He goes, no, I hit the foreman over the head with a shovel for shagging my wife.

GREGORY BURKE, *Gagarin Way*, 2001.

THE IMAGE O' GOD

Crawlin aboot like a snail in the mud,
  Covered wi' clammie blae,
Me, made after the image o' God—
  Jings! but it's laughable, tae.

Howkin' awa' 'neath a mountain o' stane,
  Gaspin' for want o' air,
The sweat makin' streams doon my bare back-bane
  And my knees a' hackit and sair.

Strainin' and cursin' the hale shift throu,
    Half-starved, half-blin', half-mad;
And the gaffer he says, "Less dirt in that coal
    Or ye go up the pit, my lad!"

So I gi'e my life to the Nimmo squad*
    For eicht and fower a day;
Me! made after the image o God—
    Jings! but it's laughable, tae.

JOE CORRIE

SCOTTISH PRIDE

It's fine when ye stand in a queue
at the door o' the "Dole"
on a snawy day,
To ken that ye leive in the bonniest
land in the world,
The bravest, tae.

It's fine when you're in a pickle
Whether or no'
you'll get your "dough",
To sing a wee bit sang
o' the heather hills,
And the glens below.

It's fine when the clerk says,
"Nae 'dole' here fir you!"
To proodly turn,
and think o' the bluidy slashin'
the English got
at Bannockburn.

JOE CORRIE

*When Corrie read the poem for the BBC, the broadcasting authorities did not challenge his reference to the pit owner Nimmo, assuming that 'Nimmo' was a Scots word beyond their comprehension.

FOR JOE CORRIE

"Arise, ye sleepy-heids, dawin is the day,
the coal is derned doun deep," said Jenny Gray,
"It's liggin in its lair, aw weet an cauld,
it's bidin on brave lads, baith strang and bauld."
The wyndin gear o Glencraig girned and roared,
"Wha'll delve and howk ma kist and treisure hoard?
It's spreid out in the yirth ablo for miles,
the fuel that gars an empire blaw and bile."

The Happyland woke up and steeked its lums,
the dozy miner's raws yawned reeky thrums.
Syne Mary moaned, "for fire there's aucht a feu…"
and Nelly threiped and craiked, "wha'll pey whit's due?"
But Lindsay sabbed and shook his airn heid,
"The price o coal is nine puir miners deid."

WILLIAM HERSHAW

From *REBUS'S SCOTLAND: COURT AND SPARK*

John Rebus grew up in Cardenden. In fact, he grew up in Bowhill, in the same cul-de-sac as me, if the books are to be believed:

> Rebus had been born in a pre-fab but brought up in a terrace much like this one *(Dead Souls,* p 36).

In *The Black Book* we learn that Rebus's father was born in a miners' row. My own father's family had lived in just such a house, built quickly and in long rows to identical designs. These were thrown up in order to get as many men into the area as possible early in the twentieth century, when the demand for coal seemed insatiable:

> Cardenden had grown up around coal, hurried streets constructed in the twenties and thirties to house the incoming miners. These streets hadn't even been given names, just numbers. Rebus's family had moved into 13th Street. Relocation had taken the family to a pre-fab in Cardenden, and from there to a terraced house in a cul-de-sac in Bowhill *(Dead Souls,* p 306).

This was my family's own trajectory, though I think my father had actually lived on 17th Street rather than 13th. I was born in a pre-fab in Cardenden, my parents moving us to Craigmead Terrace immediately after it was built. All the same, Rebus's past is inextricably linked to my own, and this can some-times cause problems. For example, in *The Black Book* I say that Rebus went to school in Cowdenbeath. By the time we reach *Dead Souls,* some six years later, we find that he actually attended Auchterderran Secondary School, and left at fifteen to enlist in the Army. Both cannot be true, and comprise a conflation of my own education. I spent the first two years of my high school education at Auchterderran, then was offered a place at Beath Senior High in Cowdenbeath. (The brightest few kids were decanted from all the Junior Highs in the area: one friend, cleverer than me in most subjects, chose not to switch, a decision which surely coloured his whole life thereafter.) In using my own life as a template for some of Rebus's background, errors sometimes do creep in. I even had to be careful over the naming of Auchterderran: in Rebus's time, it was a Secondary School; by the time I arrived there, its status had been altered to Junior High—a blessing, in that the badge on the breast-pocket of the school blazer no longer bore the letters ASS.

Here is Rebus on the west-central Fife of the early 1990s:

Like the towns and villages around it, Cowdenbeath looked and felt de-pressed: closed down shops and drab chainstore clothes. But he knew that the people were stronger than their situation might suggest. Hardship bred a bitter, quickfire humour and a resilience to all but the most terminal of life's tragedies. He didn't like to think about it too deeply, but inside he felt like he really was "coming home". Edinburgh might have been his base for twenty years, but he was a Fifer. "Fly Fifers" some people called them. Rebus was ready to do battle with some very fly people indeed *(Dead Souls,* p 127).

I've said in the past that I started writing the Rebus books in order to make sense of Edinburgh, my adopted home. But Fife plays a major role in several of Rebus's adventures, and comprises the majority of his memories. I wonder now if all this time, I've really been trying to make sense of my own upbringing, in order better to understand myself.

Not that Rebus is me, of course, and the title of this book—*Rebus's Scotland*—is a trick typical of a novelist. Since Rebus is not real, how can the country where he lives be real? The only way to make sense of my fictional universe is to say something of myself, showing how my autobiography merges with his, and how my sense of Scotland and Scottishness becomes his. This then is a story of the relationship between Rebus, his creator, and the country called Scotland.

IAN RANKIN. *Rebus's Scotland*, 2005.

Auchtertool to Kirkcaldy, Dysart, Wemyss, Methil, Buckhaven and Leven

ST. ANDREW IN THE WINDOW

Written while walking by Auchtertool Kirk on Easter Monday morning.

As I walked out last Monday morn,
thought I felt the winter pass
the sun shone on an empty kirk
I saw St. Andrew in the glass.
While here the lilting sunlight fell
that warms the seed
that grows the wheat
the fruitless harvest o' the gun
leases men
like litter
in the street.

Still the peesie takes the air
sees the spring sun melt the snow
will we ever, ever learn
St. Andrew in the window?

They say the simple are the sick,
They say the wounded are the lost
and worthless is the refugee!
They hide the scars that hide the cost.
So if the gun robs you of choice
then you've nothing left to choose
but join St. Andrew on the road
with only burdens left to lose.

They walk the streets of Bosnia
Chile and El Salvador
their M16's, the barrels hot
take the recoil, count the score.

So when the pressure is too high
When the spirit starts to crack
St. Andrew feels the rough-hewn wood
of the cross upon his back.

Still the peesie takes the air
See the spring sun melt the snow
Will we never, ever learn
St. Andrew in the window?

ANDY SHANKS and JIM RUSSELL

LETTERS FROM AUCHTERTOOL AND EDINBURGH*

On 5th November 1844 Jane Welsh Carlyle wrote to her cousin Mrs. Russell about her cousins:

> Jeannie and Maggie are at Auchtertool with Walter, leading a good-for-nothing life there, according to their own account of it—engaged in perpetual tea-drinkings with "people whom they take no pleasure in," and "making themselves amends in sitting at home with their feet on the fender talking over the absurdities of the said people." Whereupon I have written Jeannie a very scolding letter, which it is to be feared will share the common fate of all good advice in the world—make her angry at me without putting a stop either to tea drinkings with people "we can take no pleasure in" or the idle practice of sitting with her feet on the fender, and still worse practice of laughing at one's neighbours' absurdities rather than one's own.

Whilst in Kirkcaldy in 1849 Jane Carlyle was stung by a wasp at Whytehouse but she went out to Auchtertool to see her Uncle John at the manse and whom she had described as "John, sole uncle of my house and heart!". A letter describes the suffering that wasp imposed upon her:

> I suffered horribly in silence and all night; the trophies of the world would not let me sleep—not one wink. However, I went next day to Auchtertool with my hand in a poultice, being still determined to come out of that on Monday, and unwilling to go without saying farewell to my poor uncle, whom it is likely enough I shall never see again.

On 7th August 1856, from Edinburgh, she wrote to her husband:

*Jane Carlyle, the wife of Thomas, was staying at the manse of Auchtertool, where her cousin was minister; he lived in the manse with his two unmarried sisters.

63

The day before yesterday I bathed at Kirkcaldy and walked to Auchtertool after, and the fatigue was too much, and I was up to nothing but lying on the sofa all the evening, which delayed my packing till yesterday morning; and I got up at half after six to leave time for a letter, and it was not till "prayers" were over and breakfast ready that I was ready to sit down. Immediately after breakfast the dogcart came round to take me to the half after eleven boat...

In 1857 her Auchtertool visit again included some bad health:

Oh heaven! Or rather, oh, the other place! I am degenerating from a woman into a dog, and feel the inclination to bark—bow-bow!wow! Ever since I came here I have been passing out of one silent rage into another at the things in general of this house. Viewed from an invalid point of view they are enough to make one not only bark but bite, were it not that in other people's houses one has to assume the muzzle of politeness... Is it possible that the change of a cook can make the difference betwixt now and last summer, or is it the increased irritability of my nerves that makes it? Or are my cousins getting stupefied for want of something to stir their souls, on this hill-top?

In August 1859 both Mr. and Mrs. Carlyle were at Auchtertool House:

Whether it be that the air of Auchtertool suits me better than that of Aberdour, or that my having my kind little cousins within cry is a wholesome diversion, or that I required a continuance of country air to act upon my feebleness, I am not competent to say, nor is it of the slightest earthly consequence what the cause is, so that the effect has been as I tell you.

JANE WELSH CARLYLE

SCHOOL IN LINKTOWN, KIRKCALDY

Ae storie, ruifed wi' reddish tile,
Some shuttered windows an' a door.
The inside juist as plain in style—
The Maister's desk an' three legg'd stule,
A press, a kist, a big blackboard,
A clock, some shelves whaur slates were stored.

Quoted by **JAMES W BEALE** in *A History of the Burgh and Parochial Schools of Fife*, edited by Donald J. Withrington, 1983.

Kirk Wynd, Kirkcaldy

From *ISRAEL POTTER: HIS FIFTY YEARS OF EXILE*

This was Sunday. The ships held on. During the afternoon, a long tack of the *Richard* brought her close towards the shores of Fife, near the thriving little port of Kirkaldy.

"There's a great crowd on the beach, Captain Paul," said Israel, looking through his glass. "There seems to be an old woman standing on a fish-barrel there, a sort of selling things at auction to the people, but I can't be certain yet."

"Let me see," said Paul, taking the glass as they came nigher. "Sure enough, it's an old lady—an old quack-doctress, seems to me, in a black gown, too. I must hail her."

Ordering the ship to be kept on towards the port, he shortened sail within easy distance, so as to glide slowly by, and seizing the trumpet, thus spoke:

"Old lady, ahoy! What are you talking about? What's your text?"

"The righteous shall rejoice when he seeth the vengeance. He shall wash his feet in the blood of the wicked."

"Ah, what a lack of charity. Now hear mine:—God helpeth them that help themselves, as Poor Richard says."

"Reprobate pirate, a gale shall yet come to drive thee in wrecks from our waters."

"The strong wind of your hate fills my sails well. Adieu," waving his bonnet—"tell us the rest at Leith."

Next morning the ships were almost within cannon-shot of the town. The men to be landed were in the boats. Israel had the tiller of the foremost one, waiting for his commander to enter, when just as Paul's foot was on the gangway, a sudden squall struck all three ships, dashing the boats against them, and causing indescribable confusion. The squall ended in a violent gale. Getting his men on board with all dispatch, Paul essayed his best to withstand the fury of the wind, but it blew adversely, and with redoubled power. A ship at a distance went down beneath it. The disappointed invader was obliged to turn before the gale, and renounce his project.

To this hour, on the shores of the Firth of Forth, it is the popular persuasion, that the Rev. Mr. Shirrer's (of Kirkaldy) powerful intercession was the direct cause of the elemental repulse experienced off the endangered harbor of Leith.★

> **HERMAN MELVILLE**, from *Israel Potter: His Fifty
> Years of Exile*, 1855.

KIRKCALDY OF GRANGE

Upone the thrid day of august the year of god mccclxxiii yearis the laird of graunge foirsaid captane of the castell of Edinburgh with his broder James Kirkcaldy quha was tane at the blacknes as I have schawin and eftir none thay war hangit schamfullie as traittouris to the kings grace. The laird of graunge himsellff was brocht furth of the abbay backwart in ane cok-cairt to the mercat croce quhair the scauffauld was and thair asked god forgivenes for his rebellioun bayth aganes god and the king and so was hangit with his broder Mr. James Kirkcaldy with ane that struik the cunyie [coins] callit Cok and syn thay war heiddit and quarterit and thair heidis and quarteris set upone sindrie portis, and also the secretar was tane furth of the stipill of leith quhair he lay deid the space of fourtie dayes and was brunt and quarterit be requeist of the quein of Ingland.

ROBERT LYNDSAY OF PITSCOTTIE

AT SEAFIELD, FIFE (1984)

I staun at the tour,
The mines are ahent an ablow me.

Here I'm maist intimate wi oor nation's past:
Minstrels made music within thae waas

★The Reverend Robert Shirra, a minister of Kirkcaldy, led his congregation to the town's sands to pray that the American naval adventurer John Paul Jones would fail in his attempt to invade the Scottish Coast. In his essay ' The Coast of Fife', Robert Louis Stevenson claims that Shirra's intervention took place on Burntisland beach: see *Stevenson's Scotland*, Tom Hubbard & Duncan Glen ed., Mercat Press, 2003, p.63.

Whaur noo the wind sings; deep, deep in the erd
Hae coalliers warslt ti create, as nou—
But sall they jyne the minstrels in oblivion?

Here I'm maist intimate wi oor nation's present:
Dame Scotland nurtures coalliers in her wame
That they maun nurture us, an bards unborn:
A process as organic as the cleckin
o that rich gress that growes aboot this tour's
Lang-tummilt stanes.
    —Oh ay! Are we sae shair o't?
Heid-makars still an on fail ti tak tent
o haun-makars: we maun nae assume
Destruction aye owretaen by we creators
Ettlin as yin. Fir certes, we are riven,
Riven apairt: waik makars, wichter brakkers.

Wad I were intimate wi oor nation's future.
The yin Seafield faces anither:
Inti the Forth there thrusts, crackit an snell,
A stany finger: it is the beldame Scotland
Pyntin ti Embro—Europe— an ayont.
I turn awaa in dreid:
Aroun, aiblins inby, the blinterin firth,
The gear that warks oor wrack, we're cosh ti thole.
An I micht scrieve, an coalliers micht howk,
An aa gang on firever, as we think it,
But there sail be some tummles, mair nor this tour kent;
An unco mirk, mair awesome nor thae mines;
Whan thae, whase hale delyt is in destroyin
—Wha lippen oor thowlessness—
Sall wi an artistry maist consummate
Rive the aareadies riven ti th'ultimate…

The ocean an the lift mell in a scaum,
Buirdlie but lythe: anither sain sae vaudie
At daith o day, sall hecht nae resurrection—
But gin I'm intimate wi sic a future
An wad be mair nor intimate wi anither,
I maun unite the present an the past,

Mysel wi ithers, heid, an haun, an hert,
Scotland an furth o Scotland.

I descend fae the tour,
Wi the mines ahent an ablow me.

Sall Scotland owretap her eild,
An a fresh seed stir in her wame?

TOM HUBBARD

KIRKCALDY VENNEL

not wide but
not narrow this
tiny
massive wilderness
where sun
falls most intensely
early evening when
longing
for silence and difference
peaks and I lean into
and look over
the soft sigh of the garden wall
watching
for the thrush
far away beneath fallen branches:
I hear before I see him
rush

along the closed off lane
where once
lovers walked,
between two walls,

where now the neighbourhood cats
ease their silky suppleness
beneath the entanglements
of low twisted branches

lost
to the map, this right of way
is now returned
to wildness
soothes
alleviates the stone
the carparked

our roots live

MAUREEN SANGSTER

MICHAEL SCOT (OR SCOTT)

To become Court Astrologer to King Frederick II of Sicily in the early part of the 15th Century was an extraordinary achievement for a young Scotsman; but Michael Scot was an extraordinary man. Such was his brilliance that after being educated at a Scottish grammar school and at Paris University, he went on to become the leading scholar of Western Europe.

Michael Scot was born probably between 1175 and 1180. His birthplace is not known for certain. One early historian, a Principal of Aberdeen University, stated that he was a member of the family of Scot of Balwearie near Kirkcaldy. Others hotly dispute this claim and maintain that he was born in the Border country. If the authority of the Aberdeen Principal is accepted, it is possible to consider him as a Fifer. What cannot be disputed, however, is the fact that he was certainly one of the most brilliant Scotsmen who ever lived. At Paris University, where his main interest lay in mathematics, he gained the distinction of "Supreme Master". His travels next took him to the University of Bologna in Northern Italy. From there he moved to the royal court in Sicily where he was appointed Court Astrologer and tutor to the young King Frederick II because of his knowledge of astronomy and his outstanding scholarship. (In those far-off days, there was not the same distinction as exists today between astronomy and astrology.)

Some years later, in order to widen his studies, he moved to Toledo in Spain, then a great centre of learning. The Moors, who were an Arab people, had conquered Spain. The Arab scholars were outstanding at that time, having made greater advances in knowledge than European scholars, particularly in science and philosophy. In Toledo, therefore, Scot studied under, and read, the works of the most famous of these Arab scholars. Through their influences he became interested in two further branches of science, namely chemistry and medicine. Because of his skill in languages, he readily learned Arabic. He then set about the

69

translation of many important scientific works from Arabic into Latin, which was the common language of educated Europeans. These translations, along with his own observations, have been described as some of the most important literary masterpieces of all time.

After spending ten very active years in Spain, he returned to Sicily, bringing with him a wealth of knowledge of science and philosophy acquired during his studies. He was re-appointed Court Astrologer to King Frederick II. During this period, he also translated into Latin the works of famous Greek scholars.

His fame had now spread throughout the western world and he travelled to the chief universities of Europe to give lectures. After a visit to Oxford University, he may have set out to revisit his native land. It is also possible that he died on his way to Scotland about the year 1235. Melrose Abbey is said to be his last resting-place, but there is no firm proof of this claim.

Michael Scot was not only a very industrious student; he also applied his brilliant mind to practical experiments in order to widen his knowledge. He was also a very religious man and included theology in his studies. At one stage, he was offered an important post in the church in Ireland, but this he refused because he felt that he could not fulfil his duties properly since he did not speak Erse, the Irish language.

Scot's biographers describe his work as a teacher, as a translator and as an original thinker. His extraordinary range of knowledge and interests was proved to the world by the books he wrote on astronomy (including astrology), medicine, sociology, psychology, chemistry (with alchemy), meteorology—and magic.

His interest in magic may seem surprising, but the practice of magic flourished in those days. He therefore studied the art and practices of the so-called magicians largely to warn people of the dangers arising from taking part in these activities. The art of magic was, he wrote, "the mistress of all evil, often deceiving and seducing the souls of its practitioners and injuring their bodies."

Unfortunately, many legends were told about his magical powers. These grew and were passed down through the centuries. These arose partly no doubt from his open but critical interest in magic, but in the main they were first told by his enemies and by those jealous of his great ability. The fact that he came to be called "The Wizard" or "The Magician" has created a false picture of this great genius. Sir Walter Scott is partly to blame for Scot's reputation as a magician in this country because of his references to Michael Scot as "The Wizard of the North" in his long narrative poem, "The Lay of the Last Minstrel."

The following story shows the kind of tale which was told about him. Michael Scot had an attendant spirit which he could turn into any creature that he wished. On one occasion, while his master was at war with France, King Frederick asked Scot to try to arrange a peace treaty with the French king. Turning his attendant spirit into a black horse, he jumped on its back and flew straight to Paris. When the King of France refused his request for peace, Scot asked him not to make his final decision until he had heard the black horse stamp three times. At the first hoof-stroke, all the bells in Paris started ringing. This extraordinary happening failed to move the king. At the second hoof-stroke, three towers in the king's palace crashed to the ground. By now the king was less confident and when the black horse raised its leg to stamp for the third time, the king cried, "Hold"—and agreed to sign a peace treaty with King Frederick.

This bald outline of the life and works of a very gifted man, whom the Pope described as "burning from boyhood with love of science" cannot do justice to his importance in the field of scholarship. Though knowledge has increased enormously since his day in all the sciences in which he was interested, due credit must be given to this brilliant scholar for the important part he played in leading the progress of the human mind in the search for knowledge.

RONNIE WOOD, *Famous Fifers*, 1977. Written for
use in schools.

MEPHISTOPHELEAN BALLANT-SCHERZO ON ANE FIFE LEGEND

—See that boy Faust? He scunners me,
    The toffee-nebbit cratur;
Aye on at me ti dae the wark
    That's richt agin my natur.

Says I, "You're fir the warkin fowk—
    Fine words, Faust! I'll be blunter:
Thae schemes o yours are faur abune
    The heid o your avrage punter.

"Time wis, a stair that wad unrowe
    As you'd gang up or doun;
A walin o my pliskiest deils
    Paradin throu the toun;

"Time wis, that saired the masses weill—
    Christ! Hit wis aa they kent!
They're better aff, but still they want
    The-day's equivalent.

"Like bairns that, gie thaim wine or juice,
    Be shair they'll tak whit's sweetest;

71

It's as it wis and aye'll be!
>   Faust, son, you're an élitist!"

I tak the doktor doun the shore
>   And scoop intil his haund
Whit's cheengeless as the fowk theirsel—
>   And common tae—the saund.

"Leuk there", says I, "fir nae twa grains
>   'll ever byde thegither;
Ilkane will think itsel unique
>   Though we canna tell ane frae the t'ither."

This Faust says I'm a clever deil;
>   Mony a ferlie I've wrocht;
Is there some darg I canna dae?
>   He canna think o ocht.

"I'm shair that Mephistopheles
>   Is the dabbest o dab haunds
At makkin me the finest raip
>   Frae the grains o Scotlan's saunds."

Weill! Hit's eneuch ti gar the deil
>   Defect at last ti Gawd:
I wove, and still I better wove,
>   But the stuffie wadna haud.

Hit gars an honest deil ti wish
>   He'd bade at hame in Hell!
—*Sae if Faust still wants his raip o saund*
>   *He can dae 't his bluidy sel.*

TOM HUBBARD

Some says the Deil's daid
An burraid in Kirkcaldy.
Some says he'll rise again,
An flegg the Hielant laudie.

ANONYMOUS

72

From *REMINISCENCES*

The beach of Kirkcaldy, in summer twilights, a mile of the smoothest sand, with one long wave coming on, gently, steadily, and breaking in gradual *explosion,* accurately gradual, into harmless melodious *white,* at your hand all the way (the *break* of it, rushing along like a mane of foam, beautifully sounding and advancing, ran from south to north, from West-burn to Kirkcaldy Harbour, through the whole mile's distance): this was a favourite scene; beautiful to me still, in the far-away. We roved in the woods, too, sometimes till all was dark. I remember very pleasant strolls to Dysart; and once or twice to the Caves and queer old Saltworks of Wemyss. Once, on a memorable Saturday, we made pilgrimage, to hear Dr. Chalmers at Dunfermline on the morrow. It was on the inducting a young *Mr.* Chalmers as Minister there (Chalmers *minimus,* as he soon got named); the great Chalmers was still in the first flush of his long and always high popularity: "Let us go and hear him, once more!" said Irving. The summer afternoon was beautiful; beautiful exceedingly our solitary walk by Burntisland and the sands and rocks to Inverkeithing, where we lodged, still in a touchingly beautiful manner (host the Schoolmaster, one Douglas from Haddington, a clever old acquaintance of Irving's, in after years a Radical Editor of mark; whose wife, for thrifty order, admiration of her husband, etc. etc., was a model and exemplar) four miles next morning to Dunfermline and its crowded day; Chalmers Maximus *not* disappointing,—and the fourteen miles, home to Kirkcaldy, ending in late darkness, in rain, and thirsty fatigue, which were cheerfully borne.

Another time, military tents were noticed on the Lomond Hills (on the eastern of the two): "Trigonometrical Survey!" said we: "Ramsden's Theodolite, and what not: Let us go!" and on Saturday we went. Beautiful the airy prospect from that eastern Lomond, far and wide: five or six tents stood on the top, one a black-stained cooking one, with a heap of coals close by ; the rest all closed, and occupants gone,—except one other, partly open at the eaves, through which you could look in, and see a big circular mahogany box (which we took to be the Theodolite), and a saucy-looking cold official gentleman diligently walking for exercise, no observation being possible, though the day was so bright. No admittance, however... ★

THOMAS CARLYLE, *Reminiscences*, 1881.

★Carlyle was schoolmaster at Kirkcaldy from 1816 to 1818; a plaque in Kirk Wynd marks the site of the now-demolished school. His walking companion was Edward Irving (1792-1834), a charismatic and influential preacher who was also based in Kirkcaldy at the time.

MARJORIE FLEMING, THE WONDER CHILD

She was born in Kirkcaldy in 1803, and she died when she was eight years and eleven months old. By the time she was five years old she was become a devourer of various kinds of literature—both heavy and light—and was also become a quaint and free-spoken and charming little thinker and philosopher whose views were a delightful jumble of first-hand cloth of gold and second-hand rags.

When she was six she opened up that rich mine, her journals, and continued to work it by spells during the remainder of her brief life… Her little head was full of noble passages from Shakespeare and other favorites of hers, and the fact that she could deliver them with moving effect is proof that her elocution was a born gift with her, and not a mechanical reproduction of somebody else's art, for a child's parrot-work does not move…

She spent the whole of her little life in a Presbyterian heaven; yet she was not affected by it; she could not have been happier if she had been in the other heaven.

She was made out of thunderstorms and sunshine, and not even her little perfunctory pieties and shop-made holiness could squelch her spirits or put out her fires for long. Under pressure of a pestering sense of duty she heaves a shovelful of trade godliness into her journals every little while, but it does not offend, for none of it is her own; it is all borrowed, it is a convention, a custom of her environment, it is the most innocent of hypocrisies, and this tainted butter of hers soon gets to be as delicious to the reader as are the stunning and worldly sincerities she splatters around it every time her pen takes a fresh breath. The adorable child! she hasn't a discoverable blemish in her make-up anywhere.

Marjorie's first letter was written before she was six years old; it was to her cousin, Isa Keith, a young lady of whom she was passionately fond. It was done in a sprawling hand, ten words to the page—and in those foolscap days a page was a spacious thing:

> "My DEAR ISA— I now sit down on my botom to answer all the kind & beloved letters which you was so so good as to write to me. This is the first time I ever wrote a letter in my life.
>
> "Miss Potune, a lady of my acquaintance, praises me dreadfully. I repeated something out of Deen Swift & she said I was fit for the stage, & you may think I was primed up with majestick Pride, but upon my word I felt myself turn a little birsay—birsay is a word which is a word that William composed which is as you may suppose a little enraged. This horid fat Simpliton says that my Aunt is beautifull which is intirely impossible for that is not her nature."

MARK TWAIN, 1909.

From MARJORY'S BOOK

From SECOND JOURNAL, SUMMER 1810

The Day of my existence here has been delightful & enchantinting. On Saturday I expected no less than three well made Bucks the names of whom is here advertised Mr. Geo Crakey and Wm Keith and Jn Keith, the first is the funniest of every one of them Mr. Crakey & I walked to Crakeyhall hand by hand in Innocence and matitation sweet thinking on the kind love which flows in our tenderhearted mind which is overflowsing with majestick pleasu[re] nobody was ever so polite to me in the hole state of my existence. Mr Craky you must know is a great Buck & pretty goodlooking...

I am at Ravelston enjoying natures fresh air the birds are sining sweetly the calf doth frisk and play and nature shows her glorious face. The sun shines through the trees, It is delightful

WEDNESDAY—THURSDAY 12 JULY

I confess that I have been more like a little young Devil then a creature for when Isabella went up the stairs to teach me religion and my multiplication and to be good and all my other lessons I stamped with my feet and threw my new hat which she made on the ground and was sulky an was dreadfuly passionate but she never whipped me but gently said Marjory go into another room and think what a great crime you are committing and letting your temper git the better of you but I went so sulked that the Devil got the better of me but she never never whip me so that I thinke I would be the better of it and the next time that I behave ill I think she should do it for she never does it but she is very indulgent to me but I am very ungrateful to hir

TUESDAY & WEDNESDAY

To Day I have been very ungrateful and bad and dissobedient Isabella gave me my writing I wrote so ill that she took it away and locted it up in her desk where I stood trying to open it till she made me come and read my bible but I was in a bad homour and red it so Carelessly and ill that she took it from me and her blood ran cold but she never punished me she is as gental as a lamb, to me an ungrateful girl

Isabella has given me praise for checking my temper for I was sulkey when she was kneeling an hole hourr teachin me to write...

Yesterday I behave extreme ill in Gods most holy church for I would never attand myself nor let Isabella attand which was a great crime for she often often tells me that when to or three are geathered together G[od] is in the midst of them and it was the very same Divel that tempted Job that tempted me I am sure but he resisted satan though he had boils and many many other misfortunes which I have escaped.

SONNET
TO A PUG⋆

O lovely O most charming pug
Thy graceful air and heavenly mu[g]
The beauties of his mind do shine
And every bit is shaped so fine
Your very tail is most devine
Your teeth is whiter than the snow
You are a great buck & a bow
Your eyes are of so fine a shape
More like a christians than an ape
His cheeks is like the roses blume
Your hair is like the ravens plume
His nose cast is of the roman
He is a very pretty weomen
I could not get a rhyme for roman
And was obliged to call it weoman.

MARJORY FLEMING

INVITATION TO THE VOYAGE: FIFE CHILD IN THE FIFTIES

They've long demolished the side-street by the Links
That set me journeying when I was six or so:
In my grandmother's room I sensed the East—
Willow-pattern tea-chest, ottoman, divan, I know

As concepts now, mere concepts. Then, I gasped
At the elephant knick-knack carried from Ceylon
By her brother. From her window to the Forth
I saw Pacific islets, sunset deepening on

Silhouettes of palms. Later, I lifted the mask
To a scene of funeral pyre, volcanic pit:

⋆By pug Marjory means an ape, rather than a dog.

The gong of a metal tub filled for my grandad
Black from the back-shift, coal-dust in his spit.

TOM HUBBARD

BY THE SEA

"I had a luve walked by the sea"
Sydney Goodsir Smith

We're back in the Lang Toon for the Links Market
for oor bairns, we say.

I mind takin you aince a year
in oor courtin days. An annual celebration
we walked haund in haund the haill lang length
and were on awthing.

The steamboats near swingin richt owre
and the dive-bombers daein juist that. The dodgems
to show what a deevil I was at the wheel
haein nae caur to drive you hame. And elaborate
new-fangled stomach-turners
noo forgotten. I shot an air-gun at wee pipes being
a crack-shot and threw
pingpong balls into gold-fish bowls nae bother at aw.
We bought candy floss and hot dogs
and rolled pennies doon wee slides
till aw oor money was gone.
Still we *were* laden wi prizes!

Prizes soon forgotten as we walked by the sea
and stood close thegither in the daurk
doon by the sea-waw.

Noo the bairns canna be kept back. I face the horror
o the steamboat but aince, and disgrace mysel
being seik ahint a caravan. I'm grounded.
I dinna quite live up to my Buffalo Bill image
and suspect the hot-dog stall to be unhygienic.
Still I'm a whizz-kid on the dodgems
and I can cairry aw the prizes the bairns are winnin.

77

The trouble is their money disnae seem to be runnin oot
and we'll be back themorrow nicht.

They can cairry their ain prizes.
Wan thing husnae cheynged
—we can still walk by the sea!

DUNCAN GLEN

KUNST = KAPITAL, ART = WEALTH

The world of Adam Smith is all around us, not so much in the buildings or streets we should like to associate with his life in the Central Lowlands of Scotland where he lived and worked as a leading figure of the Scottish Enlightenment, but in the very lie of the landscape, seascape and townscape which constitute the reality of his birthplace where we have gathered to honour him this day.

Despite the fact that Kirkcaldy, as his birthplace, has been transformed from a small port with 1500 inhabitants through the Industrial Revolution into a town with almost a 100% increase in population, its essential geographical features remain today those that he would recognise. There is the wide expanse of the Firth of Forth with Edinburgh and its Castle clearly discernible, the far horizon between the land mass of both the Lothians and Fife still beckoning sailors out into the North Sea towards Europe and beyond into the wide world.

Did living his boyhood on the sea's edge help make him that type of Scotsman who felt himself thoroughly and naturally at "home" in Europe? We have all been altered in some degree by the power of his thinking and writing for two centuries since his death. His spirit is surely urging us to follow his example and feel "at home" in Europe.

Unfortunately his physical presence is not as sharply focused as it must have been to those who knew and respected him in his lifetime. Despite his world fame he is a shadowy figure. We do not have an oil painting as a portrait. We have to make do with a profile in the form of a medallion of a man in the full maturity of his years, bewigged with a face characterised by a prominent aquiline nose, and the trace of a bemused smile around his mouth expressing his essentially benign nature, but not his legendary absent-mindedness and his awkward habits of speech...

He lived his life, it would appear, as a contented bachelor. We do not know his date of birth, although we do know his baptismal date—5th June 1723. He was named after his father, an esteemed Controller of Customs in Kirkcaldy, who sadly died before the birth of his son. His mother, Margaret Douglas, was the daughter of a local landowner and therefore able to live comfortably with her son in a fine imposing house, just off the High Street and within easy reach of the seashore. Alas, the house was demolished halfway through the 19th century. Little is known of what must have been a traumatic experience for him as a four-year-old when he was abducted for some unknown reason by gypsies. He was abandoned by them and found by a search party, thus saving him from the entirely unsuitable role as a gypsy boy—a mind-boggling thought!

RICHARD DEMARCO*

From *THE WEALTH OF NATIONS*

This great increase of the quantity of work, which, in consequence of the division of labour, the same number of people are capable of performing, is owing to three different circumstances: first, to the increase of dexterity in every particular workman; secondly, to the saving of the time which is commonly lost in passing from one species of work to another; and lastly, to the invention of a great number of machines which facilitate and abridge labour, and enable one man to do the work of many.

First, the improvement of the dexterity of the workman necessarily increases the quantity of the work he can perform, and the division of labour, by reducing every man's business to some one simple operation, and by making this operation the sole employment of his life, necessarily increases very much the dexterity of the workman. A common smith, who, though accustomed to handle the hammer, has never been used to make nails, if upon some particular occasion he is obliged to attempt it, will scarce, I am assured, be able to make above two or three hundred nails in a day, and those too very bad ones. A smith who has been accustomed to make nails, but whose sole or principal business has not been that of a nailer, can seldom with his utmost diligence make more than eight hundred or a thousand nails in a day. I have seen several boys under twenty years of age who had never exercised any other trade but that of making nails, and who, when they exerted themselves, could make, each of them, upwards of two thousand

*In 1995 the artist and impresario Richard Demarco became the first person from an arts background to deliver the annual Adam Smith Lecture at the then Fife College. In the course of his lecture Professor Demarco stressed the original meaning of 'wealth' as referring to the quality of life, and regretted that Smith's *The Theory of Moral Sentiments* was not as well-known as his most famous book. Demarco drew striking connections between the thought of Smith and that of the German artist Joseph Beuys (1921-86), whose interdisciplinary interests embraced an economics that was centred on human creativity rather than on profit. In the light of *The Wealth of Nations*, Demarco unpacked the implications of Beuys's description of his work as 'social sculpture'.

(Beuys's refusal to accept rigid boundaries between academic disciplines, and his insistence on the unity of art and life, have much in common with the active philosophy of Patrick Geddes, particularly as regards the latter's vision for Dunfermline – see p.27. In the same year, 1995, Demarco was also championing Geddes's ideas.)

three hundred nails in a day. The making of a nail, however, is by no means one of the simplest operations. The same person blows the bellows, stirs or mends the fire as there is occasion, heats the iron, and forges every part of the nail: In forging the head too he is obliged to change his tools. The different operations into which the making of a pin, or of a metal button, is subdivided, are all of them much more simple, and the dexterity of the person, of whose life it has been the sole business to perform them, is usually much greater. The rapidity with which some of the operations of those manufactures are performed, exceeds what the human hand could, by those who had never seen them, be supposed capable of acquiring.★

ADAM SMITH, *The Wealth of Nations*, 1776.

WHALING: THE MARITIME HISTORY OF KIRKCALDY DISTRICT

It was not until 1813 that Kirkcaldy sent its first whaling ship, the *Earl Percy,* to join the fleet. By this time whaling had reached the Davis Straits and it was here that Kirkcaldy and Burntisland sent their whalers during the summer months. During the rest of the year some were used as traders, like N. & N. Lockhart's barque the *Ravenscraig,* which traded in flax to the Baltic. Between 1813 and 1866, sixteen whalers sailed from the two ports. In 1835 nine made the arduous journey north—a small number when compared with Hull's fleet which peaked at over sixty ships.

The whalers set out in March with *"great crowds assembled on the quay"* to see them off. Each ship had to carry all it needed for the next eight months including whaleboats, harpoons, flensing, or cutting, tools and casks for the blubber, as well as food and clothing. The crew of about fifty included a doctor, blacksmith and carpenter as well as the harpooners and flensers needed for the actual whaling.

In the ship's log the daily routine, bearings, weather report and any special incidents were noted. Traditionally, on May-day they "Put up the Garland". This was made of ribbons taken from wives and sweethearts on departure and was left on the mast throughout the voyage for luck.

On 1st May 1831 the *Undaunted* log notes "At 7 saw an ice Berg... the first seen on the voyage". Once in the Straits the crow's nest was put up to allow for the watch to be kept for whales. The tell-tale double spout, caused by the whale expelling breath, was known as a "loose fall". At this signal the captain *"called all hands and sent away all the Boats"*. Once within range the harpoon would be thrown, or fired from a gun, from the prow of the rowing boat. When 'fast' to the whale, the boat gave chase as it struggled to get free. Other lines might be

★Smith had in mind the nailworkers of Pathhead, a district now in the north-east part of Kirkcaldy.

attached to the harpoon or other boats might try to get fast too. Occasionally a harpoon would not hold and the whale could escape…

Conditions in the Arctic could be treacherous. While navigating through ice floes and along the edge of the pack ice, it was common for ships to be frozen in. The ice could be broken up in various ways or a 'dock' could be cut round the ship to prevent it being crushed. Inevitably, however, this happened to some. Even if a ship remained intact it could be trapped for days or weeks. Then frostbite took its toll and scurvy developed as food supplies ran low. Some crews supplemented their diets by fishing, hunting, and collecting birds' eggs.

The 1835-36 season was a disastrous one for the Davis Straits' whaling fleet. The *Viewforth* was one of three ships trapped together in the ice. She was imprisoned for four appalling months. By the time she reached Kirkcaldy at the end of February 1836, of her 55 strong crew, six were dead and few were in a fit state to man the ship.

The weather posed other dangers. In 1851 a blizzard cut off the *Regalia* from the crew of one of her boats, and on 12th May 1831 the *Undaunted* of Burntisland recorded sighting the wreck of a ship *"who had suffered from the late Gale"*. It turned out to be the *Rambler* of Kirkcaldy. Her crew was saved and carried home by other whalers in the fleet. This happened with the crews of most of the ships that were lost.

While in the Straits many ships came into contact with Inuit people (Eskimos). The sailors traded food and tobacco with them for sealskin and other goods. In 1846 the *Caledonia* brought a fourteen year old Inuit boy named Aukotook Zininnuck back to Kirkcaldy. He was given lessons in English, drawing and bible studies before being taken home the following season, laden with gifts and seen off by over 8,000 townspeople.

Around early October, the whalers began their long voyage home. Arriving, at times *"with Esquimaux curiosities and white bears, like collies, chained to the decks"*, they were given a hearty welcome on the quayside. After unloading, the crews were paid, with extra bounties according to the cargo they had brought back. Despite all the dangers and hardships the rewards could be high.

As whaling intensified and stocks were depleted, ships more often returned "clean"—with no catch. It became more risky to meet the high costs of fitting out a ship and paying the crew. Many whalers in other ports were converted to steam in a bid to remain profitable but most Fife ships continued to depend on sail. At the same time the need for the oil and whalebone lessened as other raw materials became available and so the prices dropped. Dundee's jute industry provided a new market for the oil brought back by its whalers. There, the whaling industry continued up till the First World War, but in Fife it steadily became less viable.

In 1862, three of Kirkcaldy's last whalers, the *Abram, Chieftain* and *Lord Gambier* were lost in another terrible Arctic winter, signalling the beginning of the end. In 1866 Kirkcaldy's last whaler, the *Brilliant*, was sold to Peterhead.

Booklet produced by **KIRKCALDY DISTRICT MUSEUMS**, 1994.

THE BOY IN THE TRAIN

Whit wey does the engine say *Toot-toot*?
    Is it feart to gang in the tunnel?
Whit wey is the furnace no pit oot
    When the rain gangs doon the funnel?
What'll I hae for my tea the nicht?
    A herrin', or maybe a haddie?
Has Gran'ma gotten electric licht?
    Is the next stop Kirkcaddy?

There's a hoodie-craw on yon turnip-raw!
    An' sea-gulls!—sax or seeven.
I'll no fa' oot o' the windae, Maw,
    It's sneckit, as sure as I'm leevin'.
We're into the tunnel! We're a' in the dark!
    But dinna be frichtit, Daddy,
We'll sune be comin' to Beveridge Park,
    And the next stop's Kirkcaddy!

Is yon the mune I see in the sky?
    It's awfu' wee an' curly.
See! there's a coo and cauf ootbye,
    An' a lassie pu'in' a hurly!
He's checkit the tickets and gien them back,
    Sae gie me my ain yin, Daddy.
Lift doon the bag frae the luggage rack,
    For the next stop's Kirkcaddy!

There's a gey wheen boats at the harbour mou',
    And eh! dae ye see the cruisers?
The cinnamon drop I was sookin' the noo
    Has tummelt an' stuck tae ma troosers...
I'll sune be ringin' ma Gran'ma's bell,

She'll cry, "Come ben, my laddie."
For I ken mysel' by the queer-like smell
That the next stop's Kirkcaddy.

MRS M. C. SMITH (1913)

MELVILLES OF KIRKCALDY AND RAITH

The Melvilles belonged to an Anglo-Norman family, and they had come to Raith from Midlothian about the year 1400... The first Melville of Raith was a John, and it was his son, styled "John the Malvyle of the Rath," who married Marjory, daughter of William Scott, Laird of Balwearie, the neighbouring estate on which the House of Raith looks down from its wooded heights. His grandson, the ill-fated Sir John of our story, was born at Raith in the latter part of the fifteenth century, entering into possession of the estate on 29th October, 1502. Marrying Margaret, the daughter of Sir John Wemyss, of Wemyss, he was knighted by the King the following year, in all probability on the occasion of the marriage of James IV with Margaret of England... How and when Sir John Melville espoused the Protestant cause is not known. Henry Balnaves, his protégé, who returned from the Continent fully and enthusiastically committed to the Reformed Faith, undoubtedly had something to do with it... Sir John Melville's name figured in the list of three hundred noblemen, gentlemen and burgesses accused of heretical opinions, which Cardinal David Beaton presented to the King in 1539.

When, after the death of James V, following the debacle at Solway Moss in 1542, James, Earl of Arran, was appointed Governor of the Kingdom, Archbishop David Beaton was for a time incarcerated in Blackness Castle. While he remained in disfavour the Reformed cause prospered greatly. Arran, however, changed his views, Beaton was released and restored, laws against heretics were re-enacted, persecution steadily increased, and on 1st March, 1546, George Wishart, the gifted Protestant preacher and scholar, was burned at the stake at St Andrews. It was the handwriting on the wall for all who shared his opinions!

Desperate situations are thought to call for desperate remedies, and when armed men slew Cardinal David Beaton at St Andrews on 29th May, 1546, and seized the Castle, many of Sir John Melville's intimate friends were implicated, his son-in-law, Kirkaldy, being among the chief conspirators. Melville himself was not named in the letters of summons issued, nor did he, like Balnaves, take refuge in the Castle with John Knox and the others. He cannot, however, have been ignorant of the dangers which threatened him. When the Castle fell he was still at liberty, Knox being sent to the galleys, and Balnaves and Kirkaldy to prisons in France. Within eighteen months, Melville's was to be a grimmer fate than any of theirs.

John Hamilton, Abbot of Paisley and Bishop of Dunkeld—later to be the last Pre-Reformation Archbishop of St Andrews—was the man behind his arrest. Hamilton and Sir John were travelling together to Burntisland, in what appeared to be a friendly conclave, when suddenly, on Clayness Sands, the Laird of Raith was violently seized at Hamilton's instigation and hurried to Edinburgh Castle, where he was confined without any charge being preferred against him, and with no access to any means of information or defence... Ten days after his incarceration in the Castle, Sir John was brought to trial, and on December 13th he was found guilty on six charges, being executed the same day. His lands and goods were then declared forfeit, but his widow and family were allowed to stay on for some time at Raith.

What was the indictment against Melville? He was accused of having written a letter in the January previous, to his son John, then an emissary of the Protector Somerset in England, a man bitterly hated by the Scots. In it he had told him of the chief military events in Scotland, giving him vital information to pass to his master about the disposition of military forces north of the Border.

Opinion in Scotland had hardened greatly since the fall of St Andrews Castle, and what might have passed for far-sighted statesmanship a few years earlier was now branded unhesitatingly as treason. A jury composed chiefly of Fife lairds had no difficulty in finding Melville guilty. It was zero hour for the Protestant cause in Scotland.

Eleven years later the tide turned completely, and in 1563, Helen Napier, Sir John's widow, and her elderly children successfully petitioned the Government to have the condemnation and forfeiture rescinded... Thus ended a case unique in Scottish legal annals, and Raith came back into the possession of the family which was to hold it for another hundred and forty years, and from which so many famous men were to spring.

D. P. THOMSON, *Raith and Kirkcaldy*, 1952.

THE ST CLAIRS OF RAVENSCRAIG CASTLE AND ROSLIN CHAPEL

The refined architectural taste of the Earl of Caithness would doubtless lead him to make many important additions to Ravenscraig Castle, though these cannot now be identified. He was the builder of the magnificent Collegiate Church of Roslin, near Edinburgh, which he founded in 1441, and which is still regarded as "a noble pile of building and a masterpiece of architecture". His notions of right and wrong, however, were not perfect. He was twice married, and he strove to disinherit the son of his first wife that he might favour the two sons

Ravenscraig Castle

of his second. With the connivance of the King he conferred the Earldom of Caithness upon the eldest son of his second marriage, whilst William Saintclair of Newburgh, his true heir apparent, was forced to remain content with a very small portion of the estate. After the death of the father a dispute arose betwixt the three sons on this subject, and was finally adjusted after lengthened litigation. William Saintclair of Newburgh obtained the Castle of Ravenscraig and the lands of Dysart, and was ancestor of the Barons Sinclair. He is now represented by John Austruther-Thomson, Esq. of Charleston, Fife. William Saintclair, the eldest, son of the second wife, retained the title of Earl of Caithness, and was ancestor of the present holder of that title; whilst Sir Oliver Sinclair, the youngest son, obtained the lands of Roslin, and founded the family of Sinclair of Roslin, which became extinct about the middle of last century.

The Castle of Ravenscraig was in possession of James, Lord Sinclair, in 1606, and the last trace which we have found of it in public documents is in the Rebotir of Sir Francis Kinloch of Gilmerton, Bart., who was served heir of his father in "the castle, dovecot, orchard, and rabbit-warrens of Ravenscraig" in 1099. The property afterwards came into the hands of that branch of the Sinclair family represented by the present proprietor, the Earl of Rosslyn.

There seems a strong probability that Magister David Boys, the original builder of Ravenscraig Castle in 1463, was related to the family of Boys of Panbride, and was therefore a kinsman of the famous Dundee historian, Hector Boece,

85

the first Principal of King's College, Aberdeen. On this point, however, extant records are silent, and the matter is merely a plausible conjecture.

A. H. MILLAR, *The Castles and Mansions of Fife and Kinross*, 1890.

AT RAVENSCRAIG CASTLE

On the far side of Stirling Firth lies the little town of Kirkcaldy. There, on a wooded mountain stood a huge old ruin; gulls flew round it and, screeching, dipped their wings in the water.

...The actual ruin with its gloomy prison vaults and the luxuriant evergreens covering what remained of the walls like a close carpet and clinging to the rock which jutted out over the sea, was especially picturesque and strange, for the tide had ebbed and the sea retreated. The view from there across to Edinburgh was so magnificent as to be unforgettable.

HANS CHRISTIAN ANDERSEN, who visited in 1847.

ROSABELLE
From *The Lay of the Last Minstrel*

O listen, listen, ladies gay!
    No haughty feat of arms I tell;
Soft is the note, and sad the lay
    That mourns the lovely Rosabelle.

—"Moor, moor the barge, ye gallant crew!
    And, gentle ladye, deign to stay!
Rest thee in Castle Ravensheuch,
    Nor tempt the stormy firth to-day.

"The blackening wave is edg'd with white;
    To inch and rock the sew-mews fly;
The fishers have heard the Water-Sprite,
    Whose screams forebode that wreck is nigh.

"Last night the gifted Seer did view
    A wet shroud swathed round ladye gay;
Then stay thee, Fair, in Ravensheuch:
    Why cross the gloomy firth to-day?"

'Tis not because Lord Lindesay's heir
    To-night at Roslin leads the ball,
But that my ladye-mother there
    Sits lonely in her castle-hall.

"'Tis not because the ring they ride,
    And Lindesay at the ring rides well,
But that my sire the wine will chide,
    If 'tis not fill'd by Rosabelle."

O'er Roslin all that dreary night
    A wondrous blaze was seen to gleam;
'Twas broader than the watch-fire's light,
    And redder than the bright moonbeam.

It glar'd on Roslin's castled rock,
    It ruddied all the copse-wood glen;
'Twas seen from Dryden's groves of oak,
    And seen from cavern'd Hawthornden.

Seem'd all on fire that chapel proud,
    Where Roslin's chiefs uncoffin'd lie,
Each Baron, for a sable shroud,
    Sheath'd in his iron panoply

Seem'd all on fire within, around,
    Deep sacristy and altar's pale;
Shone every pillar foliage-bound,
    And glimmer'd all the dead men's mail.

Blaz'd battlement and pinnet high,
    Blaz'd every rose-carved buttress fair—
So still they blaze when fate is nigh
    The lordly line of high St. Clair.

There are twenty of Roslin's barons bold
    Lie buried within that proud chapelle;
Each one the holy vault doth hold—
    But the sea holds lovely Rosabelle!

And each St. Clair was buried there,
　　With candle, with book, and with knell;
　But the sea-caves rung, and the wild winds sung,
　　The dirge of lovely Rosabelle.

SIR WALTER SCOTT

VAL McDERMID

Best known as the winner of the 1995 Macallan Gold Dagger Award for Crime Fiction.

...Born in Kirkcaldy in 1955, Val was educated first at Fair Isle School in Templehall then Dunnikier Primary, and in 1966 was part of an experiment in "early classes". Pupils achieving a high enough standard were moved to Kirkcaldy High School a year earlier than normal and it was this that led to her being accepted by Oxford University when she was only sixteen. A member of the school athletic team and the hockey first XI, she played for the East of Scotland XI and was also a prize-winning debater.

Her one ambition was to become a writer and it was expected that she would go on to Edinburgh University but Val, wanting to spread her wings wider, decided to make a bid for Oxford. The High School opposed the idea, assuming that she would be rejected and this would reflect badly on the school, but she was supported by Wilf Allsop, her English teacher. He gave up free periods to give her extra coaching in texts that were needed for the entrance exam but didn't form part of the Scottish syllabus.

The exam took place in Kirkcaldy and a telephone call for her to appear in Oxford for an interview gave less than twenty four hours notice, making it impossible for Mrs. McDermid to accompany her, so sixteen year old Val went alone and was told she would be sent a telegram with the result. The local postman was primed to deliver the telegram as soon as it arrived, which it did on the day of the school concert... Val chose St Hilda's College because their prospectus looked most attractive, was the first undergraduate at that college to come from a Scottish state school and later became President of the Junior Common Room, the undergraduate student body, college darts champion and founder editor of a college newspaper. She achieved a BA degree in English Language and Literature just after her twentieth birthday.

LILLIAN KING

Dysart for coal and saut,
Pathhead for meal and maut,
Kirkcaldy for lasses braw,
Kinghorn for brakin the law.

ANONYMOUS

DYSART
From *A Lost Lady of Old Years*

The ancient town is now a very little place, unsightly with coal and dingy with stagnant traffic. But in the days of Mr. Shillinglaw it was a bustling port, where skippers from Amsterdam came with strong waters and cheeses and Lord knows what and carried away beer and tallow, hides and sea-coal. It boasted of a town-house where the noisy burgesses met, and elegant piazzas where foreign merchants walked and chaffered. In the rock-hewn harbour lay at all times two score and more of schooners, and the high red-tiled houses looked down upon an eternal stir of shipping and unlading. It was a goodly place to live, for health came with the clean sea-wind and wealth with every tide.

JOHN BUCHAN, *A Lost Lady of Old Years*, 1899.

DESERTA
From the satire *Franciscanus* (late 1580s)

Hit's a braid streetch o wastage, nae gairden ava:
Nocht fir the hairst, nor rowthieness o leafs.
Thristles straiggle, shilpit-like, frae the histy grund;
Nae coos leave their merk.
The neibours cry it Dysart. There, ablow the craigs,
Vulcan hauds coort in his palaces o coal.
Fires can stert up whaur they will, sulphur reeks oot whaur it can,
And the deep yird's mochie as taur.
The bleeze warsles thrawnly throu the Fifan labyrinth,
Jouks throu wee cleavins forenent the shore.

Yer neb tells ye straicht: this is the deevil's erse-hole.

GEORGE BUCHANAN (1506-1582)
Transcreated from the Latin by **TOM HUBBARD** for the 500th
anniversary of Buchanan's birth.

THE MAN IN THE ROCK*

This is the place; the curve of coast
where once six cottages outfaced the sea,
tiles weathered red and gold,
walls salt-encrusted, crumbling.
Small gardens melted into dunes
where seathrift grew,
and hard ridged sand ran out
to meet the insistent sea.

Now only tumbled stones remain.
No stray hen pecks among long grass,
no linen's flung to bleach
along the hawthorn hedge.
Where once boys dug for worms
below sand-casts, or solitary figures
gathered up sea coal,
a shadow creeps in on the tide.

The same tide wore away the path
that snaked along the shore, to pass
the lonely figure in the rock;
man carved from stone—
the Prisoner of Chillon—
whose hair grew white
but in another country
centuries ago.

The waves recede, and gather strength
to dash against his feet
but cannot reach the ledge
where still he gazes out to sea;
cold effigy, outlasting men,
and cottages, and coal, and path.
Whoever carved him here

---

*'The Man in the Rock' was a statue of Bonnivard, the eponymous hero of Byron's long narrative poem *The Prisoner of Chillon*. Carved by a local coalminer from the rock-face between Dysart and West Wemyss, it was enclosed behind an iron fence, adding to the sense of Bonnivard's incarceration. It was a popular feature with locals, and Tom Hubbard remembers being taken there during his childhood in the 1950s. It has long been washed away.

made him a prisoner anew,
since now no traveller can pass this way.

ELISE McKAY

HEY CA' THRO'

Up wi' the carls of Dysart,
    And the lads o' Buckhiven,
And the Kimmers o' Largo,
    And the lasses o' Leven.
      Hey ca' thro' ca' thro'
        For we hae mickle a do,
      Hey ca' thro' ca' thro'
        For we hae mickle a do.

We hae tales to tell,
    And we hae sangs to sing;
We hae pennies to spend,
    And we hae pints to bring.
      Hey ca' thro' &c.

We'll live a' our days,
    And them that comes behin',
Let them do the like,
    And spend the gear they win
      Hey ca' thro' &c.

ROBERT BURNS

GENERAL ALEX CAMPBELL TO GENERAL WEMYSS, M.P., WEMYSS CASTLE, DYSART, DATED 16TH SEPT, 1815

My dear General, I dined yesterday at Ochtertyre, and Sir Peter [Ramsay] told me that he had lately received a letter from you, intimating your intention of being soon in this country, which gave me much joy, when up spoke a thing they call a Lord, by the name of Pitmilly, *ci devant* [formerly] Davy Moneypenny, and emitted the following evidence—viz., "that the said Wemyss had been over-turned, coupt, or whumled in his carriage, to the great damage of his person, on his return from dining with a reverend clergyman, whose name he could not recollect, nor could he testify to the exact amount of damage the person of

91

the said General actually received." On being cross-examined, he admitted that the Parish of Auchtertool might be that of your entertainer, and I immediately called to mind the sage person who came upon our flank at the end of the engagement at Wemyss Castle, as Blucher did at Waterloo, and I believe, with the same success. But, seriously, I will be obliged if you will let me know how you are, and whether you are much hurt; above all, I hope you will be able to make out your purpose of visiting this country. The parsons here do not ask people to dinner, so you will be safe that way. My best wishes to all at Wemyss Castle. Believe me,

yours faithfully,

ALEX CAMPBELL

From *JOSEPH KNIGHT*

He would go to the coal tomorrow, and Ann would walk with him and the lad too. They would go their separate ways, he and Andrew climbing down the shaft and then crawling deep into the earth while Ann and the other women bore the great creels loaded with coal to the surface. And the men and women he worked with would call him Joe and laugh and girn as always and treat him as one of themselves. It was a sair, sair life but it was true, he was one of them, a collier. Colliers. The only people who had never held out against him. They knew that life was only ever a second away from disaster, from death. They saw him black, they knew him black, and it didn't make them hate him or love him, they just accepted him. And he understood why this was.

Slavery. It had set them together against their country, against the world. He remembered the time in Edinburgh, in a room in a tavern with John Maclaurin. Maclaurin said, "Joseph, there is a man here that wishes tae meet ye." A tiny, wizened man in threadbare working clothes had stood up and given him his hand. When Joseph grasped it he felt it rough and cracked and hard, and when he looked at it he saw it black, deep-grained with coal stour. That stour was never going to come out. The man said he was from the colliers at Wemyss in Fife, they had heard of his trouble and they had made a subscription for him. He said he was sorry for the smallness of the sum, but he hoped it might help. Joseph nearly wept at that. The collier said, "We aw ken, man, dinna be feart, we aw ken."

It was true. They were all free now, he and the other colliers, but there was something in them, a deep buried part, that would be slave till the day they died.

Joseph would not welcome death. The men he got on with best, they would not welcome it, hard and grinding and rotten though their lives were. They lived with death every day so they knew its face was ugly and cruel, just as he did. Maybe it was *because* of that, because of all he had been through, that it made him mad to think of not being alive, of not being on the earth to breathe any more.

Sometimes on a Saturday night his friends would queue outside the cottage and he would draw out his old scissors and razor and trim their hair, make them nice for their wives. He would not take money for it. Some of the men had wee square-rigged yawls that they raced on the sea and caught fish from, and they would give him some fish in return. They offered to take him out fishing but they could never entice Joseph to join them on the great grey waters. Others would buy him a drink, or leave a few rabbits poached from the laird's parks. *That* was life, that was heroism: friendship, and trust, and once in a while a little stolen delight. No, Joseph would not welcome death. Whether it came underground, or here in the bed, or some other way he could not imagine. Whether it took him to Africa, or to Jesus, or just into a hole in the earth. He would not hold out his hand to it. He was alive and he did not want to die. It might not be much, life, but he wanted it all the same, all he could get of it, so death would have to wait. He had beaten Wedderburn and he'd beat death as long as he was able. He was alive and here and now. He was alive.

JAMES ROBERTSON, *Joseph Knight*, 2003.

ORIGIN OF WEMYSS CAVES*

The mothers and grandmothers of the locality long garrulously told their offspring that "the caves were bigget by the Pechs—short wee men wi' red hair and long arms and feet sae broad that when it rained they turned them up ower their head, and then they served for umbrellas. Oh, ay, they were great builders, the Pechs; they built a' the auld castles in the country. They stood a' in a row from the quarry to the building stance and elka ane handed foreward the stanes to his neighbour till the hale was bigget."

JOHN SIMPSON, from *County Folklore: Fife*, 1912.

METHIL HERBURE, 1664

On 15 September 1664 Andrew Thomsone in Leiven did leade his Botte in the new Herbure of Methil wt colles from the colle of Methil being 60 leads of colles and he did tak them to Leith one 17 of Sepr. 1664. Which was the first

---

*The Wemyss Caves are well-known for their Pictish carvings. The Caves were long subject to neglect and vandalism until archaeologists pressed for their protection and conservation.

Botte yt did leade wt colles att yt Herbure. The colles was well loved att Leith & since thorrow all sea ports in Scotland. I sould them att 5li the 12 lodes & 2 sh. to the grive. I give 22d for mining them to the coller and 1sh. 2d. to the caller of them from the colle pit to the Herbure.

INVASION, 1667, AT BURNTISLAND AND BUCKHAVEN

On the last day of Aprill 1667 The hollands flitte inveadded Scottland & cam up yt day to Bruneiland wt 30 good ships sum of 60 sum of 80 gunes a peisse Beseids 10 littill ones. They did offer to land to have brunt all the Ships in Bruneiland but was beatten back and they shott above 1000 gritte sott att itt sum of 24 li. Balle and did not kille man wife or child. Shott att noe other Toune or pleasse killed one man in off Buickheavin yt day the Botte being att fishing and they would not cum abourd of them so they shott att the Botte & killed one Alex. Chirsstie… The flette went away one I May 1667 and did littill more only tuek one privattire belonging to Leith Shoe ridding in Brunelland Rode when they cam up. They head out Inglish Cullers. 3 of the Kings ships was ridding in Leith Rode whoe weayed & went above the Quinis ferrie when I shotte 3 Cannone aff the housse of Wemyss to warne them.

DAVID, SECOND EARL OF WEMYSS, *Diary.*

THE BARBAR O METHIL

Aye on daurk nichts
I wis sent fir a baldie;
I mynd the jurnay weill.
Throu Memorial Park
Wi its trees lik hauns o glore
Staved in a fower-weys' eerie snaw;
Past the liberary's wappin Xmas tree—
A chaft o squeebs ablow gless—
Ti the toyless windae
O Niven the barbar.

The shop wis aye the smell
O hair-ile an drams:
Wuid matured on thae was.
I'd sit at the end o a lang binch,
Droosy fae pipe-reek
An the draw o the waggity-wa.

94

Anly the mysterie
O five o'clock sheddae,
Styptic pensils an rubber johnnies
Kept me sober.

Hinnerly I'd wan ti ma dell;
A bleck-breisted stove, aa rid-moued
An glaizie fae the pautin o cley-davies.
Afore its ingle had slaiked ma hauns
The wird wis oot: "Nixt!"

I'd wauch i winder the wey
Niven wad faik me in lik a babby,
His epileptic tongue o aise
Aye lollin owre ma lugs,
The shears i his tap-pooch
Glowerin lik a stuffed houlit
As he combed doun ma hair.

I'd aince heard he'd pleyed
Fir East Fife i thir days o glore;
Nou the anly bas kickin roun his feet
Wur aff the heids o bauchles an bairns.

I wisnae auld aneuch ti crack o fitba,
Cuddies or ma wark;
I'd juist sit an chitter
As the razzor scraped ma nek.

Whan he wis near feenished, he'd ask me:
"Dae ye want a shed i yer hair?"
An dae it afore I'd time ti say aye or no,
Touslin ma heid i brylcreem.

I'd sclim aff thon lether chair o his,
A pund lichter i the heid,
An wauch him coont oot ma cheenge
Atween puffs on his fag.
This wis whit I wis waitin fir.
He'd leuk at me an say:
"Are ye wantin ony comics?"

95

An pou bak a blue plastick curtain
Ti shaw an Aladdin's cave o Beanos an Toppers.
"Tak whit ye want," he'd say,
An I wad, haudin thaim ti ma coat
Lik stolen jowels.

Afore I wis oot the door inti the snaw
He'd say: "Mynd yer lugs'll stick oot
Lik Clark Gable!" an I'd lauch
Athoot kennin whit fir.

Aa the wey bak up Memorial Road
I'd feel ma heid get crumpie
Lik the tappin o a burthday cake,
An ma lugs thrabbin wi the cauld.
Anly whan I got i the hoose
An sat doun fir ma biled egg tea
Did ma heid stap dirlin fae
The comic cuts o thon Barbar o Methil.

JOHN BREWSTER

TO MRS. SITWELL

17 Heriot Row, Edinburgh, Friday. September 12, 1873

I was over last night, contrary to my own wish, in Leven, Fife; and this morning
I had a conversation of which, I think, some account might interest you. I was
up with a cousin who was fishing in a mill-lade, and a shower of rain drove me
for shelter into a tumble-down steading attached to the mill. There I found a
labourer cleaning a byre, with whom I fell into talk. The man was to all appearance as heavy, as *hébété,* as any English clodhopper; but I knew I was in Scotland,
and launched out forthright into Education and Politics and the aims of one's life.
I told him how I had found the peasantry in Suffolk, and added that their state
had made me feel quite pained and down-hearted. "It but to do that," he said,
"to onybody that thinks at a'!" Then, again, he said that he could not conceive
how anything could daunt or cast down a man who had an aim in life. "They
that have had a guid schoolin' and do nae mair, whatever they do, they have
done; but him that has aye something ayont need never be weary." I have had
to mutilate the dialect much, so that it might be comprehensible to you; but I
think the sentiment will keep, even through a change of words, something of

the heartsome ring of encouragement that it had for me: and that from a man cleaning a byre! You see what John Knox and his schools have done.

ROBERT LOUIS STEVENSON

AMBULANCE DRIVER WITH THE FIFE VOLUNTARY AID DETACHMENT OF THE RED CROSS

I was born in 1907 and I come from Leven in Fife. Before the Second World War, I studied at the Royal Academy of Dramatic Art after which I taught elocution. I was married and I lived in London. My husband served in the war flying in RAF Lancaster bombers. My mother, Mrs. Reed, was very influential in the Fife Branch of the Voluntary Aid Detachment of the Red Cross and when the Polish Forces arrived in Fife in 1940 and 1941, the Red Cross were urgently looking for local drivers for the Red Cross ambulances to work with the Polish Services. I volunteered. I was given a smart navy blue uniform and I drove a large motor Field Ambulance with canvas sides. Most of the ambulances were based in Leven and we drove patients who were sick or injured in training between Taymouth Castle and Duplin Castle where the Polish Forces' hospital was based.

I was closely involved in the formation of the Scottish-Polish Society in the area. We organised concerts and drama with the members of the Polish Forces in Leven Town Hall and we had lots of fun. Having a background in elocution, I also taught English to Polish servicemen and women, all of whom were keen to learn and were eager students. I myself took the opportunity and learnt a little Polish.

As for the Polish men, they were nearly all officers, very handsome and very attractive to the local girls. I remember at the club on the seafront in Leven, there was one sergeant who used to play the piano most beautifully for the dances and entertainment evenings.

Later in the war after most of the Poles had left Fife for the D–Day landings, a lot of very young Polish recruits arrived—mainly from Silesia. Many of these had been prisoners of the Soviets and only arrived in Scotland towards the end of the war.

When VE Day came, many of the Poles could not go home to Poland, and some simply wanted to make a new life in Scotland. It was very difficult for them and there was a strong local feeling, particularly in the mining community, that they should return to their own country. I remember in particular a meeting in the town hall in Leven by the "Poles go home" campaigners where strong feelings ran high. I was not proud of my fellow Scots then.

I still have many friends in the surviving members of Scotland's Polish-

97

Scottish community and each year I go to the annual service in Leven and remember those days now so long ago.

ELIZABETH KENDZIA from Diana M. Henderson's *The Lion and the Eagle: Reminiscences of Polish Second World War Veterans in Scotland*, 2001.

LAST CHANCE

Leven, Fife is nowadays a frontier town in modern
east of Scotland style. Imaginary tumbleweed
is blown by North Sea winds that taste of salt

along the dual carriageway and past Banbeath
Industrial Estate. Some mornings you can almost hear
the rumble of the iron horse which used to ride this trail.

Now only Stagecoach battles through. The tourists come
to mosey down the Promenade where one-armed-bandits
still hold sway. These days the "Indians" are take-aways

but cowboys roam from door to door and drive hard deals
in double glazing. Meantime for the good, the bad
and others back on Main Street, music loud with drink

spills out of each saloon while cash tills play a tune
which sure ain't Bluegrass. Fivers by the fistful
buy us burgers, chips, the latest brand name trainers

for, except line dancers, no-one here wears cowboy boots.
Still, it's a wilderness beyond the 40-mile speed limit.
Night draws down the shutters and we circle round

our digital TVs, tune out the wild coyote call. But if you dare
to head out west where dust clouds gather in the next ridge
of low pressure, check the neon sign. It says:

Last Petrol to the Forth Road Bridge
Last Petrol to the Forth Road Bridge

ELEANOR LIVINGSTONE

By the Rivers Leven, Ore and Eden

LEVEN AND ORE VALLEYS

From Levenmouth, traditionally the east end of Fife's industrial coastline, the River Leven runs almost due west to its source, Loch Leven. Water power attracted labour and spawned communities along its banks. *"I grind the corn, I saw the wood, I bleach the linen and I spin the flax"*. (*The Leven*, Rankin, 1812). Apart from Sawmill Ford, the Leven was generally unpredictable and impassible in time of flood; the first upstream crossing was Cameron Bridge, 17th century, reconstructed 1870. At the Meetings, about 300m west, the Leven is joined by the Ore; the source of this tributary is Loch Ore round which crowd the former mining towns of Lochgelly, Cowdenbeath, Kelty and Ballingry.

Thornton, the first village up the Ore Valley, has been a fugitive of fortune. Virtually a creation of the railway, by the end of the 19th century four lines converged on its station. Railway wagon works had been built and two hotels served its travellers. At the end of the Second World War the new Rothes pit was being sunk and the future looked prosperous. Today the station is closed, the pit long abandoned and a trunk road bypasses the village.

GLEN L. PRIDE, *The Kingdom of Fife. An Illustrated Architectural Guide*, 1990.

THE CUT ON THE RIVER LEVEN

Questions are frequently asked about the origin and purpose of the obviously artificial course of the River Leven from its exit at the loch in a straight line to Auchmuir Bridge, and those who put the question may well be surprised to learn of the industrial activity which once existed all the way down on its banks from Leslie to the mouth at Leven, comprising flax spinning, bleaching, grain milling, distilling, coalmining, ironworks, sawmills and papermaking. All these concerns depended on water power supplied by the river, but this power could be highly irregular at times with floods after periods of heavy rain and low water during dry summers and frosty winters. So in 1824 a meeting of the millowners was held in the Plasterers Inn which stood at what is now the foot of Alburne Park in Glenrothes, and this meeting resulted in an Act of Parliament of 1827 whose preamble stated that "it has been ascertained by experienced Engineers, that by making a new Cut or Channel for the said River... and constructing proper sluices, Spillwaters, Embankments and other works… and regulating the Flow of Water… it would be of Great Benefit and Advantage to the Owners and Occupiers of the Lands and Mills, Manufactories, Bleachfields and other Works, and to the Public at large".

The proposed New Cut was to be "32 feet wide at the bottom with a slope on each side of 2 feet on every foot deep… to rise with a gradual acclivity to the Sluices at the Loch". The original outlet was dammed and sluice gates were constructed at the new exit to be 4¼ feet at their upper surface "below the Level of a Mark made on the Wall below the Churchyard in Kinross". The "Sluice-Keeper" was provided with a house. His duties included maintaining the area in good order, and keeping the cut free of ice and plant growth. Auchmuir Bridge was rebuilt, and the New Cut opened in May 1832 at a total cost of of £36,500. The work was not carried out without some problems for the mills, especially because of sand and mud in the water, so that one millowner had to construct a "philtre", a bleachfield had lost customers, and a paper mill had to change to the making of coarse paper only.

It was the opinion of mill tenants in general, however, that the supply of water had improved and in fact the improvement resulted in such an increase in power available to the mills that the use of water power by some was prolonged into this century. Of course, the various improvements had to be paid for, and the cost to Robert Kirk, the proprietor of spinning, lint and snuff mills at Leslie, of £817: 1: 7 was a factor in his bankruptcy in 1835. There are still Trustees in charge of the affairs of the river, and the three paper mills still pay their share of the wages of the "sluice-keeper".

G. P. BENNETT, *The Past at Work. Around the Lomonds,* 1982.

From *AT CHRYSTIS KIRK ON THE GRENE**

Was never in Scotland hard nor sene
Sic dansing nor deray,
Nother in Falkland on the grene,
Nor Peblis to the play,
As was of wooeris as I wene
At Chrystis Kirk on ane day.
Thair come our Kittie weschen clene
In hir new kirtill of gray,
Full gay,
At Chrystis Kirk on the grene.

*Christ's Kirk on the Green is in Leslie.

To dance the damisallis thame dicht
And lassis licht of laittis;
Thair gluvis war of the raffell richt
Thair schone war of the straitis;
Thair kirtillis war of the lincum licht
Weill prest with mony plaitis.
Thay war so nyce quehn men thame nicht
Thay squeild lyk ony gaitis,
    Ful loud,
At Chrystis kirk on the grene.

Off all thir madinis myld as mede
Was nane sa gymp as Gillie,
As ony rose hir rude was reid
Hir lyre was lyk the lillie;
Bot yallow yallow was hir heid,
And sche of luif so sillie,
Thoch all hir kin suld have bein deid
Sche wald have bot sweit Willie,
    Allane,
At Chrystis kirk on the grene

ANONYMOUS

LESLIE

When frae Leslie ye would gae,
Ye maun cross a brig and down a brae.

ANONYMOUS

MARKINCH

From far away—sometimes across rounded hills and parkland, sometimes perhaps with a pithead in the foreground—we have seen the tall tower and spire of the church of St Drostan at Markinch and the roofs of the town stepping towards it up the sides of the hill upon which it so serenely sits.

But before we go up that hill we must, if we are entering Markinch by the northern road, pause by the entrance of the town to look more closely at the stone slab which stands high on a bank above the road. It is a simple monument. A stone roughly hewn and carved with a cross. That is all. But it is the

101

evidence, the very seal of the antiquity of Markinch. We stand at the gateway of a very ancient and, indeed, a royal town. That St Drostan, in whose name that tall tower is raised and who is the patron saint of the town, was nephew of St Columba and of royal descent, and Markinch itself is reputed to have been the Pictish capital of the Kingdom. Nearby on Markinch Hill are traces of terraces which are believed to mark the fortifications of a Roman camp which were later used as galleries for spectators at mediaeval miracle plays.

This carved Cross which we are now looking at is the Stob Cross—from which the road nearby takes its name—and is one of the old "Girth stones" which marked the limits of a Sanctuary established by the statutes of the early Scottish Church. This one marked the Sanctuary of that church of Markinch given to the Culdees of Loch Leven 900 years ago.

Now we can climb uphill toward the tall church tower which has beckoned us across the hills to Markinch. It is one of the five pure Norman towers of the Scottish mainland. The octagonal spire which was added on to it about 150 years ago is not an altogether happy addition to the simple and lovely Norman tower, but it is in an unexpected way in some degree responsible for the tower's present fine state of preservation. Some years ago it was found that the great weight of the added spire was threatening the tower, and the work undertaken to remedy this resulted in a complete and meticulous renovation of the ancient building, so that it is now one of the most perfect Norman towers in existence.

We are moved, as we stand in its shadow, to attempt a fuller appreciation of the great age of these historic stones. Perhaps we succeed most vividly in that attempt by reflecting that the tower by which we stand was already half a century old when on a Sunday in August 1296 Edward I of England also halted in its shadow.

One of the church's interesting relics is the niche at the entrance. At one time the collecting plate was placed in this niche. Behind the plate was a window into the session house. And there the elders sat with the plate in view, not only seeing the growing pile of contributions but also, we can be sure, noting those who passed without an offering.

One of the strangest epitaphs to be seen anywhere is that on a memorial plaque inside the church. It is to the memory of the Reverend John Pinkerton who, for twenty-six years minister of Markinch, died in the 67th year of his age on 16th June, 1784. The plaque was erected by Mr Francis Pinkerton Drummond, one of the family of the famous Drummond of Hawthornden, and upon it is carved this story of the minister's death:

> After having spent a very Cheerful evening at Balfour House with Mr Bethune and his family, he was found in the morning in his bedroom sitting in a chair by the Fire place with one stocking in his hand *Quite Dead*.

The Balfour House at which Mr Pinkerton spent that last cheerful evening was the birthplace of James Beaton, Archbishop of St Andrews, and of his nephew Cardinal Beaton. Of this family, who held the estate for more than 500 years, was Mary Beaton—one of Queen Mary's famous "Four Maries".

Buried at Markinch Church is the famous Covenanting General, Alexander Leslie, who died at Balgonie Castle in 1661. "Old General Leslie, in Fyffe, the Earle of Leven, depairted out of this life at his own house in Balgonie, and was interred at Markinshe church in his own iyle, the 19 of Apr., in the evening," writes Lamont. Balgonie, one of the grandest memorials of past ages, stands on the banks of the Leven a mile from Markinch.

The Kingdom of Fife and Kinross-shire, edited by **THEO LANG**, 1951.

From *WALKIN IN FIFE*

Stars and hoolets and squirrels

We are oot haund in haund on the back road
by Viewforth Plantation on the stretch doon
to Newton Farm. We look at the stars sae very bricht
and I name what I ken. You are richt surprised,
the sky at nicht on country walks in winter
being new to you. Later, I say, there'll be
aurora borealis, a saftness across the sky,
and you're even mair surprised though you've lived
for years in Markinch toon,
but a mile or sae frae here, summer and winter.

I draw on the furthest extent o my astral knowledge
and risk my airm roond your waist
though it's only oor second walk oot thegither.
The stars are bricht owreheid and we tak the road
doon by Newton Farm and ancient terraces and Stob Cross
and Markinch the Pictish capital of Fife.
But these are daytime places and you were
no impressed as I try anither knowledgeable tack.

Still there's the hoolets and squirrels in Balbirnie woods
even if I tried to show you them
on oor first time walkin oot thegither!

THE UNKENT

Late at nicht we come owre the Cuinin Hill
through the trees closin in, and oot by the tinkers' camp
wi daurk bulbous tents and tethered horses.
We walk very quaitly close thegither but fast
at the soond o their howlin and wailin that's mebbe
singin. And the stirrin o horses.

The stars are bricht in a daurk black sky
and the moon castin lang hidin shadows. Feelin
the nip in the air and that singin gettin nearer
we set aff into a slaw tip-toe run
haund and haund past their tents. Quicker and
quicker but as quaitly as we can wi quick looks back
owre oor shooders. The singin cheynges key
as we turn onto the main road
and the soond o oor feet loud as drums
but there's nae thocht o stoppin wi the deil at oor heels.
Weill past noo, we laugh and are aff into a happy run thegither
doon into Star village wi its daurk windaes
and the neighin o grey mare aside North Dalginch fairm,
and soos gruntin in Bellfield's styes close to the road.
A stoat or weasel's quick across the road
and hoolets cry in the nicht air.

But what we ken
—at haund!

THOCHTS

Only three miles but seemin like ten.
You and I oot for a Sunday walk in oor courtin days
and takin the straucht wey hame across the fields
frae Teuchat Head.
Frozen stubble haurd and ruttit aneath oor feet
and bravely walked through. The quait December air
enclosin stillness aw aroond but for the crunch o frost
agin the earth. Hand in haund we lean furrit
and think only o the end o this walk
and escape frae that cauld,

104

we thocht. Haunds sculptured lumps withoot feelin
and noses cauld ayont onie pain.

The nicht is closin in fast for aw the brichtenin hoar
and aheid the sma lichts o Burnside show we've faur to gae.
But soon doon by the watterman's cottage
and the tall windaes of Carriston House oor next goal
bricht owre the reservoir unseen ahint its bank
but felt in a cheynge o air. Noo roond by the loch's faur edge
and large doocot agin the western sky. And Lomond Hill
a white Matterhorn aw day noo a distant greyness
and ither warld. We think o the sma cottage
and blazin fire, and escape frae this cauld,
we thocht.

Noo I mind the walk frae Teuchat Head to hame
and you oot walkin wi me.

KEEN

You thocht we should hae a lang walk on Sunday.
On Setterday we had sclimed East Lomond frae Falkland
and walked the taps to West Lomond and then back
hame by Leslie, Markinch and Star
a very, very twistin village.

On Sunday we set oot by Drummy Woods whaur we stoppt
the walk no being aw for a courtin couple. But soon
doon the steep brae wi meikle laughter by East Forthar
and West Forthar and a wee stop in the hay loft.
And airm and airm into Freuchie on its quaitest sabbath
but wi a kirkyaird we could doucely walk roond.
In Freuchie we ate oor sandwiches.

And on oot the road to Newton o Falkland and Falkland itsel.
We hae sclimed the Lomonds yesterday
but want to reveesit large copper beech
in the wud aneath the hill. I forget my tiredness
at the beech but mind it on the lang, lang road
to Markinch by Kirkforthar Feus
and Balbirnie Estate whaur I revive a little

on a seat aneath anither famous beech. You lead me
up and owre Cuinin Hill and through twistin Star
a very, very lang village,
and up the hill wi the evenin staur green to oor richt.

At nicht you talk o a walk oot to Drummy Wood
in the daurk
but I took to bed for a week
—alane and exhaustit!

DUNCAN GLEN

LAIRDS IN THE MARKINCH DISTRICT OF FIFE

Carriston and Pyeston
Kirkforthar and the Drum,
Are fowre o the maist curst lairds
That ever spak wi tongue.

From *Popular Rhymes of Scotland*, 1826, edited by
ROBERT CHAMBERS

KIRKFORTHAR

The sun trickles through calligraphy
on the pine-tops and the path
becomes a chess board of dark and light,
a swithering of midges
one moment there, the next,
no more, illusion performed.

A train shaves the edge of the tree-line,
shooting towards Dundee, its long
drawn out ebb more of a wind
than a wind that kneels in prayer
in a green and grand cathedral;
only a roe deer surprised,

will shatter silence, beating retreat
on dead wood, tree-root and tussock;

or a woodpecker with his rapid tattoo
at the start of work. It finishes
in a portico of light, which bottles
all of the business of beyond.

IAN NIMMO WHITE

THE MAIDENBORE ROCK*

The hole ye see cut through the stane
    Wisnae aye sae braid;
Aince she whae could pass through it
    Wis caa'd a maid.

They cam aa frimple-frample-like tae see
    Whae could pass through
An' ony lusty lass whae could
    Wis guid as new.

The puir auld stane wis pentratit
    A thousan thousan times
By hatchin hens whae's squeeze wis heezed
    Up tae the climes.

An' noo the hole is braid eneuch
    Tae tak baith man an' wife
Ye cannae tell whae's no a maid,
    Ach weel—that's life.

The lassie in her kyrtle,
    The auld yin in her shaw:
Baith hae the blessin o the hole,
    The guid rock made them aa.

ALAN BOLD

*The Maidenbore Rock is located below the western slope of West Lomond, on an outcrop of which the 'Bannet Stane' (a bonnet-shaped projection upon a natural pillar) is also part. The cave-like hole in the rock was so narrow that it was claimed only a virgin could pass through it.

107

THE HAIG DISTILLERIES

[John Haig] was born at Kincaple in 1802 and after being educated at St. Andrews University, where he gained a silver medal for mathematics, he joined his father at Seggie to learn the business of distilling.

One day in the summer of 1822 when he was still only twenty he was riding with his old servant, Alexander Berry, along the road which runs through Windygates in Fife. Windygates then, in the days before railways, was a busy posting station for travellers going to Edinburgh from the north-east. John Haig was on his way back to his home at Kincaple after visiting friends in the locality. His attention was arrested by the old Cameron Mills which lay a few yards down the road and which for two centuries had enjoyed "thirled" privileges whereby the local tenants were under obligation to have their corn ground there. It dealt with most of the grain raised on the banks of the River Leven. But the young man was not thinking of grinding corn for bread. The place seemed to him an ideal situation for a distillery. "D'ye ken, Sandy," he said, "there is money to be made here—aye, from whisky."

One of his friends was a certain Captain Wemyss, the landlord of much of the property in the district, and it was from him that he was able to acquire the lease of the ground on which Cameron Bridge distillery was to be built. As he was still a minor, the lease was acquired in his father's name and his father advanced the funds for its purchase. By the summer of 1824, the new building had been erected and one of the early entries in the ledgers under the date of October 30th records that a distillery licence was obtained for the sum of £10 2s. 6d., the 2s. 6d. being for stamp duty. On the same day the first excise duty was paid, amounting to £190 7s. 6d.

Most of the business was done by "riders", or commercial travellers, as we should call them today. These were men of great personality, willing to face wind and weather, who rode their horses, or drove their gigs, along the desolate country roads to visit the landlords of remote inns, and other customers. Much could be done to expand business in this way by a level-headed and genial man; such a man, in fact, as John Haig himself. In his early days he seems to have been his own traveller, for there is an entry in the ledger a month after he had started business: "For a horse… £12 12s. 0d." But soon he had enough to do managing the concern at headquarters.

In the first year no more than a few thousand gallons of spirit were made, but production rapidly expanded and by 1877 had risen to the prodigious figure of 1¼ million gallons. By this time the Bonded Warehouses were capable of storing 3 million gallons and the building covered fourteen acres. But we are moving ahead too fast in our story, for John Haig had scarcely started in business at

Cameron Bridge before an ingenious invention laid the foundations of a revolution in the making of whisky.

This was the Patent Still, invented in 1826 by Robert Stein, a cousin of the Haigs, who still owned the Kilbagie distillery in which so many members of the family had learned their trade. The Patent Still was much more economical than the pot stills previously in use and speeded up the process of distillation. The new apparatus was primarily adopted for the production of grain whisky and in this fact lay the seed of developments which were in the next two generations to transform the business of distilling. John Haig lost no time. He erected a Stein Still at Cameron Bridge in the year following its invention, and a premium of 1*d*. on every gallon distilled was paid to the Steins.

Within a few years, however, the Stein Still was superseded by the Coffey Patent Still, devised in 1831 by Aeneas Coffey, Inspector General of the Excise in Ireland; this is the apparatus which, with minor elaborations and improvements, is still in use. At first only malt spirit, termed "malt aqua" had been produced at Cameron Bridge, but as the Patent Still came into use, more grain spirit was produced and this was much cheaper. The consequent fluctuations in whisky prices gave John Haig much food for thought. He was a man not only of great administrative capacity but of wide grasp and vision. Less than ten years after the establishment of Cameron Bridge we find him striving to interest the Eastern Lowland distillers in a scheme to regulate prices...

In April 1877 an event occurred in the Scotch Whisky trade which was to have far reaching consequences. This was the formation of a new limited company known as The Distillers Co. Ltd, which was registered on 24 April 1877 with a nominal capital of £2,000,000. As the name implied it was a combination of various distillers, all of whom were the owners of one or more grain distilleries. One of these distilleries was that owned by the Haigs at Cameron Bridge, which thereupon became the property of The Distillers Co. Ltd. ...

It was felt necessary that the blending business of John Haig & Company should be removed from Cameron Bridge, and in consequence the firm, at first known as John Haig Sons & Co. was removed to Markinch, some three miles distant. The original partners were John Haig, Hugh Veitch Haig, W. H. Haig and Alexander Harvie Aitken.

John Haig died in the following year, at the end of an era which had witnessed such revolutionary changes in the trade as would have seemed impossible to the young man who had, in his early twenties, selected Cameron Bridge as the site of his distillery. The work which he had accomplished was to open up a new epoch in the Scotch Whisky trade.

JAMES LAVER, *The House of Haig*, 1958.

BY BALGRIEBANK AND BIGHTY, ABOVE BAINTOWN

Taking the right-of-way from Baintown by Balgriebank and Bighty (the highest hearth-stone in Fife) we reach "Kennoway Common" or the "Chappin' Caup" Moor—an old commonty, belonging to the feuars of the village. The "Chappin' Caup" or Quern itself, belonging to the hand-mill, in which the corn of the community was ground, stood till the end of last century at least, in the middle of the moor.

Today, it is silent and remote, a scene of awesome beauty. Billowing waves of bronze and silvering grasses, stirred by the breeze, ripple and flow in the summer sunshine and break into splashes of colour—the shaded crimsons and mauves of the willow-herb, the rose-red of the ling, the brown of the heather a-tip with opening purple, the yellow stars of the creeping tormentil, bracken in every shade of green—while a-wash over all this riot of colour, masses of wild wood-ruff break through like foam-fleck on the sea. Great grey boulders lie here and there, often in groups, looking like play-things that Titans of old, wearying of the game, have petulantly flung aside. At the highest point of the moor, behind Torloisk or "Cauld Hame," stands a circle of wind-vexed trees—relic of the "sacred grove" of Druidical worship, their sole use now to afford shelter for a few moorland sheep from the blasts which sweep down from the Norlands.

Far to the north-west, the Grampian peaks lie in a haze of mist-blue and grey, deepening into purple shadow. Schiehallion, Ben Ledi, and Ben More are plainly visible, and, snuggling down beside the giants, the low green-clad slopes of the Ochils. Eastward, we look over to the wooded slopes of Whalley Den (the Holy Den), with its sacred well, known as the "Brandy Well" (supposed to have been dedicated to St. Brendan), and crowned, near its summit, on the "Chapel Brae" by an old doorway with side niches, all that now remains of a building, which tradition holds was once the small religious House of Kilmux, erected when Merleswain made a grant of the adjoining lands to the Church.

Below lies the "Cadgers' Road," the old, disused loaning, along which fish cadgers were wont to drive their wares from the Royal Burgh of Earlsferry to the King's Palace at Falkland. Away to seaward, Largo Law, with its cleft summit, stands guardian over its magic bay, whose shimmering waters break gently on a long curve of golden sand.

At our feet, on its sunny hill slopes, lies our old-world parish [of Kennoway] with its roots deep in the past of glamorous Scottish history and legend, wistfully greeting the advance guards of the marvellous new age of scientific wonders which is dawning over the earth.

A. M. FINDLAY, *Kennoway:Its History and Legends*, 1946.

ARCHBISHOP SHARP'S JOURNEY FROM KENNOWAY
TO MAGUS MUIR

It was about nine o'clock on Saturday 4th May 1679 when Archbishop Sharp left Captain Seton's house in Kennoway. We can try to envisage the grand equipage drawing away from Cross House, standing gable-end to the Causeway. It must have taken considerable skill to drive the state coach with six horses, coachman, postilion, four servants and two very important passengers along the narrow causey which was cobbled not with today's even-cut setts but with round stones from the burn.

...Tradition has it that Sharp smoked his last pipe at Ceres with Alexander Leslie before setting off on the last stage of his journey to St Andrews. Sharp knew of threats to his life and he may have been aware that crossing the moors beyond Ceres was potentially dangerous. He obviously did not, however, consider the number of servants with him as important, as he sent one of them to pay his respects to the Earl of Crawford. In Ceres kirkyard is the burial chamber of the Lindsays which now has a Victorian tomb of John Lindsay, Earl of Crawford, who died in 1749. The Lindsay vault is now detached but was probably once attached, in the late sixteenth century, to an earlier church.

At Ceres Archbishop Sharp was not much more than halfway from Kennoway to St Andrews and ahead of him lay the route, in reverse, that the Duke of Rothesay may have been taken on his way to his imprisonment and death in Falkland Tower. The road may have been straight enough to Pitscottie but the country was rising to the moors beyond Blebo Craigs.

This hurrying party may have been aware of shadows cast by Drumcarrow Craig but, unlike the captive Duke of Rothesay who was forced to travel at night and into driving rain, when Archbishop Sharp reached the village of Magus it was near enough noon on a bright day, and despite the gloomy atmosphere that many visitors have said they sensed at Magus Muir, in fact it was probably a pleasant enough scene until the coachman saw men riding fast towards them. A pleasant landscape on a sunny May day but suddenly a dangerous place to be even with a coach pulled by six rested and fed horses.★

DUNCAN GLEN, *Historic Fife Murders*, 2002.

★James Sharp (1618-1679), Archbishop of St Andrews, was murdered by Covenanters on 3 May 1679 by the roadside near Magus Muir, between Ceres and St Andrews.

111

AN ACCOUNT OF THE MURDER OF ARCHBISHOP SHARP
written by JAMES RUSSELL, who was one of the murderers

John Balfour said follow me:

...whereupon all the nine rode what they could to Magus Muir, the hills at the nearest, and Andrew Henderson riding afore, being best mounted, and saw them when he was on the top of the hill, and all the rest came up and rode very hard, for the coach was driving hard; and being come near Magus, George Fleming and James Russell riding into the village, and James asked at the goodman if that was the bishop's coach? He fearing, did not tell, but one of his servants, a woman, came running to him and said it was the coach, and she seemed to be overjoyed; and James riding towards the coach, to be sure, seeing the bishop looking out at the door, cast away his cloak and cried, Judas be taken! The bishop cried to the coachman to drive; he firing at him, crying to the rest to come up, and the rest throwing away their cloaks except Rathillet, fired into the coach driving very fast about half a mile, in which time they fired several shots in at all parts of the coach, and Alexander Henderson seeing one Wallace having a cocked carrabine going to fire, gript him in the neck, and threw him down and pulled it out of his hand. Andrew Henderson outran the coach, and stroke the horse in the face with his sword; and James Russell coming to the postilion, commanded him to stand, which he refusing, he stroke him on the face and cut down the side of his shine, and striking at the horse next brake his sword, and gripping the ringeses of the foremost horse in the farthest side: George Fleming fired a pistol in at the north side of the coach beneath his left arm, and saw his daughter dight [prepare or clean] of the furage [wadding for gun or pistol] and riding forward gripping the horses' bridles in the nearest side and held them still, George Balfour fired likewise, and James Russell got George Fleming's sword and lighted off his horse, and ran to the coach door, and desired the bishop to come forth, Judas. He answered, he never wronged man: James declared before the Lord that it was no particular interest nor yet for any wrong that he had done to him, but because he had betrayed the church as Judas, and had wrung his hands these 18 or 19 years in the blood of the saints, but especially at Pentland; and Mr. Guthrie and Mr. Mitchell and James Learmonth; and they were sent by God to execute his vengeance on him this day, and desired him to repent and come forth; and John Balfour on horseback said, Sir, God is our witness that it is not for any wrong thou hast done to me, nor yet for any fear of what thou could do to me, but because thou hast been a murderer of many a poor soul in the kirk of Scotland, and a betrayer of the church, and an open enemy and persecutor of Jesus Christ and his members, whose blood thou hast shed like water on the earth, and therefore thou shalt die! and fired a pistol; and James Russell desired him again to come forth and make him for death, judgment, and eternity; and the bishop said, Save my life, and I will save all yours. James answered, that he knew that it was not in his power either to save or to kill us, for there was no saving of his life, for the blood that he had shed was crying to heaven for vengeance on him, and thrust his shabel at him. John Balfour desired him again to come forth, and he answered, I will come to you, for I know you are a gentleman and will save my life; but I am gone already, and what needs more? And another told him of keeping up of a pardon granted by the king for nine persons at Pentland, and then at the back side of the coach thrust a sword at him, threatening him to go forth; whereupon he went forth, and falling upon his knees, said, For God's sake, save my life; his daughter falling on her knees, begging his life also. But they told him that he should die, and desired him to repent and make for death. Alexander Henderson said, Seeing there has been lives taken for you already, and if ours be taken it shall not be for nought; he rising of his knees went forward, and John Balfour stroke him on the face, and Andrew Henderson stroke him on the hand and cut it, and John Balfour rode him down; whereupon he, lying upon his face as if he had been dead, and James Russell hearing his daughter say to Wallace that there was life in him yet, in the time James was disarming the rest of the bishop's men, went presently to him and cast of his hat, for it would not cut at first, and haked his head in pieces.

Having thus done, his daughter came to him and cursed him, and called him a bloody murderer; and James answered they were not murderers, for they were sent to execute God's vengeance on him; and presently went to the coach, and finding a pair of pistols, took them, and then took out a trunk and brake it up, and finding nothing but women's furniture, and asked what should be done with it; and it was answered, that they would have nothing but papers and arms; and Andrew Henderson lighted, and took a little box and brake it up, and finding some papers, which he took; and opening a cloak-bag they found more papers and a Bible full of porterers [portraits], with a little purse hung in it, a copper dollar, two pistol ball, two turners, two stamps, some coloured thread, and some yellow coloured thing like to pairings of nails, which would not burn, which they took. At this time James Russell was taking the rest of his men's arms, and Wallace, as he would have resisted, came roundly forward, and James Russell smote him on the cheek with his shabel and riped all their pockets, and got some papers and a knife and fork, which he took; and crying to the rest to see that the bishop be dead, William Dalziel lighted, and went and thrust his sword into his belly, and the dirt came out; turning him over, ript his pockets, and found a whinger and knifes conform, with some papers, which he took. James Russell desired his servants to take up their priest now. All this time Andrew Guillan pleaded for his life. John Balfour threatening him to be quiet, he came to Rathillet, who was standing at a distance with his cloak about his mouth all the time on horseback, and desired him to come and cause save his life, who answered, as he meddled not with them nor desired them to take his life, so he durst not plead for him nor forbid them.

Then they all mounted, and going west gathered up some pistols which they had thrown away after fired.

JAMES RUSSELL, from **JAMES KIRKTON**, *The Secret and True History of the Church of Scotland*, 1678.

THE MURDERERS AT MAGUS MUIR

I still see Magus Muir two hundred years ago; a desert place, quite unenclosed; in the midst, the primate's carriage fleeing at the gallop; the assassins loose-reined in pursuit, Burley Balfour, pistol in hand, among the first. No scene of history has ever written itself so deeply on my mind; not because Balfour, that question-able zealot, was an ancestral cousin of my own; not because of the pleadings of the victim and his daughter; not even because of the live bum-bee that flew out of Sharpe's 'bacco-box, thus clearly indicating his complicity with Satan; nor merely because, as it was after all a crime of a fine religious flavour, it figured in Sunday books and afforded a grateful relief from *Ministering Children* or the *Memoirs of Mrs. Katharine Winslowe*. The figure that always fixed my attention is that of Hackston of Rathillet, sitting in the saddle with his cloak about his mouth, and through all that long, bungling, vociferous hurly-burly, revolving privately a case of conscience. He would take no hand in the deed, because he had a private spite against the victim, and 'that action' must be sullied with no suggestion of a worldly motive; on the other hand, 'that action,' in itself, was highly justified, he had cast in his lot with 'the actors,' and he must stay there, inactive but publicly sharing the responsibility. 'You are a gentleman—you will protect me!' cried the wounded old man, crawling towards him. 'I will never lay a hand on you,' said Hackston, and put his cloak about his mouth. It is an old temptation with me, to pluck away that cloak and see the face—to open that bosom and to read the heart. With incomplete romances about Hackston, the drawers of my youth were lumbered. I read him up in every printed book that I could lay my hands on. I even dug among the Wodrow manuscripts, sitting shame-faced in the very room where my hero had been tortured two centuries before, and keenly conscious of my youth in the midst of other and (as I fondly thought) more gifted students. All was vain: that he had passed a riotous non-age, that he was a zealot, that he twice displayed (compared with his grotesque companions) some tincture of soldierly resolution and even of military common sense, and that he figured memorably in the scene on Magus Muir, so much and no more could I make out. But whenever I cast my eyes backward, it is to see him like a landmark on the plains of history, sitting with his cloak about his mouth, inscrutable. How small a thing creates an immortality! I do not think he can have been a man entirely commonplace; but had he not thrown his cloak about his mouth, or had the witnesses forgot to chronicle the action, he would not thus have haunted the imagination of my boyhood, and today he would scarce delay me for a paragraph. An incident, at once romantic and dramatic, which at once awakes the judgment and makes a picture for the eye, how little do we realise its perdurable power!

ROBERT LOUIS STEVENSON, *The Coast of Fife*, 1888.

THE MURDER OF DAVID, DUKE OF ROTHESAY*

Far different had been the fate of the misguided Heir of Scotland, from that which was publicly given out in the town of Falkland. His ambitious uncle had determined on his death, as the means of removing the first and most formidable barrier betwixt his own family and the throne. James, the younger son of the King, was a mere boy, who might at more leisure be easily set aside. Ramorny's views of aggrandizement, and the resentment which he had latterly entertained against his master, made him a willing agent in young Rothsay's destruction. Dwining's love of gold, and his native malignity of disposition, rendered him equally forward. It had been resolved, with the most calculating cruelty, that all means which might leave behind marks of violence were to be carefully avoided, and the extinction of life suffered to take place of itself, by privation of every kind acting upon a frail and impaired constitution. The Prince of Scotland was not to be murdered, as Ramorny had expressed himself on another occasion,—he was only to cease to exist.

Rothsay's bedchamber in the Tower of Falkland was well adapted for the execution of such a horrible project. A small narrow staircase, scarce known to exist, opened from thence by a trap-door to the subterranean dungeons of the castle, through a passage by which the feudal lord was wont to visit, in private, and disguise, the inhabitants of those miserable regions. By this staircase the villains conveyed the insensible Prince to the lowest dungeon of the Castle so deep in the bowels of the earth, that no cries or groans, it was supposed, could possibly be heard, while the strength of its door and fastenings must for a long time have defied force, even if the entrance could have been discovered. Bonthron, who had been saved from the gallows for the purpose, was the willing agent of Ramorny's unparalleled cruelty to his misled and betrayed patron.

This wretch revisited the dungeon at the time when the Prince's lethargy began to wear off and when, awaking to sensation, he felt himself deadly cold, unable to move, and oppressed with fetters which scarce permitted him to stir

*Here Scott follows his common practice of fictionalising an actual historical event.

from the dank straw on which he was laid. His first idea was, that he was in a fearful dream—his next brought a confused augury of the truth. He called, shouted, yelled at length in a frenzy,—but no assistance came, and he was only answered by the vaulted roof of the dungeon. The agent of Hell heard these agonizing screams, and deliberately reckoned them against the taunts and reproaches with which Rothsay had expressed his instinctive aversion to him. When, exhausted and hopeless, the unhappy youth remained silent, the savage resolved to present himself before the eyes of his prisoner. The locks were drawn, the chain fell; the Prince raised himself as high as his fetters permitted,—a red glare, against which he was fain to shut his eyes, streamed through the vault; and when he opened them again, it was on the ghastly form of one whom he had reason to think dead. He sunk back in horror. "I am judged and condemned!" he exclaimed; "and the most abhorred fiend in the infernal regions is sent to torment me."

"I live, my lord," said Bonthron; "and that you may live and enjoy life, be pleased to sit up and eat your victuals."

"Free me from these irons," said the Prince,—"release me from this dungeon,—and, dog as thou art, thou shalt be the richest man in Scotland."

"If you would give me the weight of your shackles in gold," said Bonthron, "I would rather see the iron on you than have the treasure myself—But look up—you were wont to love delicate fare—behold how I have catered for you." The wretch, with fiendish glee, unfolded a piece of raw hide covering the bundle which he bore under his arm, and, passing the light to and fro before it, showed the unhappy Prince a bull's head recently hewn from the trunk, and known in Scotland as the certain signal of death.

SIR WALTER SCOTT, from *The Fair Maid of Perth*, 1828.

NAE BIELD IN FALKLAND

Dinna bide in yon chaumer
Wi the wee, clorty winnock
At the tap o the hoose
Up the kypie stair
I tell ye, ye'll no ken yersel
Aince up in yon chaumer
An the door steekit efter ye.

Aiblins ye'll try a canny keek oot the pane
Dichtin the gless wi yer thoum
A'thing unco quaet—deil's wark doon the wynd
Syne, ower the causey, tae yer frichtit een

The gantin Palace wa', rowed in deid–licht,
The peelie mune blintin owre cauld stane,
Ower wally een o beast or hoodie craw
Or halie kists o kings—
Tak tent—ye'll catch them keekin at ye—back!

Nae warm bield beddin doon in yon chaumer
Ye may hap yer heid nicht lang atween the sheets
Stappin yer lugs tae the wun's wersh chunnerin,
They'll aye come for ye, loupin oot their kists
Een bleezin as het coals,
Corbies wi knablick nebs,
Stookie saunts o the kirk,
Queer wizzent carls an quines
An a hail smarrich o Stuarts.

LILLIAS SCOTT FORBES

From *THE DREME*

TO KING JAMES V

Quhen thow wes young, I bure thee in myne arme
Full tenderlie, tyll thow begouth to gang,
And in thy bed oft happit thee full warme
With lute in hand, syne, sweitlie to thee sang!
Sum tyme, in dansing, feiralie I flang,
And, sum tyme, on myne office takkend cure
And, sum tyme, kyke ane feind, transfegurate;
And, sum tyme, lyke the greislie gaist of gye:
In divers formis, oftymes, disfigurate;
And, sum tyme, dissagyist full pleasandlye.
So, sen thy birth, I have continewalye
BeNe occupyt, and aye to thy plesoure;
And sum tyme, seware, coppare, and caruoure...

Fare weill Falkland, the fortalice of Fife—
Thy polite park under the Lomond low
Sum tyme in thee I led ane busy life
Thy fallow deer to see them raike in row.

SIR DAVID LYNDSAY of the Mount, c. 1526.

117

THE LAST DAYS OF KING JAMES V

He passit to Edinburgh and thair tairit viij dayis witht great dollour and lamen-
tatioun of the tinsall and schame of his lieges quhilk was be misfortoun and evill
goverment brocht to schame and dishonour quhilk pat the kingis grace in dispair
that he could never recover his honour againe. This being done the king passit
out of Hallieruidhouse to Falkland and thair became so heavie and so dolarous
that he nether eit nor drank that had good degestioun, and so he became so
vehement seik that no man had hope of his lyffe. Than he send for certane of
his lordis baith sperituall and temporall to have thair consall bot or they come
he was nearhand strangled to death be the extreme melancollie.

. . .

Be this the post came out of Lythgow schawing to the king goode tydingis that
the quene was deliverit. The king inquyrit "wither it was man or woman." The
messenger said "it was ane fair douchter." The king ansuerit and said. "Adew,
fair weill, it come witht ane 'lase, it will pase witht ane lase,'" and so he recom-
mendit himself to the marcie of Almightie god and spak ane lyttill then frome
that tyme fourtht, bot turnit his bak into his lordis and his face into the wall. At
this tyme David Bettoun cardienall of Scottland standing in presentis of the king,
seing him begin to faill of his strength and naturall speiche held ane through
of papir to his grace and caussit him subscryue the samin quhair the cardenall
wrait that plessit him for his awin particular weill, thinkand to have autorietie
and prehemenence in the goverment of the countrie bot we may knaw heirbe
the kingis legacie was verie schort, ffor in this maner he depairtit as I sall now
tell. He turnit him bak and luikit and beheld all his lordis about him and gaif
ane lyttill smyle and lauchter, syne kissit his hand and offerit the samyn to all
his lordis round about him and thairefter held upe his handis to god and yeildit
the spreit. This nobill king depairtit in this manner as I have schawin to yow, at
Falkland in his awin palice the xx day of the monetht of December in the yeir
of god I^m v^o xlij yeiris and that verie quyetlie for few was at his depairting except
the cardinall the erle of argyle the erle of rothus the lord askyne the lord Lyndsay
the Doctour Mr Michall Dury schir David Lyndesay of the Mont Lyone herauld
the laird of graunge andro wood of largow Normond leslie maister of rothus.
The rest war bot his awin secreit serwandis…

ROBERT LYNDSAY OF PITSCOTTIE

Och, awa to Freuchie and fry mice.

ANONYMOUS

The Lomond Hills

LOMOND HILLS

These hills are very dear to the people of Fife. Not by virtue of their height, for although they are the highest hills in the Kingdom they are not high as Scottish hills go, and the highest, the West Lomond, is only 1713 feet above sea level. But they stand in grand isolation between the valleys of the Eden and the Leven, and their handsome skyline is visible from nearly every part of the Kingdom. "My own blue Lomonds", Fife's artist David Wilkie called them… At the end of the 18th century a lead mine was worked near the farm of Hangingmire and record has it that silver was extracted from the ore. The English manager of the mine convinced the proprietor, who was working the place at his own expense, that it would be more profitable to sell the ore in England. Six tons were sent to Perth for shipment. Then the English manager disappeared and so did the ore. In 1852 came news of a find on West Lomond richer than silver. Gold! The hill became the scene of a gold rush. But the gold was as difficult to locate as is the ghost of poor Jenny Nettles, the fair-haired, blue-eyed maiden who, betrayed by a soldier of Falkland's Palace garrison, died with her child on the Lomonds.

The Kingdom of Fife and Kinross-shire, edited by **THEO LANG**, 1951.

JENNY NETTLES

Saw ye Jenny Nettles,
Jenny Nettles, Jenny Nettles,
Saw ye Jenny Nettles
Coming frae the Market;
Bag and Baggage on her Back,
Her Fee and Bountith in her Lap;
Bag and Baggage on her Back,
And a Babie in her Oxter.

I met ayont the Kairny,
Jenny Nettles, Jenny Nettles,
Singing till her Bairny,
Robin Rattles' Bastard;
To feel the Dool upo' the Stool,
And ilka ane that mocks her,
She round about seeks Robin out,
To stap it in his Oxter.

Fy, fy! Robin Rattle,
Robin Rattle, Robin Rattle;
Fy, fy! Robin Rattle,
Use Jenny Nettles kindly:
Score out the Blame, and shun the Shame,
And without mair Debate o't,
Take hame your Wain, make Jenny fain,
The leal and leesome Gate o't.

ANONYMOUS

From *A DRUNK MAN LOOKS AT THE THISTLE* (1926)

And as at sicna times am I,
I wad ha'e Scotland to my eye
Until I saw a timeless flame
Tak' Auchtermuchty for a name,
And kent that Ecclefechan stood
As pairt o' an eternal mood.

HUGH MACDIARMID

From *THE PRIVATE MEMOIRS AND CONFESSIONS OF A JUSTIFIED SINNER* (1824)

"It was but the year afore the last, that the people o' the town o' Auchtermuchty grew so rigidly righteous, that the meanest hind among them became a shining light in ither towns an' parishes. There was nought to be heard, neither night nor day, but preaching, praying, argumentation, an' catechising in a' the famous town o' Auchtermuchty. The young men wooed their sweethearts out o' the Song o' Solomon, an' the girls returned answers in strings o' verses out o' the Psalms. At the lint-swinglings [flax-beatings], they said questions round; and read

120

chapters, and sang hymns at bridals; auld and young prayed in their dreams, an' prophesied in their sleep, till the deils in the farrest nooks o' hell were alarmed, and moved to commotion. Gin it hadna been an auld carl, Robin Ruthven, Auchtermuchty wad at that time hae been ruined and lost for ever. But Robin was a cunning man, an' had rather mae wits than his ain, for he had been in the hands o' the fairies when he was young, an' a' kinds o' spirits were visible to his een, an' their language as familiar to him as his ain mother tongue. Robin was sitting on the side o' the West Lowmond, ae still gloomy night in September, when he saw a bridal o' corbie craws coming east the lift, just on the edge o' the gloaming. The moment that Robin saw them he kenned, by their move-ments, that they were craws o' some ither warld than this; so he signed himself, and crap into the middle o' his bourock. The corbie craws came a' an' sat down round about him, an' they poukit their black sooty wings, an' spread them out to the breeze to cool; and Robin heard ae corbie speaking, an' another answer-ing him; and the tane said to the tither: 'Where will the ravens find a prey the night?'—'On the lean crazy souls o' Auchtermuchty,' quo the tither.—'I fear they will be o'er weel wrappit up in the warm flannens o' faith, an' clouted wi' the dirty duds o' repentance, for us to mak a meal o',' quo the first.—'Whaten vile sounds are these that I hear coming bumming up the hill?' 'O these are the hymns and praises o' the auld wives and creeshy louns o' Auchtermuchty, wha are gaun crooning their way to heaven; an' gin it warna for the shame o' be-ing beat, we might let our great enemy tak them. For sic a prize as he will hae! Heaven, forsooth! What shall we think o' heaven, if it is to be filled wi' vermin like thae, amang whom there is mair poverty and pollution, than I can name.' 'No matter for that,' said the first, 'we cannot have our power set at defiance; though we should put them in the thief's hole, we must catch them, and catch them with their own bait too. Come all to church to-morrow, and I'll let you hear how I'll gull the saints of Auchtermuchty. In the mean time, there is a feast on the Sidlaw hills tonight, below the hill of Macbeth,—Mount, Diabolus, and fly.' Then, with loud croaking and crowing, the bridal of corbies again scaled the dusky air, and left Robin Ruthven in the middle of his cairn.

"The next day the congregation met in the kirk of Auchtermuchty, but the minister made not his appearance. The elders ran out and in, making inquiries; but they could learn nothing, save that the minister was missing. They ordered the clerk to sing a part of the 119th Psalm, until they saw if the minister would cast up. The clerk did as he was ordered, and by the time he reached the 77th verse, a strange divine entered the church, by the *western door,* and advanced solemnly up to the pulpit. The eyes of all the congregation were riveted on the sublime stranger, who was clothed in a robe of black sackcloth, that flowed all around him, and trailed far behind, and they weened him an angel, come to exhort them, in disguise. He read out his text from the Prophecies of Ezekiel, which consisted of these singular words: 'I will overturn, overturn, overturn it; and it shall be no more, until he come, whose right it is, and I will give it him.'

"From these words he preached such a sermon as never was heard by human ears, at least never by ears of Auchtermuchty. It was a true, sterling, gospel sermon—it was striking, sublime, and awful in the extreme. He finally made out the IT, mentioned in the text, to mean, properly and positively, the notable town of Auchtermuchty. He proved all the people in it, to their perfect satisfaction, to be in the gall of bitterness and bond of iniquity, and he assured them, that God would overturn them, their principles, and professions; and that they should be no more, until the devil, the town's greatest enemy, came, and then it should be given unto him for a prey, for it was his right, and to him it belonged, if there was not forthwith a radical change made in all their opinions and modes of worship.

"The inhabitants of Auchtermuchty were electrified—they were charmed; they were actually raving mad about the grand and sublime truths delivered to them, by this eloquent and impressive preacher of Christianity. 'He is a prophet of the Lord,' said one, 'sent to warn us, as Jonah was sent to the Ninevites.' 'O, he is an angel sent from heaven, to instruct this great city,' said another, 'for no man ever uttered truths so sublime before.' The good people of Auchtermuchty were in perfect raptures with the preacher, who had thus sent them to hell by the slump, tag, rag, and bobtail! Nothing in the world delights a truly religious people so much, as consigning them to eternal damnation. They wondered after the preacher—they crowded together, and spoke of his sermon with admiration, and still as they conversed, the wonder and the admiration increased; so that honest Robin Ruthven's words would not be listened to. It was in vain that he told them he heard a raven speaking, and another raven answering him: the people laughed him to scorn, and kicked him out of their assemblies, as a one who spoke evil of dignities; and they called him a warlock, an' a daft body, to think to mak language out o' the crouping o' craws.

"The sublime preacher could not be heard of, although all the country was sought for him, even to the minutest corner of St. Johnston and Dundee; but as he had announced another sermon on the same text, on a certain day, all the inhabitants of that populous country, far and near, flocked to Auchtermuchty. Cupar, Newburgh, and Strathmiglo, turned out men, women, and children. Perth and Dundee gave their thousands; and from the East Nook of Fife to the foot of the Grampian hills, there was nothing but running and riding that morning to Auchtermuchty. The kirk would not hold the thousandth part of them. A splendid tent was erected on the brae north of the town, and round that the countless congregation assembled.

"When they were all waiting anxiously for the great preacher, behold, Robin Ruthven set up his head in the tent, and warned his countrymen to beware of the doctrines they were about to hear, for he could prove, to their satisfaction, that they were all false, and tended to their destruction!

"The whole multitude raised a cry of indignation against Robin, and dragged him from the tent, the elders rebuking him, and the multitude threatening to resort to stronger measures; and though he told them a plain and unsophisticated tale of the black corbies, he was only derided. The great preacher appeared once more, and went through his two discourses with increased energy and approbation. All who heard him were amazed, and many of them went into fits, writhing and foaming in a state of the most horrid agitation. Robin Ruthven sat on the outskirts of the great assembly, listening with the rest, and perceived what they, in the height of their enthusiasm, perceived not,—the ruinous tendency of the tenets so sublimely inculcated. Robin kenned the voice of his friend the corby-craw again, and was sure he could not be wrang: sae when public worship was finished, a' the elders an' a' the gentry flocked about the great preacher, as he stood on the green brae in the sight of the hale congregation, an' a' war alike anxious to pay him some mark o' respect. Robin Ruthven came in amang the thrang, to try to effect what he had promised; and, with the greatest readiness and simplicity, just took haud o' the side an' wide gown, an' in sight of a' present, held it aside as high as the preacher's knee, and behold, there was a pair o' cloven feet! The auld thief was fairly catched in the very height o' his proud conquest, an' put down by an auld carl. He could feign nae mair, but gnashing on Robin wi' his teeth, he dartit into the air like a fiery dragon, an' keust a reid rainbow our the taps o' the Lowmonds.

"A' the auld wives an' weavers o' Auchtermuchty fell down flat wi' affright, an' betook them to their prayers aince again, for they saw the dreadfu' danger they had escapit, an' frae that day to this it is a hard matter to gar an Auchtermuchty man listen to a sermon at a', an' a harder ane still to gar him applaud ane, for he thinks aye that he sees the cloven foot peeping out frae aneath ilka sentence."

JAMES HOGG

THE WEE COOPER OF FIFE

There was a wee cooper that leeved in Fife,
Nickety-nackety, noo, noo, noo;
And he has gotten a gentle wife,
Hey Willie Wallacky, hoo John Dougal;
Alane, quo' Rushity, roue, roue, roue.

She wadna bake, nor she wadna brew,
Nickety-nackety, noo, noo, noo;
For the spoiling o' her comely hue,

Hey Willie Wallacky, hoo John Dougal;
Alane, quo' Rushity, roue, roue, roue.

She wadna card, nor she wadna spin,
Nickety, Nackety, noo, noo, noo,
For the shamin' o' her gentle kin,
Hey Willy Wallacky, hoo John Dougal,
Alane, quo' Rushity, roue, roue, roue.

She wadna wash, nor she wadna wring,
Nickety, Nackety, noo, noo, noo,
For the spoiling o' her gowden ring,
Hey Willy Wallacky, hoo John Dougal,
Alane, quo' Rushity, roue, roue, roue.

The Cooper has gane to his woo' pack,
Nickety, Nackety, noo, noo, noo,
And he's laid a sheep's skin on his wife's back,
Hey Willy Wallacky, hoo John Dougall,
Alane, quo' Rushity, roue, roue, roue.

It's I'll no thrash ye for your gentle kin,
Nickety, Nackety, noo, noo, noo,
But I will skelp my ain sheep's skin,
Hey Willy Wallacky, hoo John Dougal,
Alane, quo' Rushity, roue, roue, roue.

Oh I will bake, and I will brew,
Nickety, Nackety, noo, noo, noo,
And nae mair think o' my comely hue,
Hey Willy Wallacky, hoo John Dougal,
Alane, quo' Rushity, roue, roue, roue.

Oh I will card, and I will spin,
Nickety, Nackety, noo, noo, noo,
And nae mair think o' my gentle kin,
Hey Willy Wallacky, hoo John Dougal,
Alane, quo' Rushity, roue, roue, roue.

Oh will wash, and I will wring,
Nickety, Nackety. noo, noo, noo,

And nae mair think o' my gowden ring,
Hey Willy Wallacky, hoo John Dougal,
Alane, quo' Rushity, roue, roue, roue.

A ye wha ha'e gotten a gentle wife,
Nickety, Nackety, noo, noo, noo,
Just you send for the wee Cooper o' Fife,
Hey Willy Wallacky, hoo John Dougal,
Alane, quo' Rushity, roue, roue, roue.

ANONYMOUS

JIMMY (SHAND) IN A NUTSHELL

Bill McCue did a brave thing on Monday night. In the first of a BBC Scotland series, The Scottish Tradition, he attempted to interview the band leader Jimmy Shand. It was gratifying to learn that the legendary octogenarian, last seen in typically lugubrious form during the BBC's Hogmanay show, is capable of the occasional shy smile. Where Bill McCue went wrong was in imagining that he could break down the verbal defences of Auchtermuchty's best-known citizen. Jimmy fully justified his reputation for elevating the humble monosyllable to the status of an art form.

McCue, imprisoned in a set that might have been designed for Anthony Hopkins in Silence of the Lambs, tried every trick in the book: flattery, gentle teasing, encouraging laughter. At one desperate moment he even dared to suggest that he and Jimmy had a lot in common. It was difficult to tell if Jimmy agreed; Jimmy wasn't saying. But Jimmy wasn't saying much about anything.

About his musicianship, the lovely man had least of all to say. "It was a new technique you were developing," Bill reminded him. "Ah wouldna' say it was new," Jimmy mumbled darkly. So the conversation turned to the places he had been during his long career. "All over," Jimmy replied. Indeed: all over in more ways than one. But with another 20 minutes to fill somehow, Bill had no alternative but to press on. How about hobbies? Hadn't he been a keen motor-cyclist? He had.

"Ay," said Bill, "there's no' many hedges you havenae been over in Auchter-muchty."

"I wouldna' say that," Jimmy replied.

"What were your other hobbies?"

"No' many."

Now this was the point at which a lesser interviewer might have been dragged from the cell, screaming for mercy. But not the intrepid McCue: far

125

from pleading for early parole, he was determined to see out his time like a man.

"Where did you keep your boat?" he persisted.

"Wormit."

"Where did you sail?"

"In the Tay."

"You never ventured into the deep blue sea?"

"Nut."

Well, that seemed to be Jimmy's hobbies all wrapped up; in a nutshell, as it were.

KENNETH ROY

MACDUFF'S CROSS*

Nay, smile not, Lady, when I speak of witchcraft,
And say that still there lurks amongst our glens
Some touch of strange enchantment.
  Mark that fragment,
I mean that rough-hewn block of massive stone,
Placed on the summit of this mountain-pass,
Commanding prospect wide o'er field and fell,
And peopled village and extended moorland,
And the wide ocean and majestic Tay,
To the far distant Grampians. Do not deem it
A loosen'd portion of the neighbouring rock,
Detach'd by storm and thunder,—'twas the pedestal
On which, in ancient times, a Cross was rear'd,
Carved o'er with words which foil'd philologists;
And the events it did commemorate
Were dark, remote, and undistinguishable
As were the mystic characters it bore.
But, mark,—a wizard, born on Avon's bank,
Tuned but his harp to this wild northern theme,
And, lo! the scene is hallow'd. None shall pass,
Now, or in afterdays, beside that stone,
But he shall have strange visions; thoughts and words,

---

*As featured in the play from which this extract was taken, Macduff's Cross, on the hill above Newburgh, served as an unusual sanctuary; according to legend, members of the Clan Macduff who had killed in anger would be immune from justice if they managed to reach the cross and then hold on to one of the nine rings which were once attached to it.

That shake, or rouse, or thrill the human heart,
Shall rush upon his memory when he hears
The spirit-stirring name of this rude symbol;
Oblivious ages, at that simple spell,
Shall render back their terrors with their woes,
Alas! and with their crimes; and the proud phantoms
Shall move with step familiar to his eye.

SIR WALTER SCOTT, 1823.

LINDORES LOCH

No traveller can survey the loch of Lindores, when it opens at once on his view, without being both surprised and pleased. The small wood of Wood-Mill, just showing its northern extremity on the S.W., the manse, church, and church-yard, standing solitary on the W., and the old mansion-house of Old Lindores, with the trees that surround it on the N., have a very fine effect. Taken together they justify the following lines occasioned by the death of the late minister, Mr. Millar:

'Tis not the site that fixes my regard,
Nor lake, nor grove, nor hills, inspire the bard;
Though nature here might warm a Thomson's lay,
Or a Salvator Rosa's powers display;
And richly grants, as genius may choose,
Helvetian manners, and Helvetian views;
Another hour may note the varying face
Of vale and mountain, and their beauties trace;
Our morning walks renew and frequent stand,
To mark that Abdie is a Switzerland.

From **ANONYMOUS**, 'Parish of Abdie' [1791-93], *The Statistical Account of Scotland*, Vol. X, Fife.

TWO RURAL RUINED CHURCHES

St Magridin's (Old Parish) Church, Abdie

The roofless remains of old Abdie Church are close to Lindores Loch and to stand on the shore of the loch on a still summer's morning, with only the lightest of ripples on the water, is an excellent prelude to a visit to St Magridin's.

This old church has been linked to a Culdee settlement dedicated to St Magridin. It was rededicated by Bishop David de Bernham in 1242 but later adapted for Reformed worship. The best of what has survived since the 13th

127

century can be seen at the east end of the roofless remains. The building was in use until 1827 when the new building, some 500 metres to the north, was completed. The original narrow rectangle can be envisaged if the north transept, porch and birdcage bellcote on the west gable are ignored. They belong to the 17th century. The building was repaired in 1803, abandoned in 1827 and, as an inscription informs, "Repaired 1856, DW" with the cross on the east gable belonging to that date.

The Statistical Account (1791-93) for the parish of Abdie was written not by the minister, as the parish was then vacant, but by "a Friend to Statistical Inquiries" who wrote that it was "situated between Abernethy and Monimail on the S. of the river Tay, in the heart of the range of high lands, which, to westward, is known by the name of Ochil Hills". This anonymous contributor to the *Account* was critical of the manse's site and not much enamoured by the old kirk, "The situation of the minister's manse is, perhaps, as unfavourable to health, as any other house in the parish; for it stands close by a lake of considerable extent in low and wet ground... The parish is at present vacant. Earl Mansfield is patron. The church is an old narrow building, low in the walls, and poorly lighted. The manse is lately repaired, and tolerably commodious."

From the Rev. Laurence Miller, who wrote *The New Statistical Account* in March 1836, we learn, "The old church, which is now in ruins, may be traced to the beginning of the fifteenth century. There still remains in the porch the basin for the holy water, and, till lately, the steps that led to the altar." We may now date some parts of the church from the thirteenth century.

From Mr. Miller we learn that a new "church was built in 1827. It may accommodate 500 or 600. It is a plain substantial building, planned by [William] Burn, and cost about L.1200. The manse was built in 1721. The offices are new." This church of 1827 is passed on the way to the old building and somehow seems more isolated than St Magridin's, although it is only a few minutes' walk from the village of Grange of Lindores and in sight of the railway line to Perth.

Here also close to the entrance to the kirkyard, is a Gig House which today shelters a very interesting pre-Christian Symbol Stone which once stood on a low hill overlooking the village of Lindores. This Stone is incised with abstract symbols, the meanings of which we can only guess at, although a map-maker's benchmark is all too evident, as are marks made recently when this stone was used as a sundial.

Monimail Old Parish Church

The two parish church buildings of Monimail can be reached by climbing the hill from Collessie which passes Halhill Farm, or the hill from Letham which sits off the A92 Glenrothes to Dundee road.

The *Statistical Account*, 1791, was written by Rev. Samuel Martin who wrote bluntly, "The church is a long narrow building, rather old and incommodious. The manse being very old, and insufficient, a new and more commodious one is about to be erected... The Earl of Leven is patron." Martin added a footnote, "The bell is on the east end of the church. It was erected about 40 years ago, when the former one became insufficient: that bell had been used from the days of Robert the Bruce, as appeared by an inscription on it. The church was new-roofed about 50 years ago."

Mr. Martin was minister for 53 years, dying in 1829 aged 89 years. It was during his time that the old church was vacated and a new one built in 1792. Mr. Martin was the first to be buried in that part of the old kirkyard known as the "minister's ground" and it is appropriate that the minister who was the last one to conduct services in the old church was buried within the walls of the kirk. His wife and some of his children are also interred there.

Mr. Martin was succeeded by his grandson, Rev. James Brodie, who was at Monimail until 1843 when he 'came out' with about one-third of the ministers of the Church of Scotland to form the Free Church. With Brodie went 130 members of his congregation and together they built the Free Church at Bow of Fife. It is pleasing, however, that he is buried in Monimail near his grandfather.

The New Statistical Account of 1836 was written by Brodie who was able to describe the new parish church built in 1796 as "rather a handsome building, with a tower at the east end, and is in thorough repair. It affords accommodation for nearly 600 persons... The manse was built in 1790, and is still in excellent condition." Today the manse is no longer in Monimail as the Rev. Mitchell Collins is also minister for Creich and Kilmany and, indeed, the old parish of Flisk.

No record of the ruined Monimail Church seems to exist before 1298 when Edward I of England, believing the See of St Andrews to be vacant, presented Robert de Carteret "to the church of Monymel". It could be that when Bishop William Lamberton returned from his consecration at Rome he replaced this English intruder. It could have been Bishop Lamberton who began building an Episcopal palace at Monimail. Today the tower over the wall from the old kirkyard is a fragment of a later palace of the archbishops of St Andrews. For those who like visiting kirkyards this is a fascinating place. The ruins of the old church are complex, but the ruined walls of the chancel are discernible. We can see a round-arched tomb recess in the north wall and beside it a sacrament house with an ogee-arched aumbry under two shields; these may be fifteenth-century. The right shield is carved with the royal arms and surmounted by a crown. The early-seventeenth century north, or Melville, aisle is in good condition; its south gable could have been built up when the church was left to ruin in 1797; on it is the coroneted monogram of George, Earl of Melville, dating from about 1700.

The north lodge of Melville House is near the entrance to the old kirkyard. Currently unoccupied, the classically-styled Melville House was built between 1697 and 1703 for the first Earl of Melville who died in 1707. The next Earl, David Melville, also became Earl of Leven on the death of his mother, Katherine Leslie, grand-daughter of General Sir Alexander Leslie, first Earl of Leven. The Earls of Leven and Melville remained at Melville House into the twentieth century; some of their memorials can be seen in the Parish Church of 1796.

Another minister buried in the old kirkyard is Rev. James Brunton who came to Monimail in 1882 and died in 1905. His wife, Emily Douglas, was the daughter of an Edinburgh lawyer who rented Melville House during the summer months. Mrs Brunton died in 1901 and, like her husband, is buried in the enclosure. In addition to those of the ministers, there are many interesting old memorials and headstones in the old kirkyard, including those of the Balfours of Fernie Castle. There is the elaborate memorial of David Langdale Lindiferon who died on 9th December 1860 aged 67 years. His wife, Isabella Russell, had died in 1842, aged 39 years. The sculptor of this elaborate piece was Anderson K. Christie, Perth.

In the north-west corner of the kirkyard is the burial ground of the Nairn family, who made a very considerable fortune out of manufacturing linoleum and other floorcloths in Kirkcaldy. Sir Michael Barker Nairn, first Baronet, had this burial area excavated from very rocky ground. Sir Michael was a member of the Free Church at Bow of Fife and his generous support of it allowed the building to be twice reconstructed. The Monimail manse is now Monimail House and in the new Monimail cemetery is the headstone of Elizabeth Livingston Spencer-Nairn, née Henderson, of Monimail House, who died in 1985. Sir Michael Nairn bought part of the Rankeillor estate which was once owned by the Hope family, and the monumental pillar on the top of Mount Hill is to the memory of Lieutenant-General John Hope who became the fourth Earl of Hopetoun. The Mount is also important for its associations with Sir David Lindsay, the poet and dramatist.

Downhill from Monimail in Collessie kirkyard is the burial ground of Sir James Melville, of Halhill, the distinguished courtier and diplomat in the time of Mary, Queen of Scots, who left papers which have been published as very readable diaries or memoirs. The outside wall of this burial ground carries a memorable inscription.

DUNCAN GLEN, *Ruined Rural Fife Churches*, 2002.

> Ye loadin pilgrims passing langs this way,
> Pans [pause] on your fall and your offences past.
> Hou your frail flesh first formit of the clay

In dust mon be dissolvit at the last.
Repent, amend, on Christ the burden cast
Of your sad sinnes, who can your sauls refresh,
Syne raise from grave to gloir your grislie flesh
Defyle not Christ's kirk with your carrion,
A solemne sait for God's service prepard
For praier, preaching, and communion.
Your byrial should be in the kirkyaird.
On your uprysing set your great regard,
When saul and body joynes with joy to ring
In Heaven for ay with Christ our Head and King.

Inscription on the roadside wall of the recently-restored Sir James Melville tomb dated 1609, which it has been suggested was written by Sir James, but it was probably written by his daughter, Elizabeth, Lady Culross.

MY DEAR BROTHER, WITH COURAGE BEARE THE CROSSE

My dear Brother, with courage beare the crosse,
Joy shall be joyned with all thy sorrow here;
High is thy hope; disdain this earthly drosse!
Once shall you see the wished day appear.
Now it is dark, thy sky cannot be clear,
After the clouds, it shall be calm anone,
Wait on his will whose blood hath bought you dear,
Extoll his name, tho' outward joys be gone.
Look to the Lord, thou art not left alone,
Since he is there, quhat pleasure canst thou take!—
He is at hand, and hears thy heavy moan,
End out thy faught, and suffer for his sake!
   A sight most bright thy soul shall shortly see,
   When store of glore thy rich reward shall be.

ELIZABETH MELVILLE, LADY CULROSS (c.1580-1640)

COLLESSIE AND MONIMAIL TO CUPAR

If you approach Collessie by road from Auchtermuchty and alight at Trafalgar Inn you have two roads immediately before you going eastward. The right fork is the main Cupar road: the left leads to Collessie and Monimail, and in

131

the angle between them stands the schoolhouse shaded with trees. When you proceed past the school by the left-hand route you know at once from the surroundings that you are on the track of rustic pursuits. Very shortly a wynd diverges going down to the Collessie hamlet which lies at the burnside. There is a verge of small thatched cottages with grass sprouting by the walls and a stray head of daffodil in a doorway plot recalling someone's bygone love of flowers. Your way then crosses the lively little stream that comes trotting out of Collessie Den. As I stood on the bridge on the day that I recall, two yellow wagtails, somewhat rare to be seen, were fly-catching farther down above the glancing water.

This way (which is undoubtedly the early and true approach to Collessie) having gone down now proceeds up again through the houses by a wynd to the kirkyard gate. In the natural disposition of this neighbourhood the land rather quaintly and suddenly has risen into a knoll about two hundred feet high, and the old village, beginning at the foot, has climbed up and arranged itself in terrace fashion about it, until its thatched or tiled roofs are very little below the tall yew hedge that encircles the place of burial on the top.

At the foot you meet a number of cottages that have long out-lived their day. Somehow they are not unpleasant in their desolation, their walls being decorated with the green tufts and small blue flowers of toad-flax. Protected perhaps by some right of ownership they linger beneath the neat houses that rise higher up. The latter have garden plots on shelving banks set with homely blossoms, and at the gable ends there are butts to catch rainwater from the roofs. Collessie is surely the quaintest inland village of Fife, and when the train stops at it on a peaceful summer day (as it once did) you feel that the world of commerce and industry is very far out of sight, and is quite out of mind. Crowning the knoll is the stone-built church, raising its firm but graceful spire into the clear sky.

It is to it that the wynd goes steeply up, and when you reach the place where the kirkyard wall impends you see above you, outwards to the wynd, the carved faces of ancient monumental stones, chief of which is the imposing one belonging to Sir James Melville of Hallhill. It is still possible to read the sonnet inscribed on its wasting stone. Sir James, a famous courtier in the reign of Queen Mary, was the son of Sir John Melville of Raith, an ardent reformer. That the monument should be set overlooking the wynd shows that this was the customary avenue of approach, a fact which is probably emphasised by the opening line of the pious verse, "Ye loadin pilgrims passing langs this way"…

From the green plot of the kirkyard you may look over a widespread scene. The whole Howe valley lies before you to the south and east, and you see it settled with little towns, enriched with woods and bounded by low opposing hills. Slightly behind you on the north side are the open braes of Dunbog and

Monimail. Melville House in white stone is well in view. This latter was the site also of old Hallhill associated with Henry Balnaves and the early Melvilles. Leaning on the churchyard wall you can overlook the red-tiled roofs of the prettily-set village beneath with the ruined cottages at the foot: it is a pleasing and most unusual setting.

The kirk itself, rising on this quiet uplifted situation, is a handsome building of brown freestone with a square tower and spire. It was built in 1839 and replaced a small narrow building of pre-Reformation times, the floor of which is said to have been sunk several feet below the kirkyard level...

We now return to the Monimail road passing Gask and its almost obliterated cairn. The way to Monimail is quiet and little-frequented. At first the wall of the grounds of Melville House obstructs the view but when it ends you can overlook the lands beyond Rankeilour down to the Eden. Looking down a side road that day we saw the smoke of the Home farm and it was as blue as the blue sky. As you travel you are bound to mark with appreciation the noble bordering trees set out in the parks and at the roadside. They are invariably the sign of neighbouring estates, and of an interest in the decorative effect of fine timber. The celandines growing by the way seemed particularly large and golden...

Just beyond a pretty cottage at Whynny Park—the scene once of a pitiful tragedy—you reach the ingoing road to the decayed clachan of Monimail. The name may describe the high country behind: the bare hill or moorland. Not very far away is the ancient burial ground with the remains of the pre-Reformation church. We entered to find the turf graced with the pure bells of springtime's snowdrops, meek and virginal as they always seem. There are antique stones and private tombs here of the former owners of Cunnoquhie, namely Paterson, Hendry, Hutchison; the Balfours of Fernie; the Maitlands, Makgills, and Crichtons of Rankeilour, and Melvilles of that ilk. And in one nook the beautifully enshrined resting-place of the family of Sir Michael Nairn, Bt.

As you look round this scene you catch sight over the southern wall of a venerable and solitary tower. You are looking at what is popularly called "Cardinal Beaton's Tower". In the Historical Monuments Record it is judged to be the remnant of the archiepiscopal "Palace" of Monimail, the country residence of the bishops of St. Andrews, and it may contain part of the actual residence of the Cardinal who was Archbishop of St. Andrews from 1539 to 1546. This historic vestige reminds us that "Melville" as applied to the adjacent grounds is a comparatively modern name, the old land name being Monimail.

An interesting incident associated with the "Palace" was the cure effected on Archbishop Hamilton by a famous Italian physician called Cardan. It is traditionally related that Cardan wrought his cure through the use of water drawn from a spring which became known as "Cardan's Spring". The well is still marked on some of the maps and was long used and regarded as a medicinal spring, but today there is scepticism about its mineral virtues, and it is suggested that the Archbishop was cured as much by his frequent exercise in getting to the spring as by taking the water when he reached it.

The manse, a house dating from 1790, is situated just across the road. Here if anyone wished he could make an unusual journey by road to Inchrye and Lindores over the Dunbog hills. This is one of these utterly abandoned ways that we have alluded to from time to time, and it runs for two and a half miles through the lonely grassy moorland.

Should you wish to follow it you go up by the manse wall and enter a natural pass into the hills. Up there you come to a disused quarry and then that vexing sight in our Fife uplands, two ruined farmhouses. The second, and last vacated, had a striking situation on a sharp rising bank. The now abandoned road which pursues a remarkably direct course between Whitefield hill (749 feet) and Dunbog hill (707 feet), reveals its ancient importance by the great stones that line its ten-foot track. Obviously it is a very old route and may have had the moot-hill at Lindores as its object in early times.

On these lovely hillsides the land is cultivated up to 400 or 500 feet, and there are a few highly-set farm-steadings, as for example Gowdie lying up at over 400 feet. We have had inspiring walks through the hummocky whins of these higher slopes, but nowadays wide areas have been afforested. The road itself must rise to at least 400 feet, and when you reach the top you look forward towards Kinnaird and Glenduckie, and into the vale of Dunbog to which a well-defined track goes off about a mile from Inchrye. The last stretch of the way goes straight down to the loch. When you think of Macduff's castle there, and that Fernie was reputed to have been another of the Thane's seats, you are intrigued by the nature of the traffic that may once have passed along this lonely connecting road through the hills.

At Monimail the present church is a short distance from the burial ground, and was built in 1796, the session-house and tower being added afterwards. The choice situation of this delightful structure is more evident when you look back at it from the Letham side. Around it is a broad green lawn on which it stands with ivy-clad walls and a square neat tower at the east end. The latter is not built into the main structure but projects and yet in no way breaks the pleasing unity either of the exterior or interior of the building. Within the church there is a recess with the Laird's loft above. This faces the pulpit which is set midway in the length of the back wall.

Nothing could be lovelier than this rural shrine on a summer day. The Table and its furnishings are of oak and the church woodwork has been treated to agree, and has cream-toned walls. The ceiling is relieved with panels in lozenge design, and the small galleries are supported by neat bottle-shaped pillars. This article describes an afternoon visit towards the end of a week and when we entered the silent church the bowl of springtime flowers was already in place. It seemed an ideal setting for worship in a Scottish country parish...

The way passes on shortly to Letham. Fife is a shire of unique villages and small towns. How different from each other are Ceres, St. Monance, Collessie, Strathmiglo. Here in Letham is a village consisting for the most part of one broad street built up on the east side. There is a short transverse street at the top, also a one-sided affair. The village lies open and slopes upward with scarcely a tree to decorate it: a rigid strip of stonework.

One of the interesting things which I have heard about Letham, told in a rich doric tongue, was recounted by an old country ploughman as one of his earliest memories. It was that as a child he was held up at a window in this village to see Tam o' Shanter ride past on his grey mare, Meg. It was of course not the original Tam but a feature of a local procession held on 25th January to celebrate the poet's birth. The time which he recalled would be about 1845. My old friend whom I found to be a keen and able debater of public and political questions was in later years a quarryman at Greenwells near the top of Maspie Den above Falkland, and lived near the elevated cottage known as "See Far".

A feature of Scotland's social history which may escape our notice is illustrated strikingly by this almost obscure village of Letham. With a population of about 150 it had sixty years ago: a shoemaker, blacksmith, saddler, cartwright, joiner, tailor, baker, grocer, and a man whose business was that of drover and pig-killer. At the head of the village it had its own small malt barn. This latter, with hand-loom weaving, and the pursuit of the individual occupations mentioned, made up its industrial activities. In some respects of course it served not only the needs of the villagers but of the surrounding farms and countryside...

Turning down we take the highway to Ferniebarns and pass on towards Cunnoquhie. In the national war effort of 1939-45, the braes around this house were being turned up by the plough; it was land that had not been tilled for perhaps sixty or a hundred years. The Cunnoquhie mansion is beautifully situated and overlooks the ancient pile of Fernie Castle. The latter place, as already mentioned, has remote association with Macduff and is evidently, even as it stands, a place of strength, although much modernised within.

When you turn over the stream at Ferniebarns you catch a striking glimpse northward of the rugged tops of Norman's Law, dark with its shadows. The Cupar road winds on for two miles towards Carslogie on one hand and Balgarvie on the other. It is an open country of pleasant farmlands overlooked by the "Mount". The route goes by Horselaw to meet the Newburgh highway and enters the county town near the Lady burn.

All along the route we have travelled we have been off the highway and away from the more heavily populated centres, away from the rush and fever of our modern ways. It is a road for loitering and looking whether you go by car or on foot, and was a highway itself once of rustic use and travel, of plodding country carts and lairds riding their cobs to do business at the market of the famous burgh. The distance in all is about seven leisurely miles.

T. G. SNODDY, *'Tween Forth and Tay*, 1966.

"PROCLAMATIOUN" ON CASTLE HILL, CUPAR

Richt famous pepill, ye sall understand
How that ane prince rycht wyiss and vigilent
Is schortly for to cum in to this land
And purpossis to hald ane parliament.
His Thre Estaitis thairto hes done consent,
In Cowpar toun in to thair best array
With support of the Lord omnipotent,
And thairto hes affixt ane certane day.

. . .

Faill nocht to be upone the castell hill
Besyd the place quhair we purpoiss to play.
With gude stark wyne your flacconis see ye fill,
And hald your self the myrieast that ye may.
Be not displeisit quhatevir we sing or say,
Amang sad mater howbeid we sumtyme relyie;
We sall begin at sevin houris of the day,
So ye keip tryist—forsuth, we sall nocht felyie.

SIR DAVID LYNDSAY of the Mount

From *MARMION*

The flash of that satiric rage
Which, bursting on the early stage,
Branded the vices of the age,
And broke the keys of Rome...
Still is thy name in high account
And still thy verse has charms,
Sir David Lyndsay of the Mount,
Lord Lion King-at-Arms.

SIR WALTER SCOTT, 1808.

CUPAR, from *LOGIE TOWN*

What did Lizzie see to afford her sufficiently pleasant and satisfactory occupation? The street was somewhat wide for the street of a small country town, and it was clean since there was little traffic to dirty it, but it was hardly grass-grown. The houses were not so picturesque as they would have been in an English town of the same age. They were all of gray stone, with roofs for the most part of cold blue slate, though here and there the warm red tiles lingered. There was an occasional gable with crow-steps to the street, and the line was broken by wynds and closes, and by a tree or a clump of bushes, where a garden abutted on the thoroughfare. As a rule the houses were without pretension, rigidly plain in their height and breadth, blinking out from formal rows of narrow windows on the causeway for the most part. Yet some of those houses, including that in which the Lindesays dwelt, were old town houses which the neighbouring gentry had occupied in the winter, when the little town figured as a miniature Edinburgh. The whole place was of far greater antiquity than might have been imagined from its general aspect. Like Rome, there was within its bounds an older Logie, of which scarcely an architectural relic remained.

The sole traces were to be found in names, traditions, and accredited history. Logie had been the scene of courts and national parliaments in its day. It had possessed monastic establishments which had vanished piecemeal. It had owned a castle, of which it might be said, as of the Temple at Jerusalem, that not one stone was left upon another. It had rejoiced in gates, of which the word "port," applied to two suburbs, was the only vestige. A renowned play, the acting of which had been an era in the spiritual and moral life of the kingdom, had been played at Logie. But all that ancient glory was long fled, and few people even wasted wonder upon it. The exception was in the case of one brooding owl of an elderly gentleman, who lived in a tiny house, presided over by a careful housekeeper, whose orderly soul he vexed by his small collection of mouldy books, worm-eaten fragments of wood, and rusty bits of iron.

Even the Logie of Lizzie Lindesay's experience was removed from the Logie of the present, alike by a racy individuality in the middle of its starched dignity, and by a vigorous stir and current of fresh life from the outer world. The last came and went with the coaches and four, which with their red-coated drivers, their pealing bugles, their clusters of passengers drew up with a flourish every forenoon and afternoon, accomplishing the great sensation of the day, and depositing a quota of travellers prepared to tarry a night, or a day or two as it might be, at the Crown Inn, a two-storied, widespread building, next door to the Lindesays.

Lizzie's view extended on the one hand as far as where two intersecting streets met. The junction received its name from the ancient market cross. The market cross itself had been hustled away bodily as an obstruction to traffic and a symbol of popish idolatry, but its very memory continued a landmark and helped to create a thoroughfare, which in the earlier part of the day was the Billingsgate of the town. There cadgers and cadgers' carts, and strapping fish-wives with their creels bringing a salt-sea flavour thus far inland, were ranged; and brisk bargaining went on between provident heads of houses and managing house-wives and the Maggie Mucklebackets of the situation.

Commanding the fish market in the morning, the corn market once a week, and the perennial high-place of Logie, the grim old jail still frowned through its barred windows, not without benefit to the prisoners within, who thus caught a glimpse of the brightest prospect in the town. Lax discipline permitted them to do more: small boxes and old stockings dangling from strings were lowered until brought within reach of charitable passers-by, who might deposit in these extempore purses, pence, or if the donors were very generous, silver coins for the solace of the unhappy wights whose faces, unwashed and unshaven for the most part, peered eagerly down to ascertain the fate of the venture. Miserable women who had stakes in the fortunes of some of the prisoners occasionally squatted, with or without children, shrouded in grey duffle cloaks, on the pavement. There the poor creatures propped themselves against the grimy walls, and waited hours in sullen patience for the chance of seeing or exchanging words with members of the branded colony in durance.

In the opposite direction, Lizzie scarcely saw beyond the Crown Inn, where the High-gate ended. The street was intersected by one of the entrances to the town, so narrow—blocked as it was by small shops on the one side, and on the other a substantial mansion house of the date of the Lindesays' dwelling—that carts heavily laden with corn or hay had been known to get wedged in the aperture, and had to be then and there unloaded before proceeding further. Facing the Lindesays was a steep, somewhat sordid-looking wynd, between poor houses and a high moss-grown garden wall, the wynd bearing the sombre name of "The Corp Wynd." It was the chief access from that quarter of the town to the crowded kirk-yard. But constant contemplation robs even the well-defined path to the grave of any particular sadness, not to say terror. The Corp Wynd had a western exposure, and Lizzie had seen its squalor, and its melancholy associations, transformed and glorified under many a fine sunset.

SARAH TYTLER (pseudonym of **HENRIETTA KEDDIE)**
Logie Town, 1888.

ENCOUNTER

It was on Kettlehill and, walkin slawly
up the brae, I stoppt, lookin back doon
at the lichts o Kingskettle and thinkin
it was fine to be alive. And then he was on me,
straucht oot o the hedgeraw. Takin my airm
and peerin into my een. And strivin to say something
but dribblin at the mooth. A giant o a man,
I feel the pain frae his grip and smell dampness
as he leans against me. I say, "It's near daurk"
for aw it's sae daurk I can haurdly see him
wi the trees closin in on baith sides
and the road bendin roond to close oot
the open view o the Howe ablow wi its freendly lichts.
I say again, "It's gettin daurk."

He leans closer against me and taks my ither airm.
"It's daurk. It's daurk!" he splutters
and looks roond owre his shooder wi a slaw turn
o the heid. I think o pushin him aff
and takin to my heels but he's tichtenin
his grip and it's a bit faur to the hoose
at the tap o the hill. He's sayin, "It's daurk!"
and leanin haurd agin me. I push him back
and stride oot up the hill. But he's on me again
slaverin and peerin aw aroond.

I think o takin aff back doon the hill.

And then a voice and a rush o feet.
"You've got him? He's from Springfield—the asylum, ye ken.
—He's feart o the daurk!"

DUNCAN GLEN

CULTS KIRK, NEAR PITLESSIE, AND SIR DAVID WILKIE

About a mile to the South East of Pitlessie, set among the fields, sheltered by a group of mature trees and alongside the Cults Burn, lies Kirkton of Cults, dominated by the simple sandstone Parish Church.

Cults Kirk

For at least 800 years there has been a church in Cults. Early documents spell it as Quilt, Quilis or Quilque and it was not until the Reformation that it assumed the more modern forms of Cultis, Cowlts and lastly, Cults. In the vernacular the Church and parish are styled "The Cult Kirk", "The Cult Parish" (as seen on a tombstone in the kirkyard erected by the Rev. T. Gillespie, Minister of Cult). In ancient times the church was a rectory in the Bishopric of St. Andrews, dedicated by Bishop de Bernham in 1234. The present building was erected in 1793, during the ministry of Rev. David Wilkie, and has undergone very little change, either internally or externally. It stands on a little mounded site, with a surrounding kirk-yard, all enclosed and supported by an ancient retaining wall. Even in these modern times, when most churches are securely locked, every door in Cults is left on the latch. The diminutive Session House, set close to the kirkyard gate, has a cap of heavy, red local tiles. The viewer has a glimpse of the last century.

The belfry, with its steep, stone stair that climbs up the front gable, catches the eye. The carved pillars are in strange contrast to the plainness of the kirk itself. Before 1983, when the belfry was declared unsafe, the thrifty heritors had used the supports of an old table-tombstone! Now new moulded pillars carry the belfry roof, which, we hope, will mellow with age. The bell, rung every Sunday, calling worshippers to church, is inscribed "John Meikle, Edinburgh, fecit for the Kirk at Cults, 1699". This year, our weathervane was damaged by the January gales. A new "Cock-a-doodle" sits proudly, shining in the sunlight. The old weathervane can be seen in the church, we are loath to part with it. On the belfry wall is a small stained glass window, "The Burning Bush", which was designed and gifted by Cara McNeil, daughter of a former elder in Cults. Once inside the church, in the passage, is a small, neat "squint", or "lepars" window. We leave you to think which it might be!

The interior presents a small, homely, pleasing sanctuary, where a sense of peace prevails. Generations of local families have worshipped here. There is a simple charm about the dark wood of the gallery, the many box pews and the 18th century pulpit. The manse pew is on the right of the pulpit, as is the "laird's pew", with its baize covered door, in the gallery. The sacred table is plain, the old baptismal font is of eastern craftsmanship, brought back to Cults by a ship's captain, a strange object to be found in a country kirk! There is one stained glass window, erected by John Marr, a former treasurer of Cults, in memory of his wife. The other large window, with coloured surrounds, was made and gifted by Andrew Garland, also a former elder. The remaining windows are plain glass, revealing the fields, trees and hills outside.

On the walls we find a few impressive memorials; the two on either side of the pulpit being of special interest. One is to the memory of the Rev. David Wilkie and his wife, Isabella Lister (of Pitlessie Mill) executed by Chantrey, the sculptor, from paintings done by their son, Sir David Wilkie, RA. The other is of Sir David, a profile in relief, by Samual Joseph, erected by Helen Wilkie, who, in 1843, gifted the clock, which exhorts for all who see it to "Redeem the Time".

On the north wall is a tablet in memory of another son of the Rev. Wilkie, Captain John Wilkie, who died at Dinapore in 1824. Captain Wilkie's two sons are also commemorated. The other tablet on this wall is to the Rev. J. R. Crystal (1829-1879). Beneath the western gallery is a small tablet in memory of the Rev. George Crawford who was succeeded by Rev. John Cook, who became Moderator of the General Assembly. He, in turn, was succeeded by Rev. D. Cook, then by Rev. Tom Crawford, younger brother of the above George, who became Professor of Divinity in the University of Edinburgh.

In the last 400 years Cults has had 33 ministers. John Rutherford (1563-77) was a most scholarly man, in 1577 he published a book "The Art of Reasoning", considered a landmark in the history of Scottish Philosophy. James Martin, his successor, was the first to receive the degree of Doctor of Divinity in Scotland after the Reformation.

Our most famous son was Sir David Wilkie, RA, born in Cults Manse, on 18th November, 1785, third son of the third wife of the Rev. David Wilkie. His birthplace was not, however, the present house, but the former manse, a dilapidated building which was 150 years old, at least, at that time. Kirkton House (no longer a manse), built in 1796, was the home of his boyhood and youth. It was in this manse he painted "Pitlessie Fair", "The Village Recruit" and earlier sketches of the "Village Politicians". For an easel he had a chest of drawers, the middle drawer being pulled out to rest his canvas on, but, if lacking "the tools of his trade", he had no scarcity of subjects. He found them in Pitlessie School, the village, the neighbouring cottages and in the manse itself. His father's kirk was also a source of models, much to the indignation of those he sketched, and others, who thought the minister's son should be better employed on the Lord's Day!...

1985 was special for us because we celebrated the Bi-centenary of Sir David Wilkie, RA (1785-1841). We had a Flower Festival in the church, the theme being the paintings of Sir David Wilkie. A "Pitlessie Fair" was held in the village, with stalls, games, etc. The village folk dressed as shown in the "Pitlessie Fair" painting, by Wilkie. The figures we have in the church were taken from a detail in this picture by Maggie Lawrie, our local artist.

KAREN GARLAND, *Cults Kirk.*

SCOTSTARVIT TOWER

Opinion is divided as to whether Scotstarvit Tower was built on the site of an older tower recorded in a charter of 1579. The estate was bought from Alexander Inglis in 1611 by John Scot, from Knightspottie (Perthshire) and in 1612 the lands were named as the Barony of Scotstarvit, combining Scot's name with the existing title of Tarvit. The date 1627 appears on a fireplace, originally in the tower's garret, which has since been transferred to Hill of Tarvit Mansion House. The same date can still be seen on a panel over the cap-house door and this may be the date the tower was completed, or it may just relate to when improvements were carried out by Sir John, which included creating a study in the attic. In *Exploring Scotland's Heritage, Fife And Tayside* Bruce Walker and Graham Ritchie think that "...Scotstarvit does not have the appearance of an earlier building converted at a later period but rather a late tower built to give the

Scotstarvit Tower

appearance of being older." Sir John was a keen historian, or antiquary, and this may give the clue to a building which was quite possibly based on his romantic notion of how earlier tower houses might have looked.

He was the Director to the Chancery and author of "The Staggering State of the Scots Statesman" which commented on the prominent administrators and politicians of the day (a kind of "Yes Minister" of its time). He was a keen geographer and sponsored work on an atlas of Scotland by a Timothy Pont which was finished by Sir Ruben Gordon of Straloch and his son. This was published by John Blaeu in Amsterdam in 1654. Another significant achievement was the editing of "Delitiae Poetarum Scotorum" in 1637, which even I can translate, as being an anthology of Latin verse by Scots poets. Sir John was married to Anne Drummond, who was the sister of the poet William Drummond of Hawthornden.

The tower was abandoned in 1696 and sold by Sir John's descendant, the Duchess of Portland, to Oliver Gourlay of Craigrothie House in the 18th century and eventually sold on by him to Colonel Wemyss of Wemyss Hall (now Hill of Tarvit Mansion House).

JOHN DEACON, *Craigrothie. Walking with History*, 2001.

TRULY CERES

You wantit a lang and truly rural walk.

I reeled aff Mill Deans to Coaltown of Burnturk
to Claybrigs to Cults and Pitlessie Lime Warks
to Paradise Farm and Chance Inn and finally
Ceres famed aw owre Fife. The maist rural walk in Fife I said
endin up in its prettiest village. You made
me tak you to prove me a deceiver and found three cottages
lackin aw mod cons at Mill Deans, seeven cottages
at Coaltown of Burnturk wi the only coal that for their grates.
And Claybrigs truly an ideal fairm wi pure spring watter
at its gates. The Lime Warks gied a blot it's true
but David Wilkie was born at Cults and made Pitlessie
Fair famous to become limner to the King.
I near made Paradise at its fairm
but you wantit to push on to the Chance Inn. A disappointment
to find a wee hamlet o cottages but still raisin up
imaginins o the auld coachin days.
And to Ceres needin nae words wi famous green

and brig and Bannockburn gemms played there still.
I hae thochts on ither gemms
and you aw woman there in Ceres.

But you (delichtit wi the pleisure I'd gien you
walkin frae Mill Deans to Ceres!)
truly woman said to me, "Mill Deans and Coaltown
of Burnturk and Claybrigs and Pitlessie
Lime Warks,
—you tried to trick me oot o it!"

DUNCAN GLEN

CERES, SCOTLAND

Here, girl, and there and yonder with a helix wynd,
The king of all the swallows slices yon slithering waver
    Of a mavis' song; surely your hair is harp strings
    Twanging to the birling of a wing, the singing
Of spray from an overhand brown arm through clear green water.

I would have the sun itself a melody of peach
And pomegranate for your hair, poem of the tingling light,
    But your eyes are splintering a sea of gray and green song,
    See, here and now and into the sharps of movement along
The air preening swallows' wings
To a world that sings beyond your hair the matter
Of keeping to the black keys to make a Scottish song, O golden daughter.

T. S. LAW

From THE HISTORIE OF ANE NOBIL AND VAILYEAND SQUYER WILLIAM MELDRUM, UMWHYLE LAIRD OF CLEISCHE AND BYNNIS

And come behind him cowartly,
And hackit on his hochs and theis
Till that he fell upon his knees.
Yet when his shanks were shorn in sunder,
Upon his knees he wrocht great wonder.
Sweipand his sword round about.

144

Not havand of the death na doubt
Durst nane approach within his bounds.
Till that his cruel mortal wounds
Bled sa, that he did swap in swoun;
Perforce behuvit him then fall doun.
And when he lay upon the ground
They gave him mony cruel wound,
That men on far micht hear the knocks,
Like butchers hackand on their stocks.
And finally without remede
They left him lyand there for dead...

And when he did decline to age
He faillit never of his courage.
Of ancient stories for to tell,
Abone all other he did precel,
Sa that everilk creature
To hear him speak they took pleasure.
Bot all his deeds honorable
For to descrive I am not able.
Of every man he was commendit,
And as he leivit, sa he endit,
Pleasandly, till he micht endure,
Till dolent death come to his door
And cruelly, with his mortal dart,
He strake the squire through the heart.
His saul with joy angelical
Past to the heaven imperial.
Thus at the Struther into Fife
This noble squire lost his life.

SIR DAVID LYNDSAY of the Mount

THE WALLED GARDEN OF KELLIE CASTLE

As is often the case, little detailed information survives about the historical development of Kellie's walled garden, although it has been cultivated for hundreds of years—changing, evolving and suffering periods of neglect. When the Lorimer family first visited in the 1870s, young Louise recalled that "the garden, still encircled by a tumbledown wall, was a wilderness of neglected gooseberry bushes, gnarled apple trees and old-world roses, which struggled through the weeds, summer after summer, with a sweet persistence". This had been a typical Scottish kitchen garden, producing fruit and vegetables for the castle but with borders containing all kinds of flowers and roses. From this scene of neglect the Lorimer family set to work to transform the garden. Cuttings would have been taken from the overgrown shrubs and plants, whilst Robert improved on the existing design by the addition of two small corner gardens, Robin's Garden and the Yew Enclosure or Secret Garden.

Other developments were the stone garden house, with its characteristic bird carved on the roof, and the central walkway with an armillary sphere sundial (known at Kellie as the "astrolabe") as a focal point. Some of these details, particularly the "gardens within a garden" and the use of yew hedges, Robert later replicated in other gardens he designed. At Earlshall and Formakin he laid out the grounds in his favourite way. He wrote:

> I always think the ideal plan is to have the park, with the sheep or beasts grazing in it, coming right under the windows of one side of the house, and the garden attached to the house at the other side. We could not quite manage that at Kellie but put as light a fence as possible between the park and the lawn.

He saw gardens as a "chamber roofed by heaven… to wander in, to cherish, to dream through undisturbed…"

The botanical development of the garden was Louise's special responsibility and she was to tend it for over twenty-five years. She wrote an essay entitled *The Final Choice—a Rose Fantasy* in which she discussed many old roses: her final choice was "The Old Blush" or "Common China". Today this is planted along the terrace wall and many of the other roses she described are found in the garden.

After the death of John Lorimer in 1936 the castle was left without a tenant and the garden again declined. By the time Hew and Mary Lorimer took up residence in 1942 it was in a sorry condition. They decided to enhance its qualities as a pleasure garden and reduce the proportion of labour-intensive kitchen garden. They laid down most of the present lawns to reduce the area under cultivation.

Hew Lorimer has contributed several artistic features to the garden. These include two distinctive wooden seats, one in Robin's Corner and the other further west where a great beech once stood, and the hand-carved stone basket which is now the focal point in the Secret Garden. Previously there was a cherub on a plinth, the subject of John Lorimer's large painting which hangs in the drawing room of the castle.

When the National Trust for Scotland took responsibility for the property in 1970 the garden was again somewhat neglected. Restoration is still continuing and older varieties of flowers, fruit and vegetables are being reintroduced.

The garden today has an ageless quality and unique peaceful charm. There are six bee boles, three still open and the same number filled in, behind the vegetable plots. Lush growth and density of planting creates the feeling of being in a series of gardens within a garden, with occasional views along paths or oblique glimpses of the castle and the trees which shelter and surround it.

KATHLEEN SAYER, HEW LORIMER and **STEPHANIE BLACKDEN**, *Kellie Castle and Garden*, National Trust for Scotland, 1993.

FROM A LETTER TO SIR WALTER SCOTT, 8 JULY 1823

...Robin Gray, so called from it being the name of the old herdsman at Balcarres, was born soon after the close of the year 1771. My sister Margaret had married and accompanied her husband to London; I was melancholy, and endeavoured to amuse myself by attempting a few poetical trifles. There was an ancient Scotch melody of which I was passionately fond,—Sophy Johnstone, who lived before your day, used to sing it to us at Balcarres: she did not object to its having improper words, though I did. I longed to sing old Sophy's air to different words, and to give to its plaintive tones some little history of virtuous distress in humble life, such as might suit it. While attempting to effect this in my closet, I called to my little sister, now Lady Hardwicke, who was the only person near me,—"I have been writing a ballad, my dear,—I am oppressing my heroine with many misfortunes,—I have already sent her Jamie to sea, and broken her father's arm, and given her Auld Robin Gray for a lover, but I wish to load her with a fifth sorrow in the four lines, poor thing! help me to one, I pray." "Steal the cow, sister Anne," said the little Elizabeth. The cow was immediately *lifted* by me, and the song completed.—At our fireside, amongst our neighbours, "Auld Robin Gray" was always called for; I was pleased with the approbation it met with, but such was *my dread* of being suspected of writing *any thing*, perceiving the shyness it created in those who could write *nothing*, that I carefully kept my own secret.

LADY ANNE LINDSAY BARNARD

AULD ROBIN GRAY

When the sheep are in the fauld, and the kye a' at hame,
When a' the weary warld to sleep are gane,
The waes o' my heart fa' in showers frae my e'e,
While my gudeman lies sound by me.

Auld Robin Gray

Young Jamie lo'ed me weel, and sought me for his bride;
But saving a croun he had naething else beside.
To make the croun a pound, my Jamie gaed to sea,
And the croun and the pound, they were baith for me.

He hadna been awa' a week but only twa,
When my mither she fell sick and the cow was stown awa';
My father brak his arm—my Jamie at the sea;
And auld Robin Gray cam a-courtin' me.

My father couldna wark, my mither couldna spin;
I toil'd day and nicht, but their bread I couldna win:
Auld Rob maintain'd them baith, and wi' tears in his e'e,
Said, "Jeanie, for their sakes, will ye marry me?"

My heart it said na—I look'd for Jamie back;
But the wind it blew hie, and the ship it was a wrack;
His ship it was a wrack—why didna Jamie dee?
And why do I live to cry, Wae's me?

My father urged me sair; my mither didna speak,
But she looked in my face till my heart was like to break.

They gied him my hand—my heart was at the sea;
Sae auld Robin Gray, he was gudeman to me.

I hadna been a wife a week but only four,
When, mournfu' as I sat on the stane at the door,
I saw my Jamie's wraith—I couldna think it he,
Till he said, "I'm come hame, my love, to marry thee."

O sair did we greet, and meikle did we say:
We took but ae kiss, and I bade him gang away.
I wish that I were dead, but I'm no like to dee;
And why was I born to say, Wae's me?

I gang like a ghaist, and I carena to spin;
I daurna think o' Jamie, for that wad be a sin.
But I'll do my best a gude wife to be,
For auld Robin Gray, he is kind to me.

LADY ANNE LINDSAY BARNARD

NEWBURN OLD PARISH CHURCH

Newburn Old Parish Church sits on a delightful back road that runs behind the A921 between Upper Largo and Colinsburgh. Thirteenth-century documents have Newburn as Nithbren, Nethbren and Nibreun but some have liked to believe that the Parish of Newburn was once Drumeldry. Today's hamlet of that name has a succession of cottages facing southwards over the splendid curve of Largo Bay. In 2002 I revisited this interesting ruin on a September day before the trees had turned, and the sun shining through the leaves onto the back road leading to the old ruined kirk made it seem like an idyllic high summer day.

   The "Rev. Mr. Lawrie" who wrote the first *Statistical Account*, 1792-3, began his section headed "Antiquities" by firmly stating the obvious, "here are vestiges of the east part of the church having been a Roman Catholic chapel." He continues, "If we may give credit to the records and traditions which have been transmitted to us of that early period, the Culdees, who are thought to have been the first regular clergy in Scotland, had a church and residence in this parish so early as the time of Malcolm Canmore... their majesties King Malcolm, and his Queen St Margaret, granted to them the village of Balchristie... in this parish. The present proprietor of the village (Mr. Christie of Balchristie) informs me, that some years ago he dug up the foundation-stones of an old edifice near the western wall of his garden, and in the very place where, according to the best accounts, the church of the Culdees stood. Some say, this was the first Christian church in Scotland; and, indeed, the name of Balchristie… and the high probability of the Culdees landing first on the adjacent inviting shore, give considerable countenance to the tradition."

The New Statistical Account of April 1836 was written by "The Rev. Thomas Laurie, D.D.," who (unlike "Mr. Lawrie") cautiously omitted claims for this being the site of the first Christian church in Scotland and modified earlier words on the site of the Culdee church, writing more cautiously on where it "is supposed to have stood." Dr. Laurie informed that the new Parish Church was built in 1815 and described it as "commodius and conveniently situated". He also states that the manse was built in 1819 but does not comment on how he regarded it. The manse is now Newburn House and the church of 1815 was converted to a house in 1970 and renamed Kirk House.

On 15th July 1243 Bishop de Bernham rededicated the church of Nithbren but the name of the patron saint has not remained in use. Substantial parts of the old ruined church have been dated by twentieth-century historians as twelfth-century, with the west part a post-Reformation reconstruction and the north aisle an early-eighteenth-century addition. On the west gable the two-tiered balustered bellcote with an urn on top may be mid-eighteenth-century.

In the south-west corner of the kirkyard is a memorial to Professor James Lorimer designed by his son Sir Robert Lorimer in an Arts and Crafts Jacobean style. Sir Robert and other Lorimers are also commemorated on this unique memorial wall.

DUNCAN GLEN, *Ruined Rural Fife Churches*, 2002.

The East Neuk

LITTLE TOWNS OF THE EAST NEUK

Of these little towns posted along the shore as close as sedges, each with its bit of harbour, its old weather-beaten church or public building… not one but has its legend, quaint or tragic.

ROBERT LOUIS STEVENSON, *The Coast of Fife*, 1888.

Crail

THE BEACHCOMBER
for Sophie

As her right foot hits the first blast
Of the North Sea's salt, she shivers,
And then runs out. Later, in a rockpool,
Her legs become more accustomed to its
Comparative warmth. She smiles, and starts
To investigate her newly-found surroundings.

First, she just pulls strands of seaweed
From the rocks, and throws them over her
Shoulders. Then, it's time for the big boulder
In the middle of the pool. And the barnacles,
That are *Lovely*. And the mussels, that are
Beautiful. And the tiny crab that she cradles,

151

For an instant, in her palm. Piece by piece,
Her mind expands to include the new wonders of
Her watery world. Talking with her, I try too,
To become more at one with it all. Like her, I go
Bare-footed, and am learning, through water, how
To love the world from the bottom of my soles.

GORDON MEADE

EAST NEUK

This huddle wracked aboot
But tidy—some hooses there
Wi' blindet een tae hide
Stramash or see aff strangers.

A man can bide inside
The kernel o' the corner
Winds, an' skliff braced up
Tae sniff the sixpenny sea—
Breathcatchin' whiles.

A ticht turf keeps things ticht,
But cacklers at the cemeteries,
The slee-slung gulls, scream
Oot the heroes, a' the shilpit an'
The obdurate shauchlin' through
Dead drunk an' roarin' fu'

Hard bitten rocks still bite,
An' auld yins that have seen
The hale thing backyairds sine
Stane coffins oan the Fisher
Dykes, gang cleekin' oot
The partins, hard as hell,
Yet lichtsome whiles, lik'
Weasels dancin'.

TOM WATSON

THE STAUNAN STANES

I. Efter Exercism

On Lundin Links there staun
Three giants petrified,
Rysan frae the yerth their dwaum
Is hapt in stane, their sleep
Is waukan aye; they mock
The deid and hate the quick.

Auld faithers, whitna ye
Micht be, or deil or priest,
We kenna, carena; historie's
Your tipple: in our livan breist
The deid is deid. God, pit
Resurgam in the room of it.

II. The Gluttons

i

Ayont the dyke staun three
Auld Stanes that speakless speak
O' man's mortalitie;
But cannae gar them greit
That lang were hemlock-stecht are free
Frae life's dreid poison, thowlessrie.

ii

Memento mori, the Stanes say,
—But daw is daw and fell is fell,
God made us glutton, nocht we hae
But in excess, of hevin or hell.
Daith dees, we wauk, God grant us three:
Luve and meat and libertie.

SYDNEY GOODSIR SMITH

THE COAST OF FIFE

Just a little beyond Leven, Largo Law and the smoke of Largo town mounting about its feet, the town of Alexander Selkirk, better known under the name of Robinson Crusoe. So on, the list might be pursued… by St. Monans, and Pittenweem, and the two Anstruthers, and Cellardyke, and Crail, where Primate Sharpe was once a humble and innocent country minister: on to the heel of the land, to Fife Ness, overlooked by a sea-wood of matted elders, and the quaint old mansion of Balcomie, itself overlooking but the breach or the quiescence of the deep—the Carr Rock beacon rising close in front, and as night draws in, the star of the Inchcape reef springing up on the one hand, and the star of the May Island on the other, and farther off yet a third and a greater on the craggy foreland of St. Abb's. And but a little way round the corner of the land, imminent itself above the sea, stands the gem of the province and the light of mediæval Scotland, St. Andrews, where the great Cardinal Beaton held garrison against the world, and the second of the name and title perished (as you may read in Knox's jeering narrative) under the knives of true-blue Protestants, and to this day (after so many centuries) the current voice of the professor is not hushed.

ROBERT LOUIS STEVENSON, *The Coast of Fife*, 1888.

ALEXANDER SELKIRK, OF LOWER LARGO

Having gone to sea in his youth, and in the year 1703, being sailing master of the ship "Cinque Ports", Captain Stradling, bound for the South Seas, he was put on shore on the island of Juan Fernandez, as a punishment for mutiny. In that solitude he remained for four years and four months, from which he was at last relieved and brought to England by Captain Woods Rogers. He had with him in the island his clothes and bedding with a firelock, some powder, bullets and tobacco, a hatchet, knife, kettle, his mathematical instruments, and Bible. He built two huts of Pimento trees, and covered them with long grass, and in

Selkirk's house, Lower Largo

a short time lined them with skins of goats which he killed with his musket, so long as his powder lasted (which at first was but a pound); when that was spent he caught them by speed of foot. Having learned to produce fire by rubbing two pieces of wood together, he dressed his victuals in one of his huts and slept in the other, which was at some distance from his kitchen. A multitude of rats often disturbed his repose by gnawing his feet and other parts of his body, which induced him to feed a number of cats for his protection. In a short time these became so tame that they would lie about him in hundreds, and soon delivered him from the rats, his enemies. Upon his return, he declared to his friends that nothing gave him so much uneasiness as the thoughts, that when he died his body would be devoured by those very cats he had with so much care tamed and fed. To divert his mind from such melancholy thoughts, he would sometimes dance and sing among his kids and goats, at other times retire to his devotion.

REV. SPENCE OLIPHANT, 'The Parish of Largo', *The Statistical Account of Scotland,* 1792.

LARGO

Ae boat anerlie nou
Fishes frae this shore,
Ae black drifter lane
Riggs the crammasie daw,
Aince was a fleet, and nou
Ae boat alane gaes out.

War ir Peace, the trawlers win
An the youth turns awa
Bricht wi baubles nou
An thirled tae factory or store;
Their faithers fished their ain,
Unmaistered; —ane remains.

And never the clock rins back,
The free days are owre;
The warld shrinks, we luik
Mair t'our maisters ilka hour—
Whan yon lane boat I see
Daith an rebellion blind ma ee!

SYDNEY GOODSIR SMITH

THE BOATIE ROW

I cast my line in Largo Bay,
    And fishes catch'd nine,
There were three to boil and three to fry,
    And three to bate the line.

O well may the boatie row,
    And better may she speed;
And lees me on the boatie row,
    That wins the bairns' breed.

ANONYMOUS

THE MESSENGER AN' ME

The wee lass deliverin' ma paper
Wi' a face fu' o Fife, seemed grim.
Examinations? Toothache?
Thae rosy cheeks bright flags
o' putrefaction? The gum's deceit?

Mebbe jist a stoor
whupped oot the Lammermuirs;
Forebye the paper's no'
The cheeriest. We dree the same
weird the messenger an' me.

Days ye canna thole it.

RUMINANT

The large and heavy pewter cow
Playing book-end to her kine
Lay down.

The weighty shiftings of a billion
Years collapsed her foggy sacking
And her shade.

Around her sweet, green fumaroles
Of Fife, old traces of funebrial
Geometry.

Her inward gaze saw oceans swelled
With clover, slick rutting deep
In byres,

The wavy, blackened tide being laid
Beside the cup marks and the silent,
Gritted castles.

TOM WATSON

A FERRY CROSSING FROM NORTH BERWICK TO ELIE, 1586

We retourned the nearest way be the Ferrie of Northe Berwick, passing the quhilk I was in the graittest perplexitie of ane that ever I was in my tyme befor, and haid the maist sudden and comfortable relief of my guid and gratius God and Father, to whase honour, as in all, I man record it.

...We hoised seall with a lytle pirhe of east wind, and lainshed furthe till almaist the thrid of the passage was past, and then it fell down dead calme. For rowing nather was ther eares meit, nor handes, the boott was sa heavie, the man auld, and the boyes young. In this mean tyme, the honest woman became sa seik with sic extremitie and preas of vomiting first, thereafter with swinings, that it was pitifull to behauld. Withe hir working, the bairn wackens, and becomes extream seik, being nane but myselff to curie tham, for Mr. Robert Durie was rowing. This dreing for the space of thrie houres, in end I becam dead seik myselff, sa that then it becam a maist pitifull and lamentable spectakle, to sie a woman, a stranger, an honest mans wyff, com fra ham to pleasure me, to be with extream pres appeirand everie minut to giff upe the ghost; an infant of thrie halff yeirs auld spreauling in the awin excrements, and father, partlie for feir and cair of mynd, and partlie for fear seikness, lifting upe pitifull handes and eis to the heavines, voide of all erdlie confort or helpe of man. ...At last the Lord luiked mercifullie on, and send, about the sune going to, a thik ear from the Southeast, sa that, getting on the seall ther was upon hir, within an houre and a halff, quhilk was strange to our consideration, na wind blawing, we arryved within the Alie [Elie], and efter a maist weirisome and sair day, gat a comfortable nights ludging with a godlie lady in Carmury.

REV. JAMES MELVILLE, *Diaries.*

ST MONANS AND SWINE

To King James VI Fife was "a beggar's mantle fringed with gold". The seaports and fertile fringe were the gold and the muirs the waste lands that produced no income. Today's fertile Howe of Fife was in James's time very boggy, with a loch, and generally suited only for hunting. Kingsmuir south of Dunino was part of that waste land and it took in the Boar's Chase that stretched in the west to Kemback north of Pitscottie to, presumably, Boarhills on the coast although there were more cows there than swine which were feared by the fishing communities. If a fisherman allowed his eye to fall on that evil beast he had to allow a tide to ebb and flow before putting to sea. Not one pig was willingly allowed in St Monans for over a century. And to hear this word of the devil was equally feared. Some protection was possible by touching "cauld iron". A much-repeated story is that of the new minister of St Monans who chose to preach around the parable of the prodigal son and announced that he would read from Luke chapter XV at the 11th verse. Even this ignorant stranger sensed a wave of unease moving through the congregation. He was aware of the apprehension growing as he read through verse fifteen towards the final dreaded word, "and he sent him into his fields to feed swine". "Touch airn" was the whisper. Startled the minister repeated the last phrase. "Touch airn" was the louder cry. The tension grew as he read verse 16 but he never reached the final evil word. The congregation panicked, those in the galleries dropped down on those below, and all rushed out into the clean sea air. For many a day few dared to cross into the kirk.

DUNCAN GLEN, *Illustrious Fife*, 1998.

ST MONANS

A broken jawline
of staggered stones
speechless
before the archaeology
of wind and wave

Here lie the bones
of St Monans
the sandworms scroll
in their coiled
calligraphy

A monastery
of marigolds shelter

the shell-capped sage
from the ruins of memory
and disconsolate sea

JOHN BREWSTER

St Monans

HOMER COUNTRY

This is Homer country.
Here by the seaside in cemetery in Fife.

Then death will drift upon me
from seaward, mild as air, mild as your hand.★

The meenister's words into the wund
aulder than time they seem.
And pop sang birlin in my heid,
Through the graves the wind is blowing.
And him of perfect physique
and not quite twenty
being lowered to be at ane wi the mool
as his stane in time
carved in immemorial leid

from seaward, mild as air, mild as your haund...

DUNCAN GLEN

★*Odyssey*, Book XXIII

159

A WITCH OF PITTENWEEM

They tied her arms ahint her back,
And twisted them wi a pin.
They tain her tae Kinneuchar Loch
And threw the limmer in
And a the swaans tak tae the hills
Scared wi the unhaley din.

ANONYMOUS

PITTENWEEM BEACH

For Jessica Crowe and Janet Cornfoot

To reach the beach the child likes best
Down to the shore they dragged you
I cradle her, rung over rung, to the shingle
To be swum and stoned at a rope's end
To plowter along the tide-line
For no belief or crime of yours, but rumour
Scouring the ground for bits of china:
Of witchcraft. You were one of the crazed
Throw–outs, shards, crazed like the faces
Refusing to die, at the mercy of men's hands
Of very old women, broken on stones:
That pressed you beneath a door, weighted with stones
Fragments she finds of vanished lives, lifting
"For a quarter of an hour or so"
Sea–weed, unearthing a piece of sky
And then they must fetch a horse and plough
With two birds flying, some writing
And drive it over what they have made
Rubbed, made smooth by the sea.
As though to efface it.
And this, we say, we will keep.

ANNA CROWE

THE PORTEOUS RIOTS

Some Pittenweem memories have retained the story of the two smugglers, Andrew
Wilson and George Robertson, who robbed an excisemen, or tax-gatherer, in an

inn which stood in Marygate along from the Tolbooth tower. A well-designed shield-shaped plaque informs interested passers-by, "Near this spot stood the Inn where the Tax Gatherer was robbed by smugglers giving rise to the Porteous Riots, 1736. Sir Walter Scott has immortalised the event in *The Heart of Midlothian.*" The two smugglers were taken to the old Tolbooth in Edinburgh where they awaited execution. When Wilson was hanged in the Grassmarket the mob almost rioted and were fired on by the City Guard, commanded by John Porteous, killing three men. Porteous was found guilty of murder and condemned to be hanged. When he was reprieved the mob took him from the Tolbooth and hanged him in the Grassmarket from a dyer's pole. As the plaque says, the story has continuing life thanks to its retelling by Sir Walter Scott in *The Heart of Midlothian.*

There is a headstone erected in Andrew Wilson's memory in Kirkcaldy in the Pathhead Feuars' Graveyard which runs alongside the grounds of Braehead House, the former head offices of Michael Nairn & Co Ltd, linoleum manufacturers, with access from Commercial Street, if you can scramble over the wall. The inscription reads: "Erected by public subscription to mark the grave of Andrew Wilson whose name associated with Sir W. Scott and the Porteous Mob has obtained a distinguished place in Scottish history. He was a native of this town and executed at Edinburgh 1736".

DUNCAN GLEN, *Illustrious Fife. Literary, Historical, &*
Architectural Pathways and Walks, 1998.

THE SPANIARDS OF THE ARMADA AT ANSTRUTHER, 1588

...earlie in the morning, be brak of day, ane of our Bailyies cam to my bedsyde, saying, (but nocht with fray,) "I haiff to tell yow newes, sir. Ther is arryvit within our herbrie this morning a schipe full of Spainyarts, bot nocht to giff mercie bot to ask." And sa schawes me that the Commanders haid landit, and he haid commandit tham to thair schipe againe till the Magistrates of the Town haid advysit, and the Spainyards haid humblie obeyit: Therfor desyrit me to ryse and heir thair petition with tham. Upe I got with diligence, and assembling the honest men of the town, cam to the Tolbuthe; and efter consultation taken to heir tham, and what answer to mak, ther presentes us a verie reverend man of big stature, and grave and stout countenance, gray heared, and verie humble lyk, wha, efter mikle and verie law courtessie, bowing down with his face neir the ground, and twiching my scho with his hand, began his harang in the Spanise toung, wharof I understud the substance, and being about to answer in Latine, he haiffing onlie a young man with him to be his interpreter, began and tauld ower againe to us in guid Einglis.

...with a guid nomber of the gentilmen of the countrey round about, gaiff the said Generall and the Capteanes presence, and efter the sam speitches in effect as befor, receavit tham in his hous, and interteined tham humeanlie, and sufferit the souldiours to com a land, and ly all togidder, to the number of threttin score, for the maist part young berdles men, sillie, trauchled, and houngred, to the quhilk a day or twa, keall, pattage, and fishe was giffen; for my advys was conforme to the Prophet Elizeus his to the King of Israel in Samaria, "Giff tham bred and water," &c. The names of the Commanders war Jan Gomes de Medina, Generall of twentie houlkes, Capitan Patricio, Capitan de Legoretto, Capitan de Luffera, Capitan Mauritio and Seingour Serrano...

In the mean tyme they knew nocht of the wrak of the rest, but supposed that the rest of the armie was saifflie returned, till a day I gat in St Andros in print the wrak of the Galiates in particular, with the names of the principall men, and whow they war usit in Yrland and our Hilands, in Walles, and uther partes of Eingland; the quhilk, when I recordit to Jan Gomes, be particular and speciall names, O then he cryed out for greiff, bursted and grat. This Jan Gomes schew grait kyndnes to a schipe of our town, quhilk he fund arrested at Calles at his ham coming, red to court for hir, and maid grait rus of Scotland to his King, tuk the honest men to his hous, and inquyrit for the Lard of Anstruther, for the Minister, and his host, and send hame manie commendationes. Bot we thanked God with our hartes, that we haid sein tham amangs us in that forme.

...About noone, ther fell a cloud of rean upon Kellie Law, and the mountains besyd, that for a space covered them with rinning water, the quhilk desending thairfra, rasit sa at ane instant the strypes and burns, that they were unpassable to the travellars, whowbeit weill horsed. The burn of Anstruther was nevir sein sa grait in mans memorie, as it rase within an hour. The reid speat off fresche water market the sea mair nor a myll and a halff. That brought grait barrenness upon the land the yeirs following.

Rev. JAMES MELVILLE, *Diaries.*

HIGH JINKS IN ANSTRUTHER

Whilst on the subject of lawlessness it would be appropriate to mention some things, which, if not exactly infringements of the penal code, were regarded as showing how much original sin continued to manifest itself, especially in Anstruther, despite the general "Hypocrisy" which, according to Thomas Carlyle (who taught in Kirkcaldy for as long as his brittle patience held out) was rampant, along with "Atheism and the Ghoul Sensuality" in the 18th century.

The Fife folk had always responded to merry-making, music, dancing and practical joking. One of the funniest poems to be found in Scots literature, which abounds in rumbustious humour, is "The Wife of Auchtermuchty," which was old in 1768, when it was universally known, and thought to have been composed by an unknown genius in the reign of Mary Queen of Scots, or earlier. The language is now too antique for our anglified generations. It was simplified and ruined by Allan Cunningham in a mealy-mouthed version entitled "John Crumlie", which entirely misses the robust language and humour of old Fife, that the presbyterian church did its best to bowdlerise or suppress. There was no such suffocation in mediaeval times: the older churchmen had their faults, but they saw to it that the natural human instinct to have a roaring good time now and again, preferably now, was associated with holy days and holy fairs. The Great St. Andrews Fair, or Senzie Fair, lasted for fifteen days. The name Senzie is the old French Seinie, meaning a synod; the fair being held in the great square of the cathedral. Two of the relics of St. Andrews' three fairs each year are still celebrated; one, indirectly, in the Kate Kennedy procession on the date of the old April fair, and the other, the Senzie, in August, when according to the local saying, "A' thing dees after the Lammas Fair," which may have a psychological as well as a natural meaning.

But, in olden times, both in St. Andrews and in Anstruther, a' things were not allowed to dee. Both of these towns had three fairs per annum. Anstruther's were in April, July and November. These were uproarious occasions, so racily described in "Anster Fair," by the poet William Tennant, in 1812. The famous Drummond of Hawthornden found time, from writing his classical masterpieces and lamenting the tragic loss of his lady-love, to go round Fife, especially the East Neuk, in the early 17th century, and note the "carrying-on" of the merrymakers there. His poem (though it has never been proved that he was the author) is a ludicrous mixture of Latin and Scots, entitled "Polemo–middinia", "or a Treatise on Middens". Anstruther is faintly disguised as Anstraea, famed for such fish as "haddocus," "codlineus," "lobster monyfootus." Some of the local worthies may still be recognised in reincarnations as "Rob Gib, wantonus homo," "plouky-faced Watty Strang," "Willie Dick heavi-arstus homo," all of whom were in the habit of tripping it lightly in jolly dances and jigs, and also keen on "bonnaeas lassas kissare."

The famous song, "Maggie Lauder," is one of the liveliest Scottish songs. It is attributed to Francis Sempill, a 17th century poet.

> Meg up and walloped ow'er the green
> For brawly could she frisk it.

She lived in the East Green of Anstruther some time before 1650; this we know, because, in the above song, reference is made to the famous piper Habbie Simson, who died and was lamented in notable stanzas by Robert Sempill, Francis' poetical father, about that period. Some mealy-mouthed writers say that

163

"Maggie practised not the most reputable of professions" which could mean almost any profession, but is meant to suggest that she was a whore, and kept a "house of ill-repute" in East Green. Others say she was related to the local aristocracy. These allegations are not necessarily contradictory, though it is gilding her character rather much to call her the "Lily of the Bass," unless this means that she had the morals of a solan goose. The site of her cottage is now a rock-garden, with benches; what was once facetiously described as a "sitooterie."

FORBES MACGREGOR, *Salt-Sprayed Burgh: A View of Anstruther,* 1980.

MAGGIE LAUDER

Wha wad na be in love
    Wi' bonny Maggie Lauder?
A piper met her gaun to Fife
    And speir'd what was't they ca'd her.
Right scornfully she answer'd him,
    "Begone, you hallanshaker,
Jog on your gate, you bladderskate,
    My name is Maggie Lauder."

"Maggie," quoth he, "and by my bags,
    I'm fidging fain to see thee;
Sit down by me, my bonny bird,
    In troth I winna steer thee;
For I'm a piper to my trade,
    My name is Rob the Ranter;
The lasses loup as they were daft,
    When I blaw up my chanter."

"Piper," quoth Meg, "hae you your bags,
    Or is your drone in order?
If you be Rob, I've heard o' you;
    Live you upo' the Border?
The lasses a', baith far and near,
    Have heard o' Rob the Ranter;
I'll shake my foot wi' right goodwill,
    Gif you'll blaw up your chanter."

Then to his bags he flew wi' speed,
 About the drone he twisted;
Meg up and wallop'd o'er the green,
 For brawly could she frisk it.
"Weel done," quoth he: "Play up," quoth she:
 "Weel bobbed," quoth Rob the Ranter;
"'Tis worth my while to play indeed
 When I hae sic a dancer."

"Weel hae ye play'd your part," quoth Meg,
 "Your cheeks are like the crimson;
There's nane in Scotland plays sae weel
 Since we lost Habbie Simson.
I've liv'd in Fife, baith maid and wife,
 These ten years and a quarter;
Gin you should come to Enster Fair,
 Speir ye for Maggie Lauder."

FRANCIS SEMPILL

From *ANSTER FAIR*

"Then come, let me my suitors' merits weigh,
 And in the worthiest lad my spouse select:—

 . . .

Then for the lairds—there's Melvil of Carnbee,
 A handsome gallant, and a beau of spirit;
Who can go down the dance so well as he?
 And who can fiddle with such manly merit?
Ay, but he is too much the debauchee—
 His cheeks seem sponges oozing port and claret;
In marrying him I should bestow myself ill—
And so, I'll not have you, thou fuddler, Harry Melvil!

There's Cunningham of Barns, that still assails
 With verse and billet-doux my gentle heart—
A bookish squire, and good at telling tales,
 That rhymes and whines of Cupid, flame, and dart;
But, oh! his mouth a sorry smell exhales,
 And on his nose sprouts horribly the wart;

165

What though there be a fund of lore and fun in him?
He has a rotten breath—I cannot think of Cunningham!

Why then, there's Allardyce, that plies his suit
    And battery of courtship more and more;
Spruce Lochmalonie, that with booted foot
    Each morning wears the threshold of my door;
Auchmoutie too and Bruce, that persecute
    My tender heart with am'rous buffets sore:—
Whom to my hand and bed should I promote!—"

WILLIAM TENNANT

ANSTRUTHER: MR THOMSON, THE 'CURAT'

Mr. Thomson, the "curat" of Anstruther Easter, was a man highly obnoxious to the devout: in the first place, because he was a "curat"; in the second place, because he was a person of irregular and scandalous life; and in the third place, because he was generally suspected of dealings with the Enemy of Man. These three disqualifications, in the popular literature of the time, go hand in hand; but the end of Mr. Thomson was a thing quite by itself, and in the proper phrase, a manifest judgment. He had been at a friend's house in Anstruther Wester, where (and elsewhere, I suspect), he had partaken of the bottle; indeed, to put the thing in our cold modern way, the reverend gentleman was on the brink of *delirium tremens*. It was a dark night, it seems; a little lassie came carrying a lantern to fetch the curate home; and away they went down the street of Anstruther Wester, the lantern swinging a bit in the child's hand, the barred lustre tossing up and down along the front of slumbering houses, and Mr. Thomson not altogether steady on his legs nor (to all appearance) easy in mind. The pair had reached the middle of the bridge when (as I conceive the scene) the poor tippler started in some baseless fear and looked behind him; the child, already shaken by the minister's strange behaviour, started also; in so doing, she would jerk the lantern; and for the space of a moment the lights and the shadows would be all confounded. Then it was that to the unhinged toper and the twittering child, a huge bulk of blackness seemed to sweep down, to pass them close by as they stood upon the bridge, and to vanish on the farther side in the general darkness of the night. "Plainly the devil came for Mr. Thomson!" thought the child. What Mr. Thomson thought himself, we have no ground of knowledge; but he fell upon his knees in the midst of the bridge like a man praying. On the rest of the journey to the manse, history is silent but when they came to the door, the poor caitiff, taking the lantern from the child, looked upon her with so lost a countenance that her little courage died within her, and she fled home screaming to her parents. Not a soul would venture out; all that night, the minister dwelt alone with his terrors in the manse; and when the day dawned, and men made bold to go about the streets, they found the devil had come indeed for Mr. Thomson.

ROBERT LOUIS STEVENSON, *The Coast of Fife*, 1888.

From *BACK-GREEN ODYSSEY*

1

The sun's oot. I sit, my pipe alunt and puff.
The claes-line's pegged wi washin. They could be
sails. (Let them) Hou they rax and thraw, and yet
caa naethin furrit. Gress growes on my deck.

Thro the wheep-cracks o my sails the blue
wine o the sea is blinkin to the bouwl rim
o the horizon whaur my classic tap
the Berwick Law hides oor nothrin Athens.

Nae watters for an odyssey ye'll think
whaur jist tankers, coasters, seine-netters ply.
Still ablow this blue roof and burst o sun

my mind moves amon islands. Ulysses—
dominie, I cast aff the tether-tow
and steer my boat sittin on my doup-end.

5

My main deck is a green. Near the foreheid
the kitchen plot. I am weel stockit wi
vittles. On the starboard gunnels, flouers
and bushes whaur the birds tulzie and skriech.

I sit here, the captain and the haill crew
and keep my sun-birsled watches dwaumin.
Whiles I scour the sky-line, whiles I scart a line
in the log-book o my tethert vaigin;

the sea has a blue doze; a raggit skirlin
o bairns rises frae the beach; a sea gull
peenges like a wean and oars the air back.

I canna read my Homer in this sun.
I feel the reid meat of my body plot.
My odyssey is jist a doverin.

11

The concrete airms o the pier clauchtin air;
and the boats plooin the herbour-mou, flat–calm
in this spell, for the runkled open loof
o the Firth or the seven seas. "Cast aff"

is the sang the engines thrum. And the nets hairst
the shoals in the cauld causeys o the fish
gut and box thro the watches o the nicht
as the bows fur hamewards wi the siller crans.

The toun's laich starns; syne the reid aster heid
o the quay-neb licht. The herbour opens
its airms and they sail intill a braid hug

and tie up whaur aince they slippit the tow.
A herbour is a tension atween twa pulls,
the beck o horizons and the rug o hame.

ALASTAIR MACKIE★

ON CEMENTING LEVEL THE STABLE FLOOR AT THE OLD MANSE, WESTER ANSTRUTHER, ST SWITHIN'S DAY, 1963

Bored with his stall, wanting he knew not what,
The minister's gelding chafed here at his lot;

★Alastair Mackie (1925-95), the son of an Aberdeen quarryman, is one of the major Scottish poets of the twentieth century. His unique Scots style, based on the Doric of his upbringing, makes him one of the finest 'makars' of all time. He was also a prolific translator, turning French, Italian and Russian poetry into superb Scots versions. His neglect in recent years is nothing short of a national disgrace.

Mackie settled in Anstruther where he was a much-admired teacher at Waid Academy; a moving obituary was written by one of his former pupils, Christopher Rush. Duncan Glen published Mackie's work under his Akros imprint, notably the collection *Clytach* (1972).

Till his old age from that he was a foal
His stamping hoof ground out this shallow hole.

With some success, penned in my cramping pew,
My soul has raged against the canting crew
And these splenetic kicks I could not quell
Have cut me out a hole as deep as hell.

FORBES MACGREGOR

FROM DARK AGE EAST FIFE TO MEDIEVAL KILRENNY

Cellardyke is a paradoxical sort of place. Despite its long history as a fishing-port, culminating in a brief period of prominence as "the cod emporium of Scotland", it has never enjoyed an independent existence. From earliest times until 1929 it hid behind the bland official title of "Nether Kilrenny"; in that year of local government reorganisation it was swallowed up by neighbouring Anstruther. Now only an incorrectly-positioned signpost on the Crail road marks its continuing existence.

The ancient parish of Kilrenny itself extends for about three miles along the coastline of the East Neuk of Fife, bounded on the west by Anstruther and Carnbee, on the north by Carnbee and Crail, on the east by Crail and on the south by the Firth of Forth. For as far back as written records go this has been a fishing community, and a romantic legend out of the Dark Ages purports to explain the origins of the rich fishing-grounds around the May Island, some five miles offshore.

Loth, pagan British king of Lothian, had a daughter, Thaney or Thenaw, who was violated and made pregnant by a prince named Ewan. Enraged by her refusal to marry her violator, her father ordered her to be hurled in a chariot from the summit of Traprain Law. Miraculously, she survived the ordeal unharmed. Loth's Christian subjects tried to intercede on her behalf, but pagan counsels prevailed. If she was worthy to live, declared Thenaw's father, let her be handed over to Neptune, and let her God free her from the peril of death if he so wished (*si vita sit digna, Neptuno tradatur, et liberat eam a mortis periculo deus ejus si vult*).

The unfortunate Thenaw was accordingly placed in a leather coracle, which was then towed out beyond the May Island and cast adrift, followed only by shoals of fish from the teeming waters of Aberlady Bay, who had taken pity on the young princess. Luckily, a favourable wind sprang up and carried the coracle up the Forth to Culross, where Thenaw's son Kentigern, the future patron saint of Glasgow, was born. The fish, however, once they saw that their mistress was out of danger, remained in the vicinity of the May, where they have flourished ever since.

This charming miracle is dated with precision to the year 518 A.D., and commemorated on the island itself in such place-names as "the Lady's Bed", "the Lady's Well" and "the Maiden Rocks".

If the story of St. Thenaw is wholly fanciful, however, the other surviving legend from Dark-Age East Fife seems to have at least some basis in fact. A Hungarian missionary named Adrian, together with six thousand, six hundred and six followers, was believed to have come on an evangelising mission to the Picts of the East Neuk sometime in the ninth century, setting up his headquarters at Caiplie Coves on the eastern fringe of Kilrenny parish. Excavations in these caves by the seashore have indeed revealed signs of human habitation, not least in the shape of crosses cut into the inner walls of the so-called "Chapel Cave". From this base the saint's ascetic followers spread out along the length and breadth of this rugged coastline, some eventually taking refuge on the May. Here, we are told, the Blessed Adrian himself suffered martyrdom at the hands of marauding Vikings on March 4th, 875.

So powerful was the tradition of the martyred saint that the May eventually acquired a rich monastic foundation, and became the goal of pious pilgrims from all classes of mediaeval Scottish society: from barren women in search of a cure for their affliction, to the Stewart kings themselves. So potent is the legend even today that a street in Anstruther was named after the saint only a few years ago.

How much substance is there in the Adrian legend? Modern scholars, from the nineteenth-century historian W. F. Skene onwards, have accepted that a mission of some kind took place at that time, but have found no evidence of any such Hungarian incursion into ninth-century Fife. The real missionary is more likely to have been the Irish St. Ethernan, from Clonfert in County Galway, and it is surely no coincidence that he and his followers arrived in East Fife shortly after Clonfert, along with many other Irish monasteries and churches, is known to have been burnt and ravaged by the Danes (i.e. between 841 and 845). Moreover, the Gaelic-speaking Scots of Dalriada, descendants of fifth century Irish invaders, had recently succeeded in conquering the warlike Picts—Kenneth MacAlpin became joint king of Dalriada and Pictland in 843—and the land that henceforth would be known as "Scotland" must have seemed a home from home to the fleeing Irish monks.

According to the Adrian legend, one of the saint's Hungarian followers was a certain Monanus, the reputed founder of St. Monans; but in fact St. Moinenn, who died in 571, was an early bishop of Clonfert, and it may well be that his ninth-century successors carried his relics with them to Fife and interred them at Inverie—the old name for St. Monans—thus creating the legend of the saint's ministry there. Another possibility is that the six-thousand-odd followers of "Adrian" are simply a folk-memory of the Scottish invasion-force itself, of the war-bands with their attendant clergy; the mythical Hungarian missionaries being a later invention designed to please the half-Hungarian Queen Margaret, wife of Malcolm Canmore.

HARRY D. WATSON, *Kilrenny and Cellardyke: 800 years of History*, 1986.

SHIPWRIGHT'S SPEHL*

When striking the first blow,
Old Rob the shipwright pointed to three spehls
That had fallen like dice away from his axe.

He said:
"Three will go down with her the first time out."
And fell to his undertaking.
The younger men shifted and smiled.

Star Jeems paid Rob a hundred pounds
and took two sons to try for herring bait.

The keel cut like a coulter
through the blue furrows of the firth.
All morning they turned over cold clods of water
that settled behind them.
Towards noon a black squall took them
and cuffed them northwards angrily
away from the shore.
For four hours they sweated
among the sudden castles—
ugly blue swellings, bastions of brine—
and fifteen times they fought free of the moving walls.

The first killer came over the gunwale
like an axe, and felled the father.
Jeems went straight through forty fettering fathoms of salt.

---

*A 'spehl' (or 'skelb' as the East Neukers often say) is the Scots term for a splinter of wood. When building a new boat, the old Fife shipwrights might foretell the boat's luck by the feel of the first blow of the axe on the keel. Alternatively, they might claim to have found an unlucky spehl in the wood, foretelling disaster for the boat and the crew. *Christopher Rush*

The second wave was like a forest
with flowering tops. It grew round John in a second.
He died swallowing hard lumps of sea

Alex went down with the boat
beneath a sea like Borneo.
A jungle of death sprung from three splinters.

Old Rob shook his beard
and studied a new keel of American elm.

CHRISTOPHER RUSH

REFLECTIONS IN CRAIL

Always I edge towards light
Like that seamew
Crow-step by crow-step in Crail,
Climbing the pantiled roof,
The pyramid gable
Rising up from the harbour.

Always I climb towards light,
Ignoring the dark when I can,
Veering from exploration
Through blind inner spaces,
Aware of terrifying tunnels,
Densities of blackness;
Always the top of the triangle,
The emptiness of light,
The disc of the sun attracts.

I move eyes from the roof
To the harbour, glance downward,
Catch reflection of space in the water
Where boats knock against solid walls
Looking, I find what I seek—
Even in reflection.

MARGARET GILLIES BROWN

High seas off the East Neuk

THE COVES OF CRAIL

The moon-white water's wash and leap,
    The dark tide floods the Coves of Crail;
Sound, sound he lies in dreamless sleep,
    Nor hears the sea-wind wail.

The pale gold of his oozy locks
    Doth hither drift and thither wave
His thin hands plash against the rocks,
    His white lips nothing crave.

Afaraway she laughs and sings—
    A song he loved, a wild sea-strain—
Of how the mermen weave their rings
    Upon the reef-set main.

Sound, sound he lies in dreamless sleep,
    Nor hears the sea-wind wail,
Though with the tide his white hands creep
    Amid the Coves of Crail.

WILLIAM SHARP

A WISH

Why am I not that raven of the steppe,
Cawing defiantly there above me?
I would fly to the fogs of the far west,
The castle's stones precipitous to the sea.
On my ancestral walls the proud shield,
The sword of my clan:
With but my wing I'd brush off the dust
For those stern splendours to be revealed.
From the minstrel's hall, I'd strum the harp
With these proud feathers; down and deep
Into the vaults, such music surely can
Call up the troubled knight from bitter sleep.

But my own dreams are idle. Alps and oceans
Bar all my claims: I breathe cold, alien air.
Why am I not a raven of the steppe?
Here was I born: my soul belongs elsewhere…

MIKHAIL LERMONTOV★

A free improvisation, via a French translation, by

TOM HUBBARD

FULMARS AT CRAIL

Two fulmars appeared last week
back from who knows where.
No fanfare, no fuss, no blare of publicity,
no twitchers' welcoming committee,
no one from the council, from welfare
or the churches… But there they were,
free aeronauts of the sea-fresh air,
their ledge on the sandstone cliff quite bare,
scoured squeaky clean below the Castle Walk
in the six months they've not been there.

Watching them glide stiff-winged across the bay
riding the updrafts of an ocean gale, I cheered.

★One of the great Russian writers, Lermontov (1814-41), renowned for his novel *A Hero of Our Time* and a considerable body of poetry, met his untimely death in a duel. He was descended from the Scottish Learmonths of Balcomie in north-east Fife.

Have they been following the fishing boats
or had a hard time of it farther north?
I listen to their crooning grunts and cackles
and watch their bowings and head-shakings
as they take the time to greet a buddy.
I look forward with pleasant anticipation
to the proper setting up of their seaside colony.

Fulmars are the only birds I can think of
that seem to fly for the sheer joy of it.
Sociable but elusive, they bother nobody
unless invaded on their nesting patch.
But once disturbed the oddest thing occurs
if you go too close. Shot from the nasal tubes
that lie along their beaks, you might receive
a squirt of stinking snot... I kid you not.

GORDON JARVIE

THE ARRIVAL OF MARY OF GUISE-LORRAINE, SECOND WIFE OF KING JAMES V, AT FIFENESS, IN JUNE 1538

...the quen landit in Scotland the viij day of Juin... in ane place callit Fywisness
besyde Ballcome [inland from Fife Ness], quhair scho remanit quhill horse come
to hir. Bot the kingis grace was in Sanctandrois for the tyme witht money of his
nobilietie waittand upoun hir hame comming. Then he sieand scho was landit
in sic ane pairt, he raid fourtht him self to meit hir. Than the kingis grace and
the hail lordis baitht spirituall and temporall, money barrouns, lairdis and genyill-
men quho was convenit at St androis ffor the tyme in thair best array raid and
ressavit the quens grace witht great honouris and mirrenes witht great treumph
and blythness of phrassis and playis maid to hir at hir hame comming. And first
scho was ressavit at the New Abbey yeit. Upoun the eist syde thair was maid
to hir trieumphant frais [pageant] be Schir David Lyndsay of the Mont, lyoun
harrot, qhilk caussit ane great clude to come out of the heivens done abone
the yeit quhair the quene come in, and oppin in two halffis instantlie and thair
appeirit ane fair lady maist lyk ane angell havand the keyis of haill Scotland in
hir handis deliverand thame unto the quens grace in signe and takin that all the
heartis of Scottland was opnit to the ressaving of hir grace; witht certane wriesuns
and exortatiouns maid by the same Schir David Lyndsay into the quens grace
instructioun quilk teichit hir to serve hir god, obey hir husband, and keep hir
body clene according to godis will and commandement. This beand done, the

quen was ressavit into hir palice and luging quhilk was callit the New Innes and was weill decoirit againe hir comming, with all necessariss perteinand to ane quen and thair scho ludgit that night, quhill on the morne at ten hours scho passit to the abbay kirk and thair scho saw money ane lustie lord and barrone and gentillmen landit all weill arayit in thair abullyementis againe hir comming; also the bischopis, abbotis, pryouris, monkis, freiris and chanounis regular maid great solemnitie in the abbay kirk witht messes [masses] songis and playin on the organis. This being done, the king ressavit the quen in his palice to the dinner quhair thair was great mirth schallmes draught trumpattis and weir [war] trumpattis witht playing and phrassis [farces] efter denner quhill tyme of supper. On the morne the quen passit throw the toune and visitit all the kirkis and colledgis and the universietie within the toun, that is to say scho vessit the blak freirs, the greyfreirs, the auld coledge and the new colledge and Sanct Leonardis, the paroche kirk and the Lady kirk of heuche, to wit. Scho was convoyit be the provost of the toune and honest burgessis thairof.

ROBERT LYNDSAY OF PITSCOTTIE

Across Country to Leuchars
and the Tay

DUNINO: THE DEN, PAGAN AND EARLY CHRISTIAN WORSHIP

We have no certain knowledge about the worship of the earliest middle Stone-age inhabitants. It is often assumed to have been centred around rather negative magic of the simplest form i.e. where some specific objects, events or animals were treated as unlucky and others as lucky totems, which were revered and protected. This culture of avoiding "bad luck" is usually associated with a "shaman" or "witchdoctor" figure, who regulated what was "taboo" rather than practised "sorcery".

By the late Stone-age, agriculture seems to have given rise to worship associated with observation, recognition or thanksgiving for the seasons and the attendant fertility. The stone circle (henge) that lay west of the Den, like others of its type, has been assumed to have had an alignment of lunar or solstitial astronomical significance. Little is agreed among scientists about stone circles as many different horizon-markers can be assumed and there is a general reluctance to impute modern ideals to prehistoric people. At the winter equinox the sun sets behind High Beley if observed from Dunino Law, and this line dissects the field where the henge was built. The site remained, what in modern terms would be called "holy", for hundreds of years of ritual burials.

The Den where the rock known as the Bel crag was excavated by the son of the manse, Charles Rogers, in 1845 is believed to be associated with Celtic druidic worship. The Den contains two pot-holes and a shallow foot print carved in the rock. The origin of the pot-holes is unknown but there is some general agreement that they are partly man-made enlargements of natural erosions. (The largest is some 4 feet wide and 2.5 feet deep although only recorded as 2.5 feet wide when first uncovered!) As Celtic ideas and people arrived in Britain around 800 BC the worship they brought was based on a calendar that was herding and stock-rearing orientated. Their festivals, although seasonal, did not coincide with lunar, solar or crop planting events. For example, "samhain" (1 November) the new year, has its origin in the timing of bringing in cattle from pasture and slaughter of those that could not be wintered, "Imbolc" (1 February) was a fertility ritual that coincided with the lactation of ewes, "Beltane" (1 May) the spring fertility ritual was related to the availability of pasture. The events show their origins in seasonal herding in Central Europe, rather than Britain, as the movement of cattle to high pasture (Alpage) is rather more regular there. This worship around stock-herding casts some doubts on the claimed alignment of the Bel crag, Kellie Law and the standing stone between Peekie and Winchester. This so-called "lay" line seems to be coincidental as the stone appears to pre-date Bel worship by a thousand years. What we do know about Bel worship is that the druids (or priests) collected dew on the first of May for ritual purposes and held an important fire festival. The fires were lit on hills and these festivals survived in Perthshire in modified forms until the middle of the 18th century. The cow herds cut a square, or round trench, to form a table on which they ate a ritual cake, one portion of which was deemed to be unlucky by size or colour. The person who drew this portion was the Beltane earl who had to leap through the bonfire three times and carried the name for the year. The origins of these activities are the earlier procession of the cattle sunwise around the fires and possible ritual sacrifices in the fires. It is supposed that at one time this widely celebrated European festival involved the burning of wicker effigies containing the sacrifice of livestock or of criminals and prisoners. We know nothing certain about our Den and it has certainly been suggested that the excavations there were part of a hoax built on local legend. Still, in its favour, are the undisputed importance of the earlier henge site, the long attachment of the name Bel, the proximity of the place called "Druids grave" Pittendriech, the Roman visit in strength and the importance attached by early Christians.

The early Christian missionaries were attracted to the sacred groves of earlier worship as part of their process of gradual conversion and because of the natural affinity with nature and open air worship of the early church. A Culdee Celtic monk scribbled this poem in the margin of the book he was copying:

> *A hedge of trees surrounds me,*
> *A blackbird's lay sings to me;*
> *Above my lined booklet*
> *The trilling birds chant to me.*

> *In a grey mantle from the top of bushes*
> *The cuckoo sings:*
> *Verily—may the Lord shield me—*
> *Well do I write under the greenwood.*

Over the years the Bel crag with the larger of the pot-holes, has been called the altar rock, with the assumption that its basin was used for baptism and its foot print for king-making. Whilst the rock immediately up stream with the smaller pot-hole became known as the pulpit rock. It has been suggested that the smaller pot-hole was used to plant the base of a wooden cross carried about by itinerant Culdee monks. A foot print at Dunadd is recorded as having been used in King-making ritual but there are no such written references to the Den being used for this purpose. Such foot prints also exist at some west coast sites (caves) associated with early Christian missionaries, including St Columba; and legends link them to the Culdee ascetic ideal (anchoritism) of travel for "seeking the place of one's resurrection".

Two sculptured stones from Dunino exist, dating from at least early Christian times. One still stands in the Church yard and was converted into a sundial in 1698. The other, which may be a fragment of the first, is in St. Andrews' Cathedral Museum and shows the intricate interwoven carving more clearly.

The only other trace of pagan worship in the Parish, not absorbed in the Church ritual, was the pan-European custom of making corn dollies. This survived in this Parish until the late 19th century, when the last stook cut was still being fashioned into a corn maiden for luck, and hung in farm houses. Unfortunately, people are more fascinated by the thought of grisly druid sacrifices in the den (like that of the English "bog man") than in the glorious thought of some 4000 years of harvest thanksgiving.

The Celtic style cross scratched in the rock-face, up-river from the Pulpit Rock, is not credited with any antiquity. However, old or not, it is a symbolic reminder of the earliest open air Christian meeting place in the Parish.

D. & L. McGILP, *Dunino: Place of Worship*, 1993.

From *DUNINO*

Fife, East Fife, the harvest stooking
gowd of grain in the rolling fields,
the hedgerows' scattered punctuation
under the height of Kellie Law;
East Neuk of Fife, the fishers' margin,
driftnet of villages pursing the shore,
the boats that fix their silver meads
over the kirk to Kellie Law.

And here the poem declared its title
before a line had yet been written:
it was a roadsign, the name of a village
—Dunino—where no village is.
A scatter of farms, a school, and one
red telephone box: but even that
a mile down the road. From the sign
there is nothing in sight. 'Dunino'—

179

and then the harvest fields.
Not a place I've ever stopped, although
for years of my life I used to drive through
on the road from St Andrews south,
the Anstruther road, up over the hill, turn
west at Drumrack farm, and home
to Carnbee. Facing out to the Forth:
my father's parish. My father's grave.

> *It is an unco orra thing*
> *tae be nae langer o the yird,*
> *tae gang nae mair the scarce-kent ways*
> *nor seek the dern sense o the burnan rose.*
> *It is an unco orra thing*
> *tae set aside yir vera name,*
> *tae lang nae mair til langin's limit*
> *but watch yir hert's benmaist desires*
> *bauchle awa like a rag on the rain.*

The dead, says Rilke, are never gone
and even the angels who move among us
cannot distinguish which we are.
In the wood of the Lorimer carving
on the pulpit of Carnbee church
(the bell-rope swings behind the window),
a pelican lances her own bright breast,
and blood is written on the leesome white.

—the Silence! and the woods are gone.★

STEPHEN SCOBIE

GOD'S OWN SCHOLAR

Many years ago a new class of preachers started suddenly up in the country. They were called the sensational school, and were not unlike a certain section of the clergy in the present day. Their motto seemed to be: "Catch the public, by dignified means if you can, but by all means catch the public." Their rules for doing this were these: "Choose as the subject of your sermon some prevalent vice; denounce it in the plainest and strongest language; threaten those who

★The italicised section is a quotation from Rilke's *The Duino Elegies*.

practise it, or even encourage it, with all the misery of this world and all the eternal woes of the next; draw your illustrations hot from ordinary life; if they are vulgar or grotesque, and excite a titter, never mind; one great end is gained if by any means they arouse the interest of the audience."

The most promising member of this school was the Rev. Jeremiah MacGuf-fog, the new parish minister at Sandyriggs. He took the most solemn view of his office. He was placed there, he felt, as an ambassador of the Most High to denounce the iniquities that were lifting their heads on every side. It was no time for smooth words. Like the martyred prophets and reformers of old, he must boldly face the transgressors, tell them of their sins in the most direct language, and warn them of the terrible doom that awaits them.

While he was a student in Glasgow, he had often heard that the most productive root of immorality in the rural districts was the Bothy System. Everyone seemed to condemn it, and not one word had been said in its defence. It was clearly his duty, therefore, to strike it down without delay. Accordingly, one Sunday not long after his settlement, he wound up his afternoon sermon with a most merciless attack upon the farmers.

"The farmers," he said, "are a most respectable class of men, and I am deeply grieved to be compelled to say anything to wound their feelings; but I am here to tell them that they are responsible for what I call *the running sore,* which is draining the life-blood of morality and religion in the rural districts. I refer to the Bothy System. You, my brethren, are really treating your fellow-men like your cattle. You lodge them in a dirty and uncomfortable outhouse, and leave them there to corrupt each other. Did I say that you treated them *like* your cattle? I should have said *worse* than your cattle. For you do not prepare food for them, you do not tie them up, you do not lock them in and prevent them from roaming abroad at night and falling into mischief. I am sorry that I am obliged to use strong language, but in the faithful discharge of my duty I am called upon to say that these bothies are nurseries of the infernal pit, and that you who keep them up are, though you may not know it, really serving the devil."

It would be impossible to describe the volcano of feeling which this onslaught roused within the souls of the farming population. They could scarcely keep their seats till the service was over; then, when they went out of church and took their way homewards in the grey winter dusk, the turmoil within them was almost too strong for expression; and for a time they could only vent it in such explosive epithets, as "nurseries o' the infernal pit!" "servants o' the deevil!" "ill-tongued cratur!" "empty-headed puppy!" "set him up!" "my certie!" But by the time they reached the foot of the Long Dykes, where the road divided into three, a group of them, both men and women, stood still to compare notes.

"Sic a desecration o' the poopit!" said Mrs Dowie of Seggie Den; "instead o' preachin' the gospel, misca'in honest folk."

181

"Eh, woman!" exclaimed Mrs. Caw of Blawearie, "ye may say that. Him to turn up his nose at bothies, that was brocht up, they tell me, in a one-roomed hoose in the wynds o' Glesky. My word, it doesna set a soo to wear a saddle."

"Low-born smaik," said Mrs. Proud of the Hill, "to scandaleese his betters!"

"I dinna ken," said Tam Bluff of Cuddiesknowes, "what they teach them at college, but it's evidently no' mainners."

"Settin' servants against their maisters," said Stables, the horse doctor, a Tory of the old school.

"What could ye expect," asked Ure, the innkeeper at Blawearie Yetts, "from a teetotaller? Did ye hear hoo he blackguarded onybody that had onything to dae wi' makin' or sellin' an honest drap o' drink. Haith! it's my opinion that when the Maister comes to the warld a second time, they'll steek in His face the door o' His ain kirk, because He ance turned water into wine."

Then Manson of the Hole, who had been standing by, red with rage, now began to splutter forth his resentment. He was a cantankerous old bachelor, greedy, miserly, and wealthy. If any bothy in the neighbourhood deserved to be tabooed, it was his. That was the reason for his feeling the most aggrieved. "By the Lord Hairy," he said, "I'll astonish the dirty cratur. I'll hae a ring in his nose before he's a week aulder. I'll ceet him before the Presbytery, and if that wunna dae, before the Synod and the General Assembly; and if I canna get Justice there, I'll gang to the Law. Don't ye think I'm richt, Gilbert Strang?"

The man who was thus addressed, and who now came up, was evidently somewhat inferior in station to the rest of the group. In fact, at first sight he looked shabby. His hat was weather-stained, his clothes were threadbare and even darned in some places, and his boots were rough and clumsy. But his well-developed figure, his clean-cut and healthy features, and his big blue eyes, gave him, in spite of his mean apparel, a look of superiority. Nay, the neat patches on his coat seemed, in some odd way, to be badges of respectability. He was the son of a small laird; but his father had recently died, a heart-broken bankrupt; the property had been sold; he had been left the sole support of his widowed mother, and had been obliged to hire himself out as an ordinary ploughman; and it was understood that he was now pinching himself to save money, in order, if possible, to redeem the little family inheritance.

Gilbert Strang, in fact, was one of those hardy human plants that can grow and flourish mentally and morally in any soil. He had been but a few years under the village teacher. The school in which he had learnt most was the world, where the lessons are undoubtedly very difficult, but, if once mastered, are most salutary. In the few books which he had, in the weekly sermons to which he listened, in the ever-varying shows of earth and sky, and in the rustic gatherings and merrymakings, he got abundant food both for mind and heart. Then, during the long quiet days when he was guiding the plough in the meadow, he found a favourite opportunity for thinking over what he had seen and read, and for forming his notions of men and things. In this way, he had made up his mind on most of the subjects that crop up in rural life, and was able to express his views, not only in the broad vernacular, but also, when occasion called, in good English. Altogether, he was a fair specimen of a man of Nature's own training, or what pious people used to call "one of God Almighty's own scholars."

"Don't you think I wad be richt, Gilbert Strang, to ceet him before the Presbytery, and if I canna get redress there to try the Law?"

"Ye wad be just playin' into his haunds, Mr. Manson."

"In what way, Gilbert?"

"Ye wad mak him staund oot before the public as a martyr, and that's what a' thae kind want to be. What I would advise wad be, to gie him rope."

"What dae ye mean, Gilbert?"

"He kens the bothies only by hearsay; and he has spoken a lot o' nonsense aboot them. Let him alane. He'll gang deeper and deeper into the mess. Then he'll find himsel in a habble and be obleeged to apologeese."

"Apologeese!" cried Manson, "catch a minister apologeese! Dod man! they're never wrang. At the time o' the Reformation, they jist shifted the doctrine o' infallibility from the Pope's shouthers on to their ain; and now, instead o' ane, we hae thousands o' Popes."

"That may be," replied Strang, "only ca' canny. Look before ye loup. Mind the proverb, 'Haste maks waste.'"

"Dod that's true," replied Manson. "But eh man! I wad gie a gude roond sum to see the gabbie body obleeged to tak back and swallow a' the nonsense he's been talkin'."

"Weel!" said Gilbert, "ye'll soon see it."

DAVID GRANT, *The Queer Folk of Fife: Tales from
the Kingdom*, 1897.

THINKIN AN DAEIN

Atween the blink o the ee an the harn,
Atween the seein an the thinkin,
Time an space whummelt in the swee.

Dykes rise,
Fields, end-rigs nae pleuchd syne,
Rummel intae the lift.

Gowd–lickit cloods
An bleck staunan aiks,
Awe the gap atween seein an thinkin.

Thinkin an daein
That wir word micht come
Speiritin oot o thon gap
Speirin at the yird an awe its cronies.

Wir ain word biggit that wi maun tak it
An yokein it, let it flee
As the finger lifts an the air
Flees oot the taem chaunter.

Chaumer pipes for dauncein
An war ains for bleedin,
Auld words for speakin
An new ains for readin;
Theres the chink atween thinkin an daein.

HARVEY HOLTON

Deal liberalye with neidful foike,
  Deny nane of them al;
For little thou knavest heir in this lyf
  Quhat chance may the defal.
A nice wyf and a back doore
Oft maketh a rich man poore.

From the painted ceiling of the Long Gallery of Earlshall, near Leuchars.

The Long Gallery, Earlshall

EARLSHALL GARDEN

The natural park comes up to walls of the house on the one side, on the other you stroll out into a garden enclosed. That is all—a house and a garden enclosed, but what a promise can such a place be made! Such surprises—little gardens within the garden, the "month's" garden, the herb garden, the yew alley. The kitchen garden, too—and this nothing to be ashamed of, to be smothered away from the house, but made delightful by its laying out. Great interesting walls of shaven grass, on either side borders of brightest flowers backed by low espaliers hanging shining apples, and within these espaliers again the gardener has his kingdom.

SIR ROBERT LORIMER

NORTHWARDS FROM ST ANDREWS

It is true that, to the north of the town [of St Andrews], beyond the estuary of the Eden, and on towards the entrance to the Firth of Tay, lies a waste and barren land, with few outstanding features and scant history—Tents Muir. But even this territory of windlestrae and sand-hills, flat foreshore and marshy pastures, is interesting as the resort of many varieties of wild fowl, and temporary place of exile of Pallas's sand-grouse, and also as formerly the abode of a race of smugglers and wreckers, who were said to be the descendants of the survivors of a Danish fleet wrecked on Abertay Sands. To reach it one has to go round by Guard Bridge, where close at hand are the Castlehill and the Kirk of Leuchars, with its double-arcaded apse—a gem of Norman architecture—and its memories of Alexander Henderson and the Covenant, and the well-preserved sixteenth-century mansion of Earlshall on the site of a castle of the Macduffs.

At the extremity of these heathery and sandy tracts we look across the Tay to Barry Links, and out to sea, where the Bell Rock is the only scrap of land between us and Jutland. Farther west, Ferry-Port-on-Craig, or Tayport, opposes Broughty Castle on the northern shore. Here, under the Craig, was the first and at one time the most famous of sea-water ferries. It has seen, and still sees, many adventurous passages between Angus and Fife. But the Tay Bridge, which, beyond Newport, strides across the Firth in many spans to where the shipping and buildings of Dundee are piled along the front and around the bases of The Law and Balgay Hill, has stripped it of its importance, which has, in part, passed over to its neighbour Newport. Scotscraig is behind it, a possession of Archbishop Sharpe, and, long before his time, of Michael Scott, from whom it may take its name. No wizardry of that ancient date, in "bridling the flood with a curb of stone", can compare with the feat of the modern engineer in flinging a structure of steel from bank to bank across more than two miles of sea-water. Yet there

185

was one wild night, in December, 1879, when the wind and the waves had their triumph, and the centre of the structure plunged into the sea with a passenger train and all that it carried.

Above Wormit and the Tay Bridge, the Firth widens, and the northern shore of Fife looks across to the rich lands of the Carse of Gowrie, a country of fertile fields and spreading woods and old castles and mansions, backed by the Sidlaw Hills, and behind these, and away to the west, the distant peaks of the Grampians. The Fife hills draw nearer the coast, and in Norman's Law and other heights show a bold front—the beginning of the Ochils; and hamlets and historic manor houses, old battlefields, churches and castles, and a couple of venerable abbeys are inserted between their steep green or forest-clad slopes and the "Broad Water".

Of the Castle of Naughton, the home of a legendary chieftain of the Hay family, whom Gawain Douglas, in his "Palace of Honour", placed alongside Robin Hood and other heroes of romance, only a few ruins are left. But the grey walls of Ballanbreich, or Bambreich, stand out boldly on a steep bank overhanging the shore, a landmark of the upper Firth.

The abbeys are Balmerino and Lindores. Of the former, founded by Queen Ermengarde, the wife of William the Lion and mother of Alexander II, and dedicated to the Virgin and St. Edward the Confessor, all that remain are some arcaded arches and vaulted apartments. There is nothing to mark the tomb of the founder before the high altar. The monks fell into bad repute before the Reformation, and the buildings went to utter decay. The lands were given to the Elphinstone family, and the latest holders of the title of Lord Balmerino won a melancholy fame for their devotion to the House of Stewart.

Lindores Abbey has a greater record behind it, and has more to show above ground. It stood near the road from the Howe of Fife, where it comes down, past Lindores Loch and the ruins of Magridrin's church and through the little glen that skirts the relics of Denmyln Castle—the home of a family of Balfours, one of whom, Sir James, the antiquary, was of the ten Lord Lyons drawn from Fife in a century—to meet the coast road on the eastern margin of the little royal burgh of Newburgh. It is ground haunted by the traditional and the real figures of Scotland's past. The foundations of yet another "Macduff's Castle" are hard by the forked ways; as has been seen, "Macduff's Cross" is hidden in the hills behind. The Sculptured Cross of Mugdrum is on the march between Fife and Perth, and ahead, the Round Tower and the poplars of Abernethy, the ancient Pictish capital, show up like the boundary marks of another province of national history. Wallace's Camp, before his victory of Blackearnside, is a little way behind us; Edward Longshanks, John Balliol, David Bruce and other royal personages sojourned in the Tyronesian Abbey, which was founded in the twelfth century by David, Earl of Huntingdon, heir to the throne and hero of the *Talisman*, and dedicated by him to St. Mary and St. Andrew, in gratitude for having taken the city of Ptolomais, and for having been saved from shipwreck. The body of his unfortunate descendant and namesake, David, Duke of Rothesay, was buried here in a stone coffin, now empty, and it wrought miracles until his brother, James I of Scots, began to wreak vengeance on his murderers, when, as Hector Boece says, they "ceassit finally". Here too, a couple of generations later, came James, ninth Earl of Douglas—"Greystiel"—to join, after a stormy life, the company of the religious, and to console himself with his stoic philosophy—"He that can do no better must be a monk".

JOHN GEDDIE, *The Shores of Fife*, 1923.

187

St Andrews

NORTHERN ROSES

It was no dream: colours and fragrances,
Not eastern spell, but north's reality.
It was late autumn, and yet the roses
Bloomed in St Andrews, above the sea.

The Gulf Stream, said my professorial friend,
Is known to visit these our Scottish shores.
Fresh lawns and sumptuous flower-beds end to end,
Reach inland from the East Sands to The Scores.

But our own souls are trembling with the blight,
The coming of a great and gloomy frost:
Oh that the Gulf could hold us, cure us quite,
Before we shrivel up and sink almost,

So we'd ignite a colour or two, going down,
And even greet the winter florally,
Just like those gardens in that snod wee town,
St Andrews, there above the northern sea.

LAJOS ÁPRILY★
Transcreated from the Hungarian by **TOM HUBBARD**
with **ATTILA DÓSA**

SCOTTISH MUID

Haar on the watter, haar in the parks,
　　River and white haar o the north.
—O wha has hushed wi her ain milk
　　This lown earth?

★Áprily (1887–1967), a leading Hungarian poet of the twentieth century, was a Scotophile who produced some of the celebrated Hungarian versions of the poems of Robert Burns. Dr Dósa, who advised Tom Hubbard during the preparation of his transcreations, is a PhD of St Andrews University and a lecturer at Miskolc University.

There's tides that swurl ayont aa sicht
    Ablow the black craig o the ness.
The drookit sheep hae couried doun,
    Dovin on the weet gress.

There's unco dreamin in this airt,
    Whaur the birks greet throu the souch:
The echo o an auld-warld ballant
    In ilka castle-neuk.

And the daurk fisher's boat
    Growes ti a ghaist-ship on the seas:
And faddoms deep, Sir Patrick Spens
    Lies in a dwam o young leddies.

The sea-maws stoiter i the lift.
    Blinly they faa ti the grey earth.
Belike I'm dreamin nou myself,
    That here I'm daunerin i the north.

And at Sanct-Aundraes, bi the haar
    Raither nor bi the müne convoyit,
There walks in sleep thon braw Scots queen,
    Her doo's-neck splattert ower wi bluid.

LAJOS ÁPRILY
Transcreated from the Hungarian by **TOM HUBBARD**
with **ATTILA DÓSA**

THE FIFE LAIRD

Ye shouldna ca' the Laird daft, though daft like he may be;
Ye shouldna ca' the Laird daft, he's just as wise as me;
Ye shouldna ca' the Laird daft, his bannet has a *bee*—
He's just a wee bit Fifish, like some Fife lairds that be.
Last Lammas when the Laird set out to see Auld Reekie's toun,
The Firth it had nae waves at a', the waves were sleepin' soun';
But wicked witches bide about gude auld St. Andrews toun,
And they steered up an unco blast, our ain dear Laird to droun.

Afore he got to Inchkeith Isle, the waves were white an' hie—
"O weel I ken thae witches wud hae aye a spite at me!"
They drove him up, they drove him doon,—the Fife touns a' they pass,
And up and round Queensferry toun, then doun unto the Bass.
The sailors row, but row in vain, Leith port they canna gain—
Nae meat or beds they hae on board, but *there* they maun remain;
O mirk and cauld the midnight hour, how thankfu' did they see
The first blush o' the dawnin' day, far spreadin' owre the sea.

Ye shouldna ca' the Laird daft, etc.

"Gae hame, gae hame," the Laird cried out, "as fast as ye can gang,
Oh! rather than wi' witches meet, I'd meet an *ourna-tang;*—
A' nicht and day I've been away, an' naething could I see
But auld wives' cantrips on broomsticks, wild cap'ring owre the sea.
I hae na' had a mouth o' meat, nor yet had aff my claes—
Afore I gang to sea again, some *folk* maun mend their ways."
The Laird is hame wi' a' his ain, below the Lomond hill,
Richt glad to see his sheep again, his dookit and his mill!

Ye shouldna ca' the Laird daft, tho' daft like he may be;
Ye shouldna ca' the Laird daft, he's just as wise as me:
Ye shouldna ca' the Laird daft, his bannet has a *bee,*—
He's juist a wee bit Fifish, like some Fife Lairds that be.

CAROLINA OLIPHANT, LADY NAIRNE

THE INHERITANCE OF A FIFE LAIRD

A wee pickle rent, a gey pickle debt,
a hantle o pride and a doocot.

ANONYMOUS

DR SAMUEL JOHNSON IN ST ANDREWS

By the interposition of some invisible friend, lodgings had been provided for us
at the house of one of the professors, whose easy civility quickly made us forget
that we were strangers; and in the whole time of our stay we were gratified
by every mode of kindness, and entertained with all the elegance of lettered
hospitality. . . .

St Andrews

The change of religion in Scotland, eager and vehement as it was, raised an epidemical enthusiasm, compounded of sullen scrupulousness and warlike ferocity, which, in a people whom idleness resigned to their own thoughts, and who, conversing only with each other, suffered no dilution of their zeal from the gradual flux of new opinions, was long transmitted in its full strength from the old to the young, but by trade and intercourse with England, is now visibly abating, and giving way too fast to that laxity of practice and indifference of opinion, in which men, not sufficiently instructed to find the middle point, too easily shelter themselves from rigour and constraint. The city of St Andrews, when it lost its archiepiscopal preeminence, gradually decayed: one of its streets is now lost; and in those that remain, there is the silence and solitude of inactive indigence and gloomy depopulation.

...Having now seen whatever this ancient city offered to our curiosity, we left it with good wishes, having reason to be highly pleased with the attention that was paid us. But whoever surveys the world must see many things that give him pain. The kindness of the professors did not contribute to abate the uneasy remembrance of a university declining, a college alienated, and a church profaned and hastening to the ground.

SAMUEL JOHNSON, *A Journey to the Western Isles of Scotland,*
1775.

From *A MONK OF FIFE*

I loved to be in the scriptorium of the Abbey, and to see the good Father Peter limning the blessed saints in blue, and red, and gold, of which art he taught me a little. Often I would help him to grind his colours, and he instructed me in the laying of them on paper or vellum, with white of egg, and in fixing and burnishing the gold, and in drawing flowers, and figures, and strange beasts and devils, such as we see grinning from the walls of the cathedral. In the French language, too, he learned me, for he had been taught at the great University of Paris; and in Avignon had seen the Pope himself, Benedict XIII, of uncertain memory.

Much I loved to be with Father Peter, whose lessons did not irk me, but jumped with my own desire to read romances in the French tongue, whereof there are many. But never could I have dreamed that, in days to come, this art of painting would win me my bread for a while, and that a Leslie of Pitcullo should be driven by hunger to so base and contemned a handiwork, unworthy, when practised for gain, of my blood.

Yet it would have been well for me to follow even this craft more, and my sports and pastimes less: Dickon Melville had then escaped a broken head, and I, perchance, a broken heart. But youth is given over to vanities that war against the soul, and, among others, to that wicked game of the Golf, now justly cried down by our laws, as the mother of cursing and idleness, mischief and wastery, of which game, as I verily believe, the devil himself is the father.

It chanced, on an October day of the year of grace fourteen hundred and twenty-eight, that I was playing myself at this accursed sport with one Richard Melville, a student of like age with myself. We were evenly matched, though Dickon was tall and weighty, being great of growth for his age, whereas I was of but scant inches, slim, and, as men said, of a girlish countenance. Yet I was well skilled in the game of the Golf, and have driven a Holland ball the length of an arrow-flight, there or thereby. But wherefore should my sinful soul be now in mind of these old vanities, repented of, I trust, long ago?

As we twain, Dickon and I, were known for fell champions at this unholy sport, many of the other scholars followed us, laying wagers on our heads. They were but a wild set of lads, for, as then, there was not, as now there is, a house appointed for scholars to dwell in together under authority. We wore coloured clothes, and our hair long; gold chains, and whingers [daggers] in our belts, all of which things are now most righteously forbidden. But I carried no whinger on the links, as considering that it hampered a man in his play. So the game went on, now Dickon leading "by a hole," as they say, and now myself, and great wagers were laid on us.

Now, at the hole that is set high above the Eden, whence you see far over the country, and the river-mouth, and the shipping, it chanced that my ball lay between Dickon's and the hole, so that he could in no manner win past it.

"You laid me that stimy of set purpose," cried Dickon, throwing down his club in a rage; "and this is the third time you have done it in this game."

"It is clean against common luck," quoth one of his party, "and the game and the money laid on it should be ours."

"By the blessed bones of the Apostle," I said, "no luck is more common. To-day to me, to-morrow to thee! Lay it of purpose, I could not if I would."

"You lie!" he shouted in a rage, and gripped to his whinger.

It was ever my father's counsel that I must take the lie from none. Therefore, as his steel was out, and I carried none, I made no more ado, and the word of shame had scarce left his lips when I felled him with the iron club that we use in sand.

"He is dead!" cried they of his party, while the lads of my own looked askance on me, and had manifestly no mind to be partakers in my deed.

Now, Melville came of a great house, and, partly in fear of their feud, partly like one amazed and without any counsel, I ran and leaped into a boat that chanced to lie convenient on the sand, and pulled out into the Eden. Thence I saw them raise up Melville, and bear him towards the town, his friends lifting their hands against me, with threats and malisons. His legs trailed and his head wagged like the legs and the head of a dead man, and I was without hope in the world.

ANDREW LANG, From *A Monk of Fife*, 1896.

From *THE LIBRARY WINDOW: A STORY OF THE SEEN AND THE UNSEEN*

I was not aware at first of the many discussions which had gone on about that window. It was almost opposite one of the windows of the large old-fashioned drawing-room of the house in which I spent that summer, which was of so much importance in my life. Our house and the library were on opposite sides of the broad High Street of St Rule's, which is a fine street, wide and ample, and very quiet, as strangers think who come from noisier places; but in a summer evening there is much coming and going, and the stillness is full of sound—the sound of footsteps and pleasant voices, softened by the summer air. There are even exceptional moments when it is noisy: the time of the fair, and on Saturday nights sometimes, and when there are excursion trains. Then even the softest sunny air of the evening will not smooth the harsh tones and the stumbling steps; but at these unlovely moments we shut the windows, and even I, who am so fond of that deep recess where I can take refuge from all that is going on inside, and make myself a spectator of all the varied story out of doors, withdraw from my watch-tower. To tell the truth, there never was very much going on inside. The house belonged to my aunt, to whom (she says, Thank God!) nothing ever happens. I believe that many things have happened to her in her time; but that was all over at the period of which I am speaking, and she was old, and very quiet. Her life went on in a routine never broken. She got up at the same hour every day, and did the same things in the same rotation, day by day the same. She said that this was the greatest support in the world, and that routine is a kind of salvation. It may be so; but it is a very dull salvation, and I used to feel that I would rather have incident, whatever kind of incident it might be. But then at that time I was not old, which makes all the difference.

MARGARET OLIPHANT, 1896.

BRAND THE BUILDER

On winter days, aboot the gloamin hour,
When the nock on the college touer
Is chappan lowsin-time,
And ilka mason packs his mell and tools awa
Under his banker, and bien forenenst the waa
The labourer haps the lave o the lime
Wi soppan sacks, to keep it frae a frost, or faa
O suddent snaw
Duran the nicht;
When scrawnie craws flap in the shell-green licht
Towards yon bane-bare rickle o trees
That heeze
Up on the knowe abuin the toun,
And the red goun
Is happan mony a student frae the snell nor'easter,
Malcolm Brand, the maister,
Seean the last hand through the yett
Afore he bars and padlocks it,
Taks yae look aroond his stourie yaird
Whaur chunks o stane are liggan
Like the ruins o some auld-farrant biggin;
Picks a skelf oot o his baerd,
Scliffs his tacketty buits, and syne
Clunters hamelins doun the wyn'.

Doun by the sea
Murns the white snaw owre the wrack ayebydanlie.

The main street echoes back his fuitfaas
Frae its waas
Whaur owre the kerb and causeys, yellow licht
Presses back the mirk nicht
As shop fronts flude the pavin-stanes in places
Like the peintit faces whures pit on, or actresses,
To please their different customers.

Aye the nordren nicht, cauld as rumour,
Taks command,
Chills the toun wi his militarie humour
And plots his map o starns wi felloun hand.

Alang the shore
The greinan white sea-stallions champ and snore.

Stoopin through the anvil pend
Gaes Brand,
And owre the coort wi the twa-three partan creels,
The birss air fu
o the smell o the sea, and fish, and meltit glue;
Draws up at his door, and syne
Hawkan his craig afore he gangs in ben,
Gies a bit scart at the grater wi his heels.

The kail-pat on the hob is hotteran fu
Wi the usual hash o Irish stew,
And by the grate, a red-haired beauty frettit thin,
His wife is kaain a spurtle roond.
He swaps his buits for his baffies but a soond.

The twa-three bairns ken to mak nae din
When faither's in,
And sit on creepies roond aboot.
Brand gies a muckle yawn
And howks his paper out.

Tither side the fire
The kettle hums and mews like a telephone wire.

"Lord, for what we are about to receive

195

Help us to be truly thankful—Aimen;
Woman, ye've pit ingans in't again!"

"Gae wa ye coorse auld hypocrite,
Thank the Lord for your meat syne grue at it!"

Wi chowks drawn ticht in a speakless sconner
He glowers on her
Syne on the quate and strecht-faced bairns:
Faulds his paper doun aside his eatin-airns,
And, til the loud tick-tockin o the nock,
Sups, and reads wi nae ither word nor look.

The warld ootside
Like a lug-held seashell, sings wi the rinnan tide.

The supper owre, Brand redds up for the nicht,
Aiblins there's a schedule for to price
Or somethin nice
On at the picters—secont hoose—
Or some poleetical meetin wants his licht,
Or aiblins, wi him t-total aa his life
And no able to seek a pub for relief frae the wife,
Daunders oot the West Sands "on the loose".
Whitever tis,
The waater slorps frae his elbucks as he synds his phiz.

And this is aa the life he kens there is?

TOM SCOTT

GOLFING AT ST ANDREWS

The natives have a pleasure of their own, which is as much the staple of the place
as old colleges and churches. This is golfing, which is here not a mere pastime
but a business and a passion and has for ages been so, probably owing to their
admirable links. This pursuit actually draws many a middle-aged gentleman
whose stomach requires exercise and purse cheap pleasure to reside here with
his family. There is a pretty large set who do nothing else, who begin in the
morning and stop only for dinner. Their meetings are very numerous and they
are rather a "guttling" population.

LORD COCKBURN, *Memorials of His Time*, 1856.
AMONG THE ST ANDREWS GOLFERS IN 1874

My friend Mr. Reginald Potts—indeed I may say my respected nephew Mr. Reginald Potts—one of the best known of its inhabitants, has at last prevailed on me to visit St. Andrews... I remembered the place had no woods to wander in—had not even a decent tree to show—and though of illustrious historical descent and full of interesting ruins, was, apart from the "melancholy ocean," not dowered with objects for the tourist to spend much time over. I inquired of Mr. Potts his designs for the morrow. He began about a Club he wished me to see, and talked in a lively manner about a "foursome" at golf he had arranged for me. "Your happiness," said he, "will be complete, if, so long, dear uncle, as you are here, you only be passive." I suspect that is the key to more happiness than can be scraped up in St. Andrews, capable as it is, now that I have seen its Club and its Links, of furnishing it in no stinted measure.

In the bright morning sunlight I found the Club-house come up to my expectations. It has no architectural pretensions to speak of, and clearly was built for comfort rather than display. It has a bow-window looking west—the window of a large room used for luncheon, for the weed, and the annual dinners. This is flanked by a billiard and a reading room, and is covered in the rear by lavatories and the steward's apartments. I don't know what is above, for I never go upstairs if I can help it, and there was no pressure of necessity in this instance... One little snuggery to the right of the entrance-door displays in a glass case the disused implements of the game, and they look like the monitory flintlocks in curious armouries, which tell of new devices. A step or two further on, and you are at the kindly steward's bar, in the principal hall, where, as in all club-houses, you get what you want, and sometimes more than is good for you. Overlooking this scene of luxury and leisure are two oil portraits—one that of the courtly Mr. Whyte-Melville (convener of the county of Fife, and absolutely the oldest member of this charming institution), by Sir Francis Grant, the other that of Sir Hugh Playfair...

But luncheon is set, and "tucking into" some hot potatoes and cold beef you observe an individual of an easy, reserved presence, and with great glistening eyes. He is in golfing deshabillé, like all the rest of them, with a brown towering wideawake. That is the Lord Justice-General of Scotland, who has just had his forenoon's round, and is now coaxing the inner man to have another...

It was at this point in the day's conversations and inquiries that Mr. Potts informed me that the hour for the foursome was come; and so behold me on the Links of St. Andrews in a tawny scarlet coat and a bonnet... It were superfluous to tell what the origin of golf is. I have just time before striking off to state that what of it is not lost in the mists of antiquity came over with

William the Conqueror. That is what my caddie tells me, and he is no less an authority than Tom Morris, who was born in the purple of equable temper and courteous habits. Well, I began my game by missing what is called "the globe" altogether, and (to anticipate events just a little) I finished it by breaking a club. I early acquired an inexplicable, undefinable, interest in my ball. I heeled it and topped it; I went under it and over it; I stood behind it and stood in advance of it; and in my multifarious endeavours, I exhausted the entire armoury of Tom's implements. Play-club and spoon, niblick and cleek, putter and heavy iron, were in constant requisition in order to get that ball to go. I followed it into the Swilcan Burn; I thrashed it out of numerous sandy bunkers; I fought with it in whinny covers; I drove it forth from grassy tufts with a zeal which, I was constantly told, was beyond all praise. At what is called "the hole across" I was extremely warm, and no doubt looked far from myself; whereupon Tom offered the polite remark—"Ye wid be nane the waur o a black strap, sir." "Certainly, Tom," I rejoined; "my performances are so miserable that I feel you cannot chastise me enough with any sort of strap." "You mistake me, sir," responded Tom; "I didn't mean that; I mean, ye wid be nane the waur o' a pint o' porter." As when the acid joins the soda there instantly arises the effervescence, so at this juncture at "the hole across" I exploded with laughter. It only wanted Tom's calling porter by the name of "black strap" to fill in, to myself, the comicality of the scene in which I was the central figure; and so, casting myself on the ground, I struck work like any miner. But it was of no use. I was compelled to resume, with the ultimate result of the club breaking, as aforesaid, and with the intimation that we had won the foursome. It seems that odds were allowed to me, a half or a whole or something—I never inquired what, seeing the issue was obtained through a conspiracy of flatterers. This conclusion was deepened in my mind at dinner—a meal in St. Andrews at which the day's games are gone over again hole by hole and stroke by stroke. Mr. Potts let fall a sentence or two then which showed me that his main object was to egg me on to that degree of fascination with the game when all self-restraint is lost, and when the enthralled novice becomes, in the choice between work and golf, quite unable to resist golf when there is a doubt existing. My nephew has so far succeeded that I have had three more rounds since and as the October Meeting is coming—to the dinner of the members of which I have received a courteous invitation—I am resolved at this writing to practise away.

The Links themselves for a walk are most enjoyable. You play, as it were, in a path of beautiful greensward, which in form is like a shepherd's crook, with the stem notched and twisted, on whose brecks of heather the bees are humming, and above which the song-birds are gyrating among the flight of balls.

Than my present situation nothing could be more agreeable or desirable; and then Mr. Potts has given me quite a ministry of useful introductions besides that to the game of golf.

"**JONATHAN OLDBUCK**", From the *Glasgow News*, September 21, 1874. Reprinted in *Golf: A Royal & Ancient Game*, edited by Robert Clark, second edition, 1893.

JO GRIMOND'S ST ANDREWS

North Street, St Andrews

...On the other side of the street lived Mr. Whyte, a St Andrews character of the days immediately before the Second World War, in a restored white harled house with curious balcony, rather like a gun emplacement.

Mr. Whyte, who appeared in St Andrews rather suddenly, was I believe brought up in America. He was a figure in one of the "Renaissances" which are recurrent features of Scottish history. The 1930s renaissance was mainly literary though, of course, with political overtones. The East Fife by-election brought Eric Linklater as the Nationalist candidate. I remember him speaking in the Temperance Hall, which was on the site of the "new cinema", a building otherwise used for sixpenny "Hops" and sales of work. I expected a romantic hero; I found a stocky figure in plus-fours over whose owl-like face rose an impressive but bald head. I later got to like and admire him. He is under-rated. His writing is easy to read, clear but full of energy: qualities out of fashion in an age which admires turgid obscurity. His book, *Juan in America,* ranks with the best of Evelyn Waugh. Mr. Whyte published a short-lived but rather good periodical, *The Modern Scot,* bound in black. He hoped to make his bookshop in South Street a meeting place for St Andrews' lecturers, students and litterateurs generally. To some extent he succeeded, but he met with the reserve with which St Andrews greets anything raffish or out of the way. The Second World War put an end to his efforts. Like Mr. Rusack, the suspicious St Andreans branded him as a spy. The top of his house does look a little like a fortification, but it is untrue that it was designed as a base from which signals were to be sent to submarines (in any case it faces the wrong way) or as a pillbox from which machine guns would sweep North Street. I remember rather little about Mr. Whyte except that he gave me rose-petal jam for tea and appeared free from the vices of which he was accused, being, as far as I could see, neither a traitor, an anarchist nor a show-off.

St Andrews Railway Station

The closing of the station was a sad blow to old St Andrews' life. Outside it stood

199

a row of cabs and buses. Until the Second World War the train was the main means of approach to the city and within it the main passenger transport was by bicycle or horse. Cars could be hired for longer journeys but I do not remember any "taxi". The station was a considerable centre. The name "St Andrews" was beautifully displayed by an arrangement of flowers and shells on the bank of the cutting in which the station lay. A hoist raised the luggage to street level; small boys could travel in it.

The railway officials were well known and respected local figures: the station master, Lees; the guard, Haddow; and Docherty, the foreman porter. Haddow was typical of the St Andrews functionaries. Immaculate in uniform and peaked cap he resembled a rather stout Sir Walter Scott. Docherty was more of Stevenson's build and colouring, and wore his cap on the back of his head. Both were men of standing and authority. I am glad that the spirit of the old railway men, helpful and humorous, still persists. Travelling recently in Fife in one of those trains laughably called Sprinters, I asked the ticket collector if it stopped at the Haymarket station in Edinburgh. "Oh yes", he replied, "it stops at every lamp-post." When a boy I was reprimanded by Haddow for crossing the line to collect a starling's egg from a nest in the wall of the cutting. That evening after dark, Haddow called at our house and taking off his cap produced four eggs out of its crown. Quite a few people commuted to and from Dundee, either to University College, Dundee, then a part of St Andrews University, or to work in Dundee offices and mills... Just beyond the station at the top of the city hill is a building, now much altered, but which seemed to carry an air of having been a chapel. Whether it once was I do not know, but it was the lair of Scott the joiner, a patriarchal figure whose dignified appearance was appropriate to the atmosphere of his workshop and his job of undertaker. He and his assistants wore long white smocks and pushed a hand-barrow. He was famous for his delays in coming to start a job and for the eternity of waiting for any repair job he removed to his sanctum. The smell of wood and glue and the deftness of his work with plane, saw or chisel fascinated children. I was also spell-bound listening to him and his assistants discussing the difficulty they would have in "boxing" a well-known citizen when he died. The poor man was twisted with rheumatism and must indeed have presented what would now be called "a challenge" to any undertaker.

JO GRIMOND,★ *Memoirs*, 1979.

★A native of St Andrews, Jo Grimond (1913-93) is best-known as the charismatic leader of the UK Liberal Party from 1956 to 1967 and again, briefly, in 1976. Under his leadership his party saw its electoral fortunes rise dramatically. He was MP for Orkney and Shetland and, during the early 1970s, Rector of Aberdeen University, where Tom Hubbard recalls him as a kenspeckle figure.

WILLA AND EDWIN MUIR IN ST ANDREWS IN THE 1930s

At first things looked as if they were going to turn out well for us at St Andrews. We liked the terrace house James Whyte had taken for us, on top of the cliffs beside the Castle, with the North Sea at our front door instead of a garden. Edwin wrote to the manager of our London bank asking for an overdraft and got it. An intelligent and sympathetic woman doctor, Dorothy Douglas, took me in hand and fixed me up so that I could at least carry on. Everything was within easy reach, a school for Gavin, shops, ancient ruins and pleasant walks by the sea. We had only to come to terms with it all, and first with James Whyte, his bookshop and his magazine, *The Modern Scot*.

We went to dine with James in his house, an old one in South Street thoroughly modernised inside. It was padded everywhere with cushions; the sitting-room ceiling had been painted blue to match them and silvered with stars. James was obviously a young man who liked to be in the fashion and could afford it, ceilings like his must have then been "the fashion", and walls outfacing each other in contrasting colours. After dinner we heard a Sibelius symphony on his gramophone, for Sibelius was in the fashion too; we did not know the symphony and felt, as we told each other later, that we were being ushered into a whole new world, since in James's house the furniture, the pictures, the lighting, as well as the music, were all fashionably *avant-garde*.

James himself was self-conscious but kindly, and arranged for us to visit his shop and look at his two new houses. The shop had been ingeniously constructed out of a barrel-vaulted room on the ground floor of another old building, a little farther along South Street. Both his house and the shop, seen from outside, were built in a traditional Scottish style with stones somewhat rough and full of character, carefully restored, a credit to their new owner. The barrel-vaulting inside the shop made an attractive setting for books, but its old-world atmosphere was startlingly contradicted by a fresco that faced one on entering; beside the end of the counter there was a large caricature of John Knox astride a beer-cask, raising high a reaming tankard, recognizably John Knox although he had a raddled nose and a wicked leer.

"We thought the young people would like it," said James, a little peevishly, "but the St Leonards girls have been forbidden to enter the shop." The fresco had been suggested by his right-hand satellite, John, whom we had not yet met. So far, James complained, very few students had come in. Perhaps when term began again more of them would venture.

The shelves were impressively well stocked, and on the counter all the most modern magazines from France and the United States were laid out, together with a copy of nearly every book one had seen recently reviewed. Only customers were lacking. The ingratiating young salesman behind the counter was filling in time by embroidering a brown silk counterpane with his own design of autumn leaves.

Edwin said little, except to remark that one would have expected the students to find it an exciting shop. He told me later that he had been struck by its sheer incongruity with the Scotland he had seen on his Journey, and that he was inclined to be sorry for James....

The magazine was better than one might have expected, for its layout was harmonious and its contents not too parochial. Christopher Grieve and F. G. Scott and Edwin were all contributing to it from time to time. One felt that it deserved to succeed. The bookshop on the other hand did not thrive at all, not even after the University term had begun...

After some years of increasing tension, during which James's bookshop went on being shunned by most people in the town and his magazine never achieved a satisfactory circulation, the near approach of the war made his position untenable. In the bar of the Royal and Ancient Golf Club he was denounced as a spy for Hitler. A picture-gallery on the roof of his North Street houses? Nonsense: that was a concrete emplacement for machine guns, commanding the bay. Innocent excursions into the bay by motor-launch? Obviously the fellow had been nosing out secret rendezvous for submarines. He had written a book about Fife, hadn't he, with special emphasis on its hills? Outlook posts for Germans, of course. If he wasn't a spy, what was he doing in St Andrews at all? These aspersions spread into the staff rooms of St Leonards and presently the town was buzzing with dark suspicions about James. He gave up the struggle. He left his super-charged car to John and departed to America, on the reasonable plea that he was tired of paying double income-tax, once in America and once in Britain. In Washington he got married and opened another up-to-date bookshop, which was presumably appreciated by that city. Meanwhile, once war had been declared, the St Andrews gossip-mongers accounted for his absence by saying that the government had very properly arrested him and put him in the Tower. I was even told that he had been beheaded. This was one aspect of the town in which I had assured Edwin we should feel at home.

We did not at once discover what St Andrews was like. The people who generated fear and disapproval of James's shop and all his doings were at the upper end of the social scale, Hugh Kingsmill's "mupples", but we began to run up against uncivilised anomalies at all levels of society...

As a student I had not been aware of social stratification in the town, although the tendency may have existed, and there had been little of it in the University. Nowadays things were different. This I learned from Dr. Drury Oeser, whose husband Oscar had just been made head of the new Psychology Department. Drury, herself a doctor of psychology and fresh from Cambridge, passed on to me her astonishment at the rigid protocol observed in the University. When she was out shopping on her bicycle she said, and saw one of Oscar's research students, of course she waved to him in a friendly manner. But the students had privately begged her not to do so, pleading that they would get into trouble, since staff and students were not supposed to recognise each other in the street. She had also been told, by a professor's wife, that she should not have invited professors' wives and lecturers' wives to the same tea-party. Some of the Top Brass were simply awful, said Drury. One old professor had found a couple of Freud's books in the library, and swore they were covered with "pornographic thumb-marks". Oscar had had to fight to keep them from being removed.

Had I not been unsuspicious, I might have guessed from an incident happening to me that the University climate had changed. A fellow-student of mine, who took her Classics degree the year after I did and had inherited my text-books and note-books was now a war-widow, with one little girl, and had come to live in St Andrews as junior assistant in the Latin Department, a post I had myself held for a year in 1914. I dressed myself in my best London clothes, took Gavin by the hand and went to call on her, expecting a warm welcome. I did not get it. Apparently I had come to St Andrews to carry on the kind of anarchic life we had been used to in pre-war days, when students lived in town lodgings, and I was likely to undermine the respectable status she had now acquired, married as I was to "a man who wrote for the papers" while she was sending her daughter to St Leonards. This unexpected rebuff hurt my feelings so much that I had taken it only as a personal matter, not as a symptom of a changed social climate.

But my one-time friend was not the only member of the University staff to high-hat us. The whole English Department, where we might have expected to meet some friendly interest, ignored us, taking its tone from the professor, who refused to admit that any contemporary work could be regarded as literature, or any contemporary writers as literary men. For Yeats he made an exception; he boasted that Yeats had once spent an afternoon on his sofa; but for an upstart like Edwin Muir, who was now labelled in the University as "a man who wrote for the'papers'" (so we were told), no exception could be made. Only the Oesers, the Greek Reader and one or two professors from the Divinity College of St Mary's were humanly friendly.

WILLA MUIR, *Belonging. A Memoir*, 1968.

ST ANDREWS, JUNE 1946

Old tales, old customs and old men's dreams
Obscure this town. Memories abound.
In the mild misted air, and in the sharp air

Toga and gown walk the pier.
The past sleeps in the stones.

Knox in his tower, bishop and priest
In the great cathedral, a queen's visit—
All traditional currency. Once there was
Meaning in the formula, gesture implied
Act. Now where's the life of the town?

Concurrence of event and sentiment
Confound perception! But look!
A small boat brings its morning catch,
Haddock and cod, plaice and mackerel.
Good sales! Landladies, hotels, hostelries,

Housefull! And America walks the street.
Today the train's spilling its complement
Down windy lanes to restaurants,
And afternoon—the beach, queues for
Cinema—or golf all day. Night—

History shrieks from the stones,
Knox, Douglas and Wishart,
Prison and torment.
Blind the eyes, broken the heart
Knox, Douglas and Wishart.

GEORGE BRUCE

AT SCHOOL

As in a film I see brown lace-up shoes
and brown lisle stockings
held by suspenders that dragged
dragged us down—
shoes that plied through dark brown leaves
along St Andrews' *Scores*
and up steps across the paving into
that cold brown house where I was kept
as if a prisoner, one of fifty.

At basement level like a moat around
the house were railings and spikes and
everywhere stone walls, my desolation.

Birds may have sung and trees flowered,
grass may have grown and weeds bloomed,
but we lived darkly in brown:
thick brown tunic, thin brown cardigan,
brown felt hat, coat and gloves,
brown paint on doors and skirtings,
furniture brown and brown linoleum.

No music except hymns,
no poetry save the Bible,
no talking, no running,
no nonny no sense.

In dull fear, sometimes acute,
we lived in solemn loneliness
yet in a crowd, like prisoners
waiting, waiting for release.

When at last it came
we were no longer children.

TESSA RANSFORD

BOB DYLAN'S HONORARY DOCTORATE

Without a word, Bob Dylan accepted his honorary doctorate from the University of St Andrews on 24 June 2004 before making his escape in a car. The last time he accepted such a degree was at Princeton in 1970. This was the blazing hot day he recalls in 'The Day of the Locusts': Two of the lines from that song are:

> There was little to say, no conversation,
> As I stepped to the stage to pick up my degree

and, with them, the precedent of the no thank-you speech was set.

Whatever this college dropout's feelings towards the academic world are now, he chose to take his doctorate of music, at the age of sixty-three, from the poets and professors of St Andrews. In complete contrast to that hot day in 1970, Dr

Zimmerman had to brave savage winds and driving rain that were more typical of winter than late June. When he left, with never a word and the car windows blacked out, it was scarcely any clearer who had been honouring whom.

SHIRLEY McKAY, *The Wee Book of Fife*, 2004.

ELEGY, ON THE DEATH OF MR DAVID GREGORY, LATE PROFESSOR OF MATHEMATICS IN THE UNIVERSITY OF ST ANDREWS

Now mourn, ye college masters a'!
And frae your een a tear lat fa',
Fam'd Gregory death has taen awa
    Without remeid;
The skaith ye've met wi's nae that sma',
    Sin Gregory's dead.

The students too will miss him sair,
To school them weel his eident care,
Now they may mourn for ever mair,
    They hae great need;
They'll hip the maist fek o' their lear,
    Sin Gregory's dead.

He could, by Euclid, prove lang sine
A ganging point compos'd a line;
By numbers too he cou'd divine,
    Whan he did read,
That three times three just made up nine;
    But now he's dead.

In algebra weel skill'd he was,
An' kent fu' well proportion's laws;
He cou'd make clear baith B's and A's
    Wi' his lang head;
Rin owr surd roots, but cracks or flaws;
    But now he's dead.

Weel vers'd was he in architecture,
An' kent the nature o' the sector,
Upon baith globes he weel cou'd lecture,

An' gar's tak heid;
Of geometry he was the Hector;
    But now he's dead.

Sae weel's he'd fley the students a',
Whan they war skelpin at the ba',
They took leg bail and ran awa,
    Wi' pith and speid;
We winna get a sport sae braw
    Sin Gregory's dead.

Great 'casion hae we a' to weep,
An' cleed our skins in mourning deep,
For Gregory death will fairly keep
    To take his nap;
He'll till the resurrection sleep
    As sound's a tap.

ROBERT FERGUSSON

JOHN KNOX ON THE MURDER OF CARDINAL BEATON IN ST ANDREWS

But early upon the Saturday, in the morning, the 29 of May, were they in sundry companies in the Abbey kirk-yard, not far distant from the Castle. First, the yetts [gates] being open, and the draw-brig down, for receiving of lime and stones, and other things necessary for building (for Babylon was almost finished)—first, we say, essayed William Kirkcaldy of Grange, younger, and with him six persons, and getting entrance, held purpose with the porter.

...While the said William and the porter talked, and his servants made them to look the work and the workmen, approached Norman Leslie with his company; and because they were no great number, they easily got entrance. They addressed them to the midst of the close, and immediately came John Leslie, somewhat rudely, and four persons with them. The porter, fearing, would have drawn the brig; but the said John, being entered thereon, stayed, and leapt in. And while the porter made him for defence, his head was broken, the keys taken from them, and he cast in the fosse; and so the place was seized.

William Kirkcaldy took the guard of the privy postern, fearing that the fox should have escaped. Then go the rest to the gentlemen's chambers, and without violence done to any man, they put more than fifty persons to the yett: The number that enterprised and did this, was but sixteen persons. The Cardinal,

207

St Andrews Castle

awakened with the shouts, asked from his window, What meant that noise? It was answered, That Norman Leslie had taken his Castle. Which understood, he ran to the postern; but perceiving the passage to be kept without, he returned quickly to his chamber, took his two-handed sword, and gart [made] his chamber child cast kists [chests], and other implements to the door. In this meantime came John Leslie unto it, and bids open. The Cardinal asking, "Who calls?, he answers, "My name is Leslie." He re-demands, "Is that Norman?" The other says, "Nay; my name is John." "I will have Norman", says the Cardinal, "for he is my friend." "Content yourself with such as are here; for other shall ye get none."

There were with the said John, James Melville [of Carnbee] a man familiarly acquainted with Master George Wishart; and Peter Carmichael [of Balmedie, or Balmaddie], a stout gentleman.

…the Cardinal or his chamber-child, (it is uncertain), opened the door, and the Cardinal sat doun in a chair and cried, "I am a priest; I am a priest, ye will not slay me." The said John Leslie (according to his former vows) strook him first, anes or twice, and so did the said Peter. But James Melville (a man of nature most gentle and most modest) perceiving thame both in choler, withdrew them, and said, "This work and judgment of God (although it be secret) ought to be done with greater gravity"; and presenting unto him the point of the sword, said, "Repent thee of thy former wicked life, but especially of the schedding of the blood of that notable instrument of God, Maister George Wishart, which albeit the flame of fire consumed before men, yet cries it a vengeance upon thee, and we from God are sent to revenge it: For here, before my God, I protest, that neither the hetterent of thy person, the luif of thy riches, nor the fear of any trouble thou could have done to me in particular, moved nor moves me to strike thee; but only because thou hast been, and remains ane obstinat enemy against Christ Jesus and his Holy Evangel." And so he struck him twice or thrice through with a stog sword; and so he fell, never word heard out of his mouth, but "I am a priest, I am a priest: fye, fye: all is gone."

And so was he brought to the east blockhouse head, and shown dead over the wall to the faithless multitude, which would not believe before it saw. How miserably lay David Beaton, careful Cardinal. And so they departed without *Requiem æternam*, and *Requiescat in pace*, song for his soule. Now, because the weather was hot (for it was in May, as ye have heard), and his funeral could not suddenly be prepared, it was thought best, to keep him from stinking, to give him great salt enough, a cope of lead, and a nuke in the bottom of the Sea-touer (a place where many of God's children had been empreasoned before) to await what exequies his brethren the Bishops would prepare for him.

These things we write merrily. But we would that the Reader should observe God's just judgments, and how they can deprehend the wordly wise in their own wisdom, make their table to be a snare to trap their own feet, and their own presupposed strength to be their own destruction. These are the words of our God, whereby he would admonish the tyrants of this earth, that in the end he will be revenged of their cruelty, what strength so ever follow they make in the contrary. But such is the blindness of man (as David speaks), "That the posterity does ever follow the footsteps of their wicked fathers and principally in their impiety"; for how little differs the cruelty of that bastard, that yet is called Bishop of Saint Andrews from the cruelty of the former, we will after hear.

JOHN KNOX

JOHN KNOX IN ST ANDREWS, 1571 AND 1574

Bot of all the benefites I haid that yeir [1571] was the coming of that maist notable profet and apostle of our nation, Mr Jhone Knox, to St Androis; wha, be the faction of the Quein occupeing the castell and town of Edinbruche, was compellit to remove thairfra with a number of the best, and chusit to com to St Androis. I hard him teatche ther the prophecie of Daniel that simmer, and the wintar following. I haid my pen and my litle book, and tuk away sic things as I could comprehend. In the opening upe of his text he was moderat the space of an halff houre; bot when he enterit to application, he maid me to grew and tremble, that I could nocht hald a pen to wryt.

...Being in St Androis he was very weak. I saw him everie day of his doctrine go hulie and fear, with a furring of martriks fur about his neck, a staff in the an hand, and guid godlie Richart Ballanden, his servand, halding upe the uther oxtar, from the Abbay to the paroche kirk; and be the said Richart and another servant, lifted upe to the pulpit, whar he behovit to lean at his first entrie; bot

or he haid done with his sermont, he was sae active and vigorus that he was lyk
to ding that pulpit in blads, and fly out of it!

Rev. JAMES MELVILLE, *Diaries*.

From *PAPISTRY STORM'D*

I sing the steir, strabush, and strife,
Whan, bickerin' frae the towns o Fife,
Great bangs of bodies, thick and rife,
  Gaed to Sanct Androis town,
And, wi John Calvin i' their heads,
And hammers i' their hands and spades,
Enrag'd at idols, mass, and beads,
  Dang the Cathedral down...

He prechit east, he preachit wast;
His voice was as the whirlwind's blast,
  That aftentimes, in days o' simmer,
Comes swirlin' sudden frae the sea,
And swoops the hay-cocks aff the lea,
  And tirls the kirks, and strips the timmer;
The vera steeples round about
Rebellow'd to his nobill shout,
And rang wi' texts baith in and out;
The dows and daws that there aboundit,
As if affrichtit and confoundit,
Out-whirr'd and whitter't at the sound o't;
The bells and bartisans reboundit,
Strang pupits flew about in blads,
Breakin' the hearers' pows wi dads;
Men, women, kirtled girls, and lads,
Were fir'd and furiated in squads;
Sae wud and wicket was their wraith...

WILLIAM TENNANT

LAST LAUCH

The Minister said it wald dee,
  the cypress buss I plantit.

But the buss grew till a tree,
    naething dauntit.

It's growan stark and heich,
    derk and straucht and sinister,
kirkyairdie-like and dreich.
    But whaur's the Minister?

DOUGLAS YOUNG

From *AN ECLOGUE. TO THE MEMORY OF DR WILLIAM WILKIE, LATE PROFESSOR OF NATURAL PHILOSOPHY IN THE UNIVERSITY OF ST ANDREWS**

'Twas na for weel tim'd verse or sangs alane,
He bore the bell frae ilka shepherd swain.
Nature to him had gi'en a kindly lore,
Deep a' her mystic ferlies to explore:
For a' her secret workings he could gie
Reasons that wi' her principles agree.
Ye saw yoursell how weel his mailin thrave,
Ay better faugh'd an' snodit than the lave;
Lang had the thristles an' the dockans been
In use to wag their taps upo' the green,
Whare now his bonny riggs delight the view,
An' thrivin hedges drink the caller dew.

ROBERT FERGUSSON

GATEWAY TO THE SEA (1)
At the East Port, St Andrews

Pause stranger at the porch: nothing beyond
This framing arch of stone, but scattered rocks
And sea and these on the low beach
Original to the cataclysm and the dark.

Once one man bent to the stone, another
Dropped the measuring line, a third and fourth

*Dr Wilkie had a farm near St Andrews in which he made remarkable improvements.

Together lifted and positioned the dressed stone
Making wall and arch; yet others
Settled the iron doors on squawking hinge
To shut without the querulous seas and men.
Order and virtue and love (they say)
Dwelt in the town—but that was long ago.
Then the stranger at the gate, the merchants,
Missioners, the blind beggar with the dog,
The miscellaneous vendors (duly inspected)
Were welcome within the wall that held from sight
The water's brawl. All that was long ago.
Now the iron doors are down to dust,
But the stumps of hinge remain. The arch
Opens to the element—the stones dented
And stained to green and purple and rust.

Pigeons settle on the top. Stranger,
On this winter afternoon pause at the porch,
For the dark land beyond stretches
To the unapproachable element; bright
As night falls and with the allurement of peace,
Concealing under the bland feature, possession.
Not all the agitations of the world
Articulate the ultimate question as do those waters
Confining the memorable and the forgotten;
Relics, records, furtive occasions—Caesar's politics
And he who was drunk last night:
Rings, diamants, snuff boxes, warships,
Also the less worthy garments of worthy men.

Prefer then this handled stone, now ruined
While the sea mists wind about the arch.
The afternoon dwindles, night concludes,
The stone is damp unyielding to the touch,
But crumbling in the strain and stress
Of the years: the years winding about the arch,
Settling in the holes and crevices, moulding
The dressed stone. Once one man bent to it,
Another dropped the measuring line, a third
And fourth positioned to make wall and arch
Theirs. Pause stranger at this small town's edge—

The European sun knew those streets
O Jesu parvule; Christus Victus, Christus Victor,
The bells singing from their towers, the waters
Whispering to the waters, the air tolling
To the air—the faith, the faith, the faith.

All this was long ago. The lights
Are out, the town is sunk in sleep.
The boats are rocking at the pier,
The vague winds beat about the streets—
Choir and altar and chancel are gone.
Under the touch the guardian stone remains
Holding memory, reproving desire, securing hope
In the stop of water, in the lull of night
Before dawn kindles a new day.

GEORGE BRUCE

Acknowledgments

The editors and publishers wish to thank the following (or their representatives) who have kindly given permission to reprint extracts and copyright material in this book.

G. P. Bennett for an extract from *The Past at Work. Around the Lomonds* (1982)

Alice Bold for Alan Bold's poem 'The Maidenbore Rock', originally published in *Summoned by Knox, Poems in Scots* (Wilfion Books, 1985)

Hamish Brown for an article 'Inchkeith: An Island of Dereliction', originally published in *Weekend Scotsman* on 5 January 1985

Margaret Gillies Brown for the poem 'Reflections in Crail', originally published in *Looking Towards Light* (Blind Serpent Press, 1988)

John Buchan, Lord Tweedsmuir, for an extract from *A Lost Lady of Old Years* (1899)

Gregory Burke for an extract from *Gagarin Way* (Faber & Faber Ltd, 2001)

Charles Beatty for extracts from *Our Admiral. A Biography of Admiral of the Fleet Earl Beatty* (1980)

John Brewster for poems 'St Monans' and 'The Barber o' Methil'. The latter poem was originally published in *Four Fife Poets: Fower Brigs ti a Kinrik* (Aberdeen University Press, 1988)

David Bruce for George Bruce's poems 'St Andrews, June 1946', originally published in *George Bruce: Selected Poems* (Oliver & Boyd, 1947), 'Gateway to the Sea (1)', originally published in *Landscape and Figures* (Akros Publications, 1967) and 'Odd On-goings in Dunfermline Toun', originally published in *Perspectives: Poems 1970-1986* (Aberdeen University Press, 1987)

V. Gordon Childe and W. Douglas Simpson for extracts from *Illustrated Guide to Ancient Monuments. Vol 6, Scotland* (1959)

Joe Corrie for 'The Image o' God' and 'Scottish Pride'

Anna Crowe for 'Pittenweem Beach'

Peter Davidson for the poem 'The Palace Lying in the Sandhaven of Culross', originally published in *Works in the Inglis Tongue* (Three Tigers Press, 1985)

John Deacon for an extract from *Craigrothie. Walking with History* (2001)

Peter and Carol Dean for an extract from *Passage of Time: The Story of Queensferry Passage and the Village of North Queensferry* (P.N. & G.C Dean, 1981)

Richard Demarco for the extract from *Kunst = Kapital, Art = Wealth*, given as the Adam Smith Lecture for Fife College in 1995.

Sally Evans for the poem 'Begging Peacock, Dunfermline', originally published in *Zed 2 O, No. 21* (Akros Publications, 2007)

A. M. Findlay for an extract from *Kennoway: Its History and Legends* (1946)

Lillias Scott Forbes for the poem 'Nae Bield in Falkland', originally published in *Turning a Fresh Eye* (Akros Publications, 1998)

A. M. Forster for 'Limekilns: Sunday May 9th, 1999'

Karen Garland for an extract from *Cults Kirk* (Howe of Fife Church, Cults. 1998)

Duncan Glen for his poems, which can all be found in his *Collected Poems 1965-2005* (Akros Publications, 2006) and for his extracts taken from *Ruined Rural Fife Churches* (Akros Publications, 2002), *Historic Fife Murders* (Akros Publications, 2002) and *Illustrious Fife* (Akros Publications, 1998)

Jo Grimond for extracts from *Memoirs* (1979)

William Hershaw for the poems 'High Valleyfield', originally published in *The Cowdenbeath Man* (Scottish Cultural Press, 1998), 'A Lakota Sioux in Cowdenbeath High Street', originally published in a pamphlet (Touch the Earth Publications, 2001), and 'For Joe Corrie', originally published in *Fifty Fife Sonnets: Coarse and Fine* (Akros Publications, 2006)

Harvey Holton for his poem 'Thinkin' and Daein', originally published in *Four Fife Poets: Fower Brigs ti a Kinrik* (Aberdeen University Press, 1988)

Tom Hubbard for the poems 'The Retour o Troilus', published in *Peacocks and Squirrels* (Akros Publications, 2007), 'Mephistophelean Ballant-Scherzo on Ane Fife Legend', originally published in *Scottish Faust* (Ketillonia, 2004), 'A Wish' (translation, via a French version, of Lermontov), originally appeared in *Markings*, double issue Nos. 20 and 21 (2005), 'Northern Roses' and 'Scottish Muid' (translation of Lajos Aprily with Attila Dósa), originally published in *Zed 2 O, No. 21* (Akros Publications, 2007), 'At Seafield, Fife', published *Four Fife Poets: Fower Brigs ti a Kinrik* (Aberdeen University Press, 1988) and 'Fife Child in the Fifties', published in *Zed 2 O, No. 19* (Akros Publications, 2005). The poem 'Deserta' (translation of George Buchanan) has its first outing here.

Alexander Hutchison for the poem 'Inchcolm', first published in *The Moon Calf* (Galliard, 1990)

Dan Imrie for an extract from *A Mining Disaster 1901-2001: 100 Years Remembered* (Bob & Helen Eadie, Inverkeithing, 2001)

Ian Jack for a piece from *The Guardian* (18th February 2006)

Gordon Jarvie for the poem 'Fulmars at Crail', originally published in *The Tale of the Crail Whale and Other Poems* (Harpercroft 2006)

Elizabeth Kendzia, quoted in Diana M. Henderson's *The Lion and the Eagle:*

Reminiscences of Polish Second World War Veterans in Scotland (Cualann Press, 2001)

Kirkcaldy District Museums for the extract from their whaling leaflet

Ian W. King for the poems '6 Cowdenbeath Koipu'

Lillian King for her profile of Val McDermid, originally published in *Famous Women of Fife* (Windfall Books, 1999)

Theo Lang for extracts from *The Kingdom of Fife and Kinrossshire* (1951)

James Laver for an extract from *The House of Haig* (1958)

John Law for T. S. Law's poems 'The Forth Brig', orginally published in *Aftentymes a Tinkler* (Fingerpost 1975), and 'Ceres, Scotland', originally published in *New Scot Volume 2, No. 10* (1946). 'The Bink' and 'Neebors Kilt in the Linday Collerie' are previously unpublished. All these poems will be published in T. S. Law, *At the Pynt o the Pick and Other Poems*, ed. Tom Hubbard and John Law (Blackford: Fingerpost Publications, 2008)

Jennie Lee for an extract from *This Great Journey: A Volume of Autobiography* (1963)

Eleanor Livingstone for the poem 'Last Chance', originally published in *The Last King of Fife* (Happenstance Press, 2005). A version of the poem had previously been published in *Seam* poetry magazine in 2001.

Carcanet Press for an extract from Hugh MacDiarmid's 'A Drunk Man Looks at the Thistle', originally published in 1926.

Forbes Macgregor for an extract from *Salt-Sprayed Burgh: A View of Anstruther* (1980) and the poem 'On Cementing Level the Stable Floor at the Old Manse, Wester Anstruther, St Swithin's Day, 1963'

Sheila Mackay for an extract from *The Forth Bridge: a Picture History* (1990)

Kate Wood for Alastair Mackie's poem 'Back-Green Odyssey', originally published in *Back-Green Odyssey and Other Poems* (Rainbow Books, 1980)

Donald and Linda McGilp for an extract from *Dunino: Place of Worship* (1993)

Elise McKay for her poem 'The Man in the Rock', originally published in *Floating Lanterns* (Envoi Publications, 1988)

Shirley McKay for an extract from *The Wee Book of Fife* (2004)

Andrew McNeil for his poem 'Mary fae Burntisland,' originally published in *Temples Fae Creels* (Ketillonia Press, 1999)

Stewart M. McPherson for an extract from *Saint Margaret: Queen of Scotland* (Akros Publications, 2007)

Gordon Meade for his poem 'The Beachcomber', originally published in *A Man at Sea* (Diehard, 2003)

James Reid Baxter for his extensive research on Elizabeth Melville, Lady Culross. The editors would not have been aware of her poetry without his work and look forward to his edition of her poems which will be published soon.

Willa Muir for an extract from *Belonging. A Memoir* (1968)

Glen L. Pride for extracts from *The Kingdom of Fife: An Illustrated Architectural Guide* (RIAS 1990)

Ian Rankin for the extract from *Rebus's Scotland* by Ian Rankin (Orion Books, 2005), © John Rebus Limited 2005.

Tessa Ransford for the poem 'At School', originally published in *When It Works It Feels Like Play* (The Ramsay Head Press, 1998)

James Robertson for the extract from *Joseph Knight* (Fourth Estate, 2003)

Christopher Rush for the poem 'Shipwright's Spehl', originally published in *A Resurrection of a Kind* (Aberdeen University Press, 1984)

Maureen Sangster for the poem 'Kirkcaldy Vennel', originally published in *Zed 2 O, No. 19* (Akros Publications, 2005)

Stephen Scobie for an extract from *Dunino* (Véhicule Press, 1989)

Heather Scott for an extract from Tom Scott's 'Brand the Builder', published in *The Collected Shorter Poems of Tom Scott* (Chapman/Agenda, 1993)

Lesley Scott-Moncrieff for an extract from *Scotland's Eastern Coast. A Guidebook from Berwick to Scrabster* (Oliver & Boyd, 1963)

Andy Shanks and Jim Russell for the lyrics to 'St Andrew by the Window', first published in the sleevenotes on their album *Diamonds in the Night* (Culburnie Records, 1997)

Eric Simpson for an extract from *Dalgety Bay: Heritage & Hidden History* (Dalgety Bay and Hillend Community Council, 1999)

Robin Smith for the extract from *Fife's Bridges* (Kirkcaldy Civic Society, 2006)

D. P. Thomson for an extract from *Raith and Kirkcaldy* (1952)

Kenneth Roy for his piece on Jimmy Shand

Kathleen Sayer, Hew Lorimer and Stephanie Blackden for an extract from *Kellie Castle and Garden* (National Trust for Scotland, 1993)

Sydney Goodsir Smith for the poems 'The Staunan Stanes' and 'Largo'

T. G. Snoddy for an extract from *'Tween Forth and Tay* (1966)

Harry D. Watson for an extract from *Kilrenny and Cellardyke: 800 Years of History* (John Donald, 1986)

Joyce Watson for Tom Watson's poems 'Ruminant', originally published in *Dark Whistle* (Akros Publications, 1997), 'The Messenger an' Me' originally published in *21st Century Poems* (Akros Publications, 2001) and 'East Neuk'

John Watt for 'The Keltie Clippy'

Ian Nimmo White for the poem 'Kirkforthar', originally published in the newsletter of the Fife Environmental Education Forum in 1997 and later in *Standing Back* (Petrel, 2000)

Betty Wood & Rhona Sragg for an extract from Ronnie Wood's *Famous Fifers* (1977)

Clara Young for Douglas Young's poem 'Last Lauch', originally published in *A Braird o' Thirstles: Scots Poems* by Douglas Young (William McLellan, 1947)

Every effort has been made to trace all the copyright holders, but if any have been inadvertently overlooked the publishers will be pleased to make the necessary arrangement at the first opportunity.